# ANGELA CAMPBELL

I read my first romance at 16 and immediately attempted to write one, too. Many attempts (and a couple of decades) later, I finally published my first novel.

A mild-mannered newspaper reporter with more than 15 years' experience as a general assignment reporter, features editor and graphic designer, I have also worked as a production assistant in TV and film. I now live in the Southeast with my rescue cat.

Learn more about my books at www.angelacampbellonline.com and follow me on Twitter @AngelaCampbel.

# Spirited Away

## ANGELA CAMPBELL

HarperImpulse an imprint of
HarperCollins*Publishers* Ltd
77–85 Fulham Palace Road
Hammersmith, London W6 8JB

www.harpercollins.co.uk

A Paperback Original 2014

First published in Great Britain in ebook format by HarperImpulse 2014



A catalogue record for this book is
available from the British Library

ISBN: 978-0-00-811346-9



Automatically produced by Atomik ePublisher from Easypress

*This book is dedicated to my wonderful critique partners, Pamela Hearon, Abby Niles, and Cynthia D'Alba. Without their encouragement and feedback, I would have never made deadline or spotted the weak points in my writing. Ladies, I love you.*

*And to my incredible editor Charlotte Ledger and the entire team at Harper Impulse, who helped me bring this series to the world, I give many, many thanks and chocolate kisses because, hey, chocolate kisses!*

*To all of my friends and family who put up with me while writing and encouraged me in the process, you guys rock! Cindy H., Cindy S., Christy, Tammatha and all my furry friends, too. Don't know what I'd do without your support.*

*Also, I dedicate this story to Felicia Day, simply for being an excellent geek ambassador for women. I doubt Spider could have existed without you first paving the way.*

*Finally, to my loyal readers — this one is for you. I hope you enjoy it!*

# Chapter 1

Oh yeah. She was gonna kill that mutt when she got her hands on him. And the cat too – just because.

Emma "Spider" Fisher rattled the locked doorknob one more time and glared at the animals watching her from the other side of the front window. Costello, the dog, panted happily and gave her a tongue-lolling, open-mouthed grin. Abbott, the cat, stood in the bay-window beside him, watching her with disinterested, narrowed eyes, as if she were the stupidest human he'd ever met – a distinct possibility.

"Ugh!" She rattled the front doorknob again and slapped the doorframe. Yeah, as if that would make it open.

It was the morning after her first night of house-sitting for Zach and Hannah, and she'd already locked herself out. Correction: one of the dogs had escaped the fence, she'd given chase in her jammies, and when she'd ran back to call for help after not being able to catch Charlie, Costello had bumped shut the door she'd left open. Locking her out. Without a key. Without a phone. Without a hope of not being killed by her boss when he returned from his honeymoon.

His beloved blind dog had disappeared after she'd chased him into some trees on the other side of the street. No telling where Charlie was now. God forbid, he could be lying dead on the highway. Might have fallen down a well somewhere. Joined a gang. Who knew?

In fact, who knew a blind dog could run so darn fast to begin with? She'd bet that dog had some cheetah in his genes.

Heaving a half-laugh, half-sob, she turned and slid down the door until her bottom met the cold concrete of the front doorstep. A quick scan of the other houses and manicured lawns lining the quiet subdivision was no comfort. Well, maybe it was. No one seemed to peek out of curtains to witness her humiliating predicament, although she'd have to start pounding on doors soon to see if someone would let her use their phone.

Who would she call? One of the so-hot-they-could-melt-her-panties-off guys she worked with? She groaned.

This could *not* be happening to her.

A flash of brown movement to her left caught Spider's attention and sent her heart thumping wildly against her ribcage again.

Charlie was sniffing the grass and following an invisible trail beside the sidewalk in front of the house. Near the freaking road! Uttering a squeak, Spider sprang to her bare feet and hurried down the driveway, muttering "owww" and "ouch" every time she stepped on a rock or something sharp in the grass.

She had a hard-and-fast policy against swearing, but she was seriously reconsidering that rule this morning.

"Charlie!" Her voice carried down the street. She clicked her tongue. "Com'ere boy!"

The dog lifted his head but kept prancing forward as a car came around the curve toward him. Panic seized her chest, releasing its grip only when the vehicle slowed and turned down a side street. The too-smart-for-his-own-good canine perked his ears up and looked in that direction. Ohmygosh, he was blind and following sounds. She had to catch him. She *had* to. If he got out of the subdivision and found a main road—

She whistled and jumped up and down, hoping the noise would divert his attention. "Charlie!"

He turned and took three slow steps toward her.

"Good boy!" She whistled again and patted the front of her thighs.

The long-legged retriever mix lowered his head, wiggled his raised butt, barked, and darted in the opposite direction.

"No, no, no!" Spider gave chase. "Charlie!"

He thought they were playing a game. Oh, for the love of—!

At least he was running in circles, not straying outside the neighbourhood. She had no idea how long they ran up and down the suburban street lined with a mixture of classic Georgian, English cottages and modern houses. It was mid-morning, and no one had come outside to see what she was causing a ruckus about. Geez. She didn't know if that was a good thing or a bad thing. What kind of neighbours were these?

"Char...Char...Charlie!" Winded, she had to slow down until she was barely moving at all. Hands on her thighs, leaning over, she watched, helpless, as Charlie plowed headfirst into a neighbour's bushes. Startled, he hunched low and took slow, careful steps around the hedge. His tongue dangled out of his mouth, but otherwise he looked ready to resume his marathon sprint. What the heck did Hannah feed that dog? Crack-cocaine?

One step. Two steps. Spider inched closer. Charlie turned, and she used all of her reserves to leap toward him.

Yes! Their bodies collided, and she rolled with him onto the grass, the forty-pound dog using her as his personal cushion – not that she cared. Not as long as she had a tight grip on him.

She laughed in triumph and then groaned when a wet tongue found her mouth. Ewww! Disgusting. Doggy slobber. So gross.

It took a few more minutes of her wrangling him on the neighbour's lawn to get into a position where she actually could pick him up. New rule. The dogs were going to wear their leashes twenty-four seven while they were under her watch.

She'd once thought she might like to have a dog, but uh-uh. Not anymore. Cats were so much easier than dogs.

The two of them lumbered back to the house and collapsed together inside the fenced yard. Oh, thank heaven. Now she just had to figure out how to get back inside the locked home she was supposed to be protecting.

Chest heaving, she sprawled on the grass for a few minutes, thinking about it.

Man, she had to pee.

Pushing herself up on her elbows, she considered each of the windows. She'd already checked most of them. Her gaze fell on one. The bathroom. Had she locked it back after cracking it open last night when someone whose name rhymed with Costello had pooped mushy stuff all over the floor?

She made a mental note to never give him part of her burrito again. Ever.

Struggling to her feet, she glared at Charlie as she made her way to that side of the house. He was happily prancing about the yard again as if the past hour had never happened. Insane dog.

Spider nearly burst into tears when she saw through the pane that the window wasn't latched. Yes! She pushed it up as far as she could, lifted herself up, and…

A pulsating siren startled her so much she squealed and fell backwards, landing flat on her butt in the grass.

"Oh, no, no, no." The house's high-tech smart alarm system was programmed to automatically arm itself after fifteen minutes if the doors and windows remained inactive. Zach had warned her about it at least a dozen times. It was a new system he was testing for clients of his private security firm.

It took Spider a few tries to pull herself up so her waist was aligned with the windowsill. A pair of almond-shaped eyes were there waiting for her when she did. Perched on the sink, Abbott's black and white feline body was drawn back and ready to spring as he stared at the opening in the window.

"No!" Spider yelled at him as she grappled to lift her left leg up. "Don't even think about it, mister."

With a growl, the cat took a leap in the opposite direction and darted through the bathroom doorway as she managed to get her leg over the windowsill. She was half-in and half-out. Basically. Almost. Her foot was inside the bathroom anyway. That was progress.

"Hello?" a man's deep voice called from not too far away. "Everything okay back there?"

Oh, for the love of Pete.

Straddling the window, Spider wiggled, trying to swing her other leg over and into the bathroom. Much harder to do than she'd expected. Her left side was pressed to the pane of glass on the outside of the house. No matter how hard she pushed, she couldn't get the window to raise high enough to let her manoeuvre inside.

The house phone began ringing and seconds later, the alarm stopped. Well, that was something at least.

Furry legs grabbed onto Spider's calf inside the house.

"Hello?" the man called again.

"Uh, yeah! We're okay." Still trying to shove the window up, she glanced down and saw Costello humping away at her leg.

*You've got to be kidding me.*

She tried to jostle the dog off, which only managed to get her stuck in a more awkward position. Uh. She was wedged in there pretty good now.

The back fence moved inward. Spider reached a hand out and screamed, "Don't let the dog out!"

A man she didn't recognize grabbed Charlie's collar just as the dog ran toward the gate. That mutt must have some superpower for detecting openings he couldn't see. She'd swear her life on it. Her body sagged against the window frame with a loud sigh of relief that he hadn't escaped again.

The stranger snapped the gate shut behind him and gave Charlie a generous rub on both ears. Spider snorted when Charlie lapped the man's face with his tongue. Some guard dog he was.

"Are you sure you don't need help?"

Seriously? He wanted to help her *now*?

The guy lifted his delicious green gaze, which widened when it found her. He swore. "Are you stuck in the window?"

She stifled a groan. He would have to be a total hottie, wouldn't he?

*Please, someone shoot me now.*

***

Noah West rubbed the playful dog behind its ears and considered the sight before him.

Young woman, scantily dressed. Half-in, half-out of the window at a house he knew she didn't live in.

He probably should have called the cops like he'd almost done when he'd looked out the window and seen the unfamiliar redhead chasing the dog up and down the street. He'd been sleeping when he'd heard someone yelling "Chaaarrrlie!" over and over outside his bedroom window. By the time he'd fumbled into his jeans and found a shirt, his neighbour's alarm had been shrieking out the formula for a migraine.

He lifted a hand and scratched at the heavy stubble on his cheek.

He'd had a late night – something that was becoming more and more common lately – or else he wouldn't have been home right now. He *wished* he hadn't been home right now.

For one, his house gave him the creeps, and he wasn't sure whether the sounds he'd been hearing, the objects he'd seen moving, meant he was roommates with Casper the not-so-friendly ghost. There was always a logical explanation for that stuff, but until he figured out what it was he preferred to avoid the place. For another, he needed to be working right now, not playing hero to a young damsel-in-distress.

He cleared his throat and approached cautiously. She'd probably locked herself out, but you never knew.

"Name's Noah. I live across the street."

Her body was shaking unnaturally, as if she were having spasms or doing something really, really naughty with that windowsill. He was afraid to ask.

"Spider."

He jerked back. "Where? What kind?"

"No, my name is Spider. I'm a friend of Zach and Hannah's. I'm house-sitting, and I got locked out."

He hurried over and shoved the window further up, giving her some extra space to move. Through the opening, he spotted a furry blond mutt humping her other leg.

A startled bark of laughter escaped his control. The girl – Spider – narrowed her eyes at him before manoeuvring the rest of her body through the widened opening. She tumbled onto the floor with a thump and a squeal.

"You okay?"

She lifted a hand and waved back at him dismissively as she found her feet and scurried out of the room. A few seconds later, the ringing telephone stopped. He could hear her talking, but he couldn't make out what she said.

The blond mutt's head popped up in front of him before he could lower the window again. Weird-looking dog, but she sure was cute. He reached a hand up to pet her, but the creature growled and showed a long snout full of some serious-looking teeth.

Whoa. The window slid down with a hiss as Noah jerked his hand back and let it fall. The dog's barking grew muffled as the animal disappeared into the house.

The back door swung open, and the ginger-haired girl poked her head out. "I'm fine. Everything's fine. Thanks for your, um, help."

He nodded and tried not to stare at her shapely legs when she stepped onto the back deck. She was only wearing skimpy shorts and a tank top that left little to the imagination. Full, perky breasts pressed against the light green shirt that read "Gamers do it all night." He focused on her feet. Blue toenails. That was kinda hot.

"Excuse me, sir," a gruff voice called out. "Do you live here?"

Noah turned and saw a uniformed officer pushing his way through the fence. He reached and constrained the other dog before it had a chance to get out again.

The gray-haired cop's face was set in grim, stern lines as he approached, one hand hovering over the gun holster at his hip.

"Eeek!"

Both men turned toward the woman who'd made the sound.

"Emma?" the officer asked.

She was doing her best to cover her front with one arm while her other hand tugged the hem of her shorts down. "Hi Jack. How's it going?" She fidgeted from one foot to the other.

Emma? He thought she'd said her name was Spider.

The officer returned his confused look to Noah. He unsnapped his holster. "This guy bothering you?"

Noah released the dog and stepped back. Last thing he wanted was to give the officer more cause for concern.

"No!" The girl risked a step forward. "He's a neighbour. He came over to help." She heaved a sigh. "I got myself locked out and the alarm went off when I was crawling through the window and—"

The officer hiked a thumb in Noah's direction. "This his house? Does your daddy know you're here?"

"What?" She shifted a look between the two men. "No. I'm house-sitting for my boss. He just got married and is on his honeymoon." She gestured toward Noah and spoke her words slowly. "This man is their neighbour. He came over to help. I already told you that."

Officer Jack settled both hands on his hips, his lips twitching as his gaze looked her up and down. "Got yourself locked out, huh?"

"*Please* don't tell my dad."

"I gotta call this in, kiddo. You know that."

"Yeah, but do you have to mention my name?"

Noah hooked his thumbs on his belt loops and hung back. If he hadn't thought the situation interesting before, he was fascinated now.

The officer shook his head, but smiled. "Alright, verify the homeowner's information for me, and I'll *try* to keep your name out of it."

She rattled off a few details about Hannah Dawson – now Hannah Collins – while the officer scribbled them down. It wasn't anything Noah didn't already know. Hannah was a pretty nurse who'd lived here for about a year. Her then boyfriend – husband now – had moved in a couple of months ago.

The cop glanced up and returned his attention to Noah. "I'm gonna need to see your identification, son."

Clenching his jaw muscles, Noah pulled out his wallet and handed over his driver's license. He'd had the ID updated a few weeks ago. He matched the dark-haired picture of himself perfectly, which was a good thing since he'd had blond highlights and glasses in the last one. While the officer jotted down his information, Noah glanced toward the girl. He tried to guess her age. Late teens, he thought. Cute. Had great legs. Probably jailbait, knowing his luck, because he didn't mess with teenagers.

He realized in a fleeting moment of self-consciousness that he was acting like a true male member of the West family, trying to judge how easy it would be to take a woman who'd caught his eye to bed. Well, so what? Something about her eyes had him rethinking she was at least early twenties. Not jailbait at all. This was a woman who stirred his blood, and there was no fighting heredity. Noah intended to find out more about her.

The officer grunted and handed the ID back. "Thanks for coming to help, Mr. West. Why don't I walk you back to your house now?"

Not that he needed the escort. Didn't take a genius to read this situation.

Noah tipped his head toward the young woman anyway. "I live in the two-storey stone house if you need anything while you're here. See you around, Spider."

She flashed him an awkward wave. "Seriously, thanks for your help!"

Officer Jack followed him to the edge of the yard before saying, "You lived around here long, Mr. West?"

Noah sighed and turned to face the man. Last thing he needed was to capture the attention of a snooping cop. "No. I'm renting the house across the street. Moved in a couple of months ago."

The officer squinted against the early afternoon sun. "Tell you what. That young woman in there is special. Make sure you don't get any ideas while she's here. Got that?"

"Sure." He held back the smile that would have betrayed the fact that it was too late.

"Good."

The officer started to move away, but Noah couldn't resist asking: "Her dad is a cop, right?" It was the only thing that made sense. It would be a helluva reason to keep his distance, but, then again, he loved a good challenge.

Jack nodded, but a smile played at his mouth as he opened his car door and looked back at Noah. "Not just any cop. Chief of police. You have a good day now, you hear?"

# Chapter 2

"Let's see how long it takes to crack their system with this baby." Smiling, Spider tapped ENTER on the script she'd spent the afternoon writing.

Leaning back on the sofa, she watched the computer code whiz past on the screen. A glance at her watch sent the thrill of victory racing through her veins. Thirty minutes earlier than she'd expected – new record. "Who's awesome?" she asked the cat stretched out on the floor watching her. "I am. Uh huh. That's right."

Call her crazy, but it looked like Abbott rolled his eyes before he looked away. His tail thumped against the carpet. Translation in kitty speak: *You're a loser.*

"Don't be a hater, cat. You know I'm awesome."

Well, except for that whole getting locked out of the house thing.

Spider loved her job, but it was still weird to think that Zachary Collins had hired her in the first place. She'd gone on the job interview to meet him and ask for his autograph more than anything. Not only had the gorgeous star of *The Psychic Detective* – now a private security guru – hired her to work as the cyber security specialist for his firm, but she was sitting on his sofa right now, drinking diet soda and about to log into Days of Adventure to kill some trolls on his big-screen TV.

Life was good.

Setting the laptop on the coffee table in front of her, she fired up the game console she'd brought with her. It only took a few minutes more while she waited for the multi-player game to connect to grab her controller and slip on the headset she used to swap insults and accolades with her guild.

No one in the house yelled for her to get the phone, do the dishes, or grab the laundry out of the dryer. There was no loud shouting at the football game on the television or chatter from the poker game going on upstairs.

Just sweet, awesome silence.

Oh yeah, she could get used to this.

Just as she was logging into her account, a knock at the door interrupted her. Yeah, but no; she wasn't expecting visitors, and that's how she wanted to keep it.

The pounding on the door intensified.

Yanking off her headset, she hurried over and peeked out. Kellan Murphy stood on the front porch.

She punched in the code to disarm the alarm and flung open the door. "What are *you* doing here?"

A brown blur whizzed past her, but Kellan snatched the dog's collar before he could escape. Again.

Spider sighed. "You heard what happened, didn't you?"

Charlie jumped up against the blond hunk in greeting, and Costello meandered over to inspect their visitor before sitting on the man's feet. Kellan, another private investigator employed by Zach's firm, glanced up from petting them, his forehead crinkled. "No. Something happened?"

Feigning ignorance, she lied. "No. Nothing happened." With a shrug, she shut the door behind him. "Nothing at all. Just me and the boys hanging out. Getting lots of work done. That's all."

He arched a brow. "Uh huh." His gaze dropped to her shirt, and he curled his sinfully gorgeous lips. "That's a good one; I like that one."

She glanced down at the royal-blue t-shirt she wore that declared: "Dear Math, I'm not a therapist. Solve your own problems." It was one of her favourites.

"So, something happened?" Kellan asked, sauntering into the room.

"Guess what?" She pointed out the laptop. "I wrote a script for our new client. It'll keep trying to log into their website with randomly-generated usernames and passwords. I should be able to run a report and tell them by tomorrow how strong their online security is, and how to fix whatever holes I find in there."

"Sounds great." The tall, muscular Adonis walked over to the couch, glancing around as if he was looking for evidence. He plopped onto the cushion beside where she'd been sitting and put his heels up on the coffee table. "So you want to order a pizza or something. Maybe watch a movie? I think *The Lord of the Rings* trilogy is on-demand."

Watching *LotR* with an Adonis would normally not be an unappealing way to spend the evening – but seriously? Spider resisted the urge to stomp her foot and scream, "No! This is my time! My privacy!"

Instead, she crossed her arms and pursed her lips. Her voice was laced with accusation when she said, "You stopped by to check on me."

His hands lifted. "Can't I stop by and check on a friend?"

"You've never stopped by my house and checked on me before."

"Well, I mean, you live with your dad…" He shifted uncomfortably. "Spider, come on. You're a young girl who—"

"I am twenty-five-years-old!" She stomped her foot. "All of you treat me like I'm twelve or something."

Each one of the hottie private eyes employed by the agency – Zach, Brian, Kellan, E.J. and even the freelancers – acted as if she was his little sister instead of another kick-butt and take-names colleague. Alexandra did too, but at least Spider had never had a crush on the woman. Truth be told, she'd always wanted a sister, so she didn't mind Alexandra's overprotectiveness quite as much as the men's.

And to be fair, there was a lot about her they didn't know. A lot that she didn't want them to know.

Kellan eyed her foot meaningfully. "Whoa. Don't get offended. It just means we all care about you. Besides, you weren't around when someone tried to kidnap Abbott and Costello. Hannah has a lot of money. You can never be too safe."

Spider tapped her foot, wishing he would leave. Her Adonis wasn't making her feel any better.

"Call me crazy, but I doubt Zach or Hannah would have left their beloved pets in my care if they thought I was incompetent." That reminded her: she'd forgotten to feed the animals their lunch. D'oh! She needed to make notes or something, like putting a reminder in her phone. Her breath came out in a huff as she moved toward the kitchen.

Kellan sighed and rolled to his feet. "Alright, I'll leave, but I'm gonna stop by every now and then. That's just a fact."

"Yeah, and I'm sure Brian and E.J. will be stopping by, too." She jerked the plastic container for the dog food out of the cabinet with more force than was necessary. Empty. Seriously?

As the only child of a cop, she'd grown up with a hundred brotherly types in the men who worked with her dad. She'd been hoping to escape all that brotherly concern with the men *she* worked alongside. Guess she'd been wrong.

Why wouldn't people just give her some credit already? She could take care of herself, and a cat and two goofy dogs too.

"I'll make sure no one stops by but me," Kellan assured her. "Although, I think Dylan is coming to spend the weekend with Alexandra soon, so Zach's little brother might drop in. I can't make any promises there."

Since Spider had an even bigger crush on Dylan Collins than she did on Kellan, she wouldn't mind a quick visit from Alexandra's hunky boyfriend. He didn't treat her with the same kid gloves everyone else did. Plus, she didn't stand a chance with him, and that somehow made him … less intimidating. Not that she stood a chance with any of them, but still.

The new forty-pound bag of dog food was heavy as she dragged it out of the pantry. A ripping sound preceded a rush of pellets scattering across the tiled floor in every direction. Darn it! She frowned and scrunched her shoulders as Charlie and Costello charged into the kitchen and gobbled up food like they were starving vultures. Abbott sprang out of somewhere and started playing soccer with the hard nuggets.

Spider took a deep breath and looked at the man watching. Amusement lit up his eyes. She pointed at the floor. "To be fair, that could have happened to anyone."

"Yep." He tiptoed around pieces. "Know where the broom is?"

She gestured to a closet. He was closer to it anyway.

Fifteen minutes later, she closed the door behind him, reset the alarm and slid down the back of the door.

She could do this. Right?

***

A loud knock jolted Noah out of the doze he'd finally succumbed to. Blinking away the blurriness from his eyes, he glanced at his clock. Eleven p.m. The only light in the room was the flickering of his television.

*Thump.*

He glanced up at the ceiling, his heart pumping like a hydraulic piston in his chest.

It was happening again.

*Thump.*

His hands squeezed the edges of the recliner. Ignoring it wouldn't make it go away, or at least it hadn't the other times. He sucked in a breath and cold air froze his lungs. When he exhaled, a white puff dissipated in front of his face.

*Thump.*

He forced himself to his feet. Even though he knew what it would read, he checked the thermostat anyway. It was still set on seventy degrees, but the room felt like a meat locker. Even the slick wood of the baseball bat he'd propped against the wall was cold to the touch, and—

*Thump. Thump.*

At the sound, he spun. This time it had come from downstairs. The kitchen? His feet felt heavy as he moved slowly in that direction.

He kept his voice loud and confident as he called out, "Hello?"

No answer.

The volume on the television jumped to a deafening level. The alarm clock in his study began screeching like a banshee. The clanging of metal-on-metal made it sound as if a marching band had invaded the kitchen. Covering his ears, he peeked into the room. All the pots and pans hung on the rack swayed to an unseen force, violently knocking into one another.

The kitchen door slammed shut in front of him. Noah was plunged into darkness as the television shut off, and seconds later the alarm clock did the same. Only a slither of moonlight penetrated the black room.

His heartbeat struggled to calm itself as he looked around. Nothing but shadows.

Soft, feminine whispering teased his ear, but for the life of him, he couldn't make out the words.

The television flickered to life again at normal volume. Warmth chased the chill on his arms away.

As quickly as it had started, it was over.

After settling the baseball bat back in its spot against the stairs, he hurried over to one of the video cameras he'd set up the day before. It still flashed red, so he removed it from the tripod and carried it into his study. He removed the memory card and inserted it into his laptop, wondering if he'd captured anything through the night vision lens.

"Come on," he muttered as he waited for the video to pull up. Rubbing at his eyes, he set the video to play at a fast speed. A pixilated version of himself sank into the chair and changed positions a few times before he jerked awake. He slowed the speed so he could watch, listening for the activity.

It was all there, caught on tape.

Noah ran a hand down his face, a breathy chuckle of laughter escaping his chest. There it was, all on tape this time. He wasn't crazy. Holy mother. He wasn't imagining it.

After rewinding the video, he stuck in earphones and jacked up the volume near the end. The soft whispers were audible. Barely.

Two explanations seemed plausible.

Either someone was pranking him, or there was some natural phenomena causing the lights and power to malfunction in the old house. Could be some kind of electromagnetic anomaly in the area that had caused his electronics to go haywire and the pots and pans to act possessed. Those type of things messed with brain waves, too. Some of the things he'd seen could have been hallucinations.

An electrician was supposed to come out tomorrow and check the wiring. That would probably explain things.

A bark outside drew his attention.

He groaned and pushed to his feet. "Don't tell me she's lost the dog again." As he peeked through the blinds, he saw the ginger-haired girl being pulled into his yard by not one, but two dogs. At least she had them on leashes; although, from the look of things, it wouldn't take much for them to get free.

They stopped at the edge of his front yard, and one of the dogs scrunched into the required catcher's position to do his business. Thankfully, the girl pulled out a bag to pick it up.

And just his luck that they'd stopped under the streetlight.

He flipped the light switch off, raised the blinds and reached for the Nikon he had set up on a tripod. The camera angled until she was in the frame, zoomed in and captured a few shots. Might come in handy later.

The zoom tightened on her face as he focused the lens.

He hadn't realized how pretty she was until now. Oh, he'd noticed she had a great body. He whistled. Girl was a looker that was for sure. And not a girl at all. She was a young and sexy woman. Exactly his type, but, then again, every woman was his type.

"Darling, too bad your daddy's the chief of police. We sure could've had fun together."

The short mutt lifted its head and glanced toward the window. Noah muttered a curse and froze. The woman – Emma – chewed at her lower lip and glanced around before bending to pick up the dog's poop.

The phone behind him rang, and dread settled in his gut. Noah had a feeling he knew who it was, so he reluctantly tore himself away from the window to answer it.

"Hello?"

"Just checking in, West," a raspy voice drawled. "I was starting to think you were avoiding my calls."

"I told you. I prefer email."

"Haven't gotten any of those from you either. You've been there more than a month. I expected to have something by now. Talk to me."

Noah closed the blinds and flipped the lights back on. His gaze fell on the collection of photos pinned to a corkboard. Photos of Hannah Dawson and Zachary Collins getting in their cars, walking their dogs and moving around inside their house across the street. Alexandra King and Zach Collins' younger brother sitting at a table at one of those sidewalk cafes.

"Collins just got married," Noah said. "He's on his honeymoon. I've been tailing King today."

The gruff voice swore. "You got anything yet?"

"No."

"If Collins isn't there—"

"So what?" Noah reviewed the pictures he'd just shot on his camera. "Give me another week or two. I'll have enough evidence to make you happy."

"We're paying you a hell of a lot of money to prove those two so-called psychic detectives are frauds. You'd better get us something soon."

The other man abruptly ended the call, but it was the paused image on his laptop that gave Noah more reason to worry. He didn't have time to figure out what was going on in this house.

He had a job to do, and the sooner he finished it, the sooner he could address the problems in this house and get a decent night's sleep.

Rubbing his eyes, he risked another look through the blinds. Emma – he preferred the name to Spider – and the dogs were still lingering in his yard. It was late. Dark. Didn't the young woman know it wasn't smart to be walking the dogs alone at this hour? Granted, it was a nice neighbourhood, but … he couldn't help but think about his sisters doing such a ridiculous thing.

With a harsh curse, he reached for the keys sitting on the desk. It would do as an excuse to go outside and see that she made it safely home.

He pretended not to notice her as he stepped out on the front porch, trotted down the steps and headed for his car. Good thing his garage was still filled with moving boxes. Otherwise, he'd have parked inside. The dogs began barking and Noah lifted his gaze in their direction, acting surprised to see them.

Strange thing was, both dogs and the woman were looking up at his house. Emma smiled, directed an awkward wave toward his second floor, and then tugged the animals back before dropping her gaze to where he stood. "Come on, guys. Our night time walk is over. Shhh!"

Noah followed her gaze up toward his bedroom window.

"Sorry," she called, drawing his attention back to her. "We didn't mean to bother you or your, er, wife."

The irony of that idea tugged at his mouth. "I'm not married."

"Oh." She glanced back toward the window. "Girlfriend?"

A chuckle tickled his windpipe. "Don't have one of those either."

If this was her idea of fishing to see if he was attached, she was doing a lousy job of being subtle.

She bit at her lower lip. "Point is, we didn't mean to bother you and your friend then." She turned and practically had to drag the growling dogs after her. "Come *on*."

Noah scratched at his neck and followed her. "Wait. What do you mean, me and my friend?"

With a nod toward his house, she seemed more preoccupied with the dogs than him now. "The woman in the window."

He jerked his gaze toward the upstairs bedroom window. The light was on. What the—? His muscles froze, rooting him to the spot. He hadn't been in the room tonight. No reason for that light to be on.

All thought of his new red-headed neighbour fled his mind as he bounded up the stairs and back into his house. This could be his best chance to catch the person who'd been messing with him.

But there was no one in the bedroom, nor any other room in the house. He searched them all. Nothing.

The house was empty.

# Chapter 3

Mornings sucked.

After letting the dogs out, Spider lumbered like a zombie from the kitchen back to bed and groaned when she saw that it was an hour-and-a-half earlier than she'd planned to get up. Only six hours since she'd fallen into blissful slumber. She faceplanted into bed and pulled the sheets over her head.

*Working from Zach's house. Can set own hours. Sleeeeep.*

A heavy weight settled against the back of her neck. She was drifting toward unconsciousness so she ignored it until, a few seconds later, the sheet tugged at her hair, exposing part of her face to cold air and the light in the room. A tiny claw nicked her scalp.

"Stop it, cat!" She swatted over her shoulder and connected with fur. "Y'all are seriously messing with my beauty sleep," she grumbled and dug deeper into the pillow.

The cat's weight shifted away from her.

She started to doze, but a sharp prick at her ear followed by "Mreeeoow" shocked her awake again.

Spider flung the sheets off her head and glared at the animal. "You have a litter box! What do you want?"

Abbott shifted on his front paws on the pillow beside her, watching her with big, rounded kitty eyes that rivaled those of Puss in Boots. "Meow."

"You're hungry?"

He stood and brushed against her. "Meow."

She glanced at the clock. "According to the note Hannah left, it's not time for you to be fed yet."

"Meow."

"Will you let me get some more sleep if I feed you?"

"Mrreeow."

"Don't make a habit of this, cat." With heavy-lidded eyes, Spider padded into the kitchen and set the cat's food out. Charlie and Costello came running, and Spider shrugged. Why the heck not? After pouring them some food, she shuffled back to bed, nudging the bedroom door shut. Darn animals could entertain themselves for a while.

She glanced at the clock again before tugging the sheets over her face and snuggling into the pillows. Ah, sleep.

Her muscles relaxed as her mind sank into a comfy dream. A lake glistened beneath bright sunlight as birds chirped in the distance. Music and singing grew closer. Wearing one of his trademark suits and over-sized glasses, Elton John sat on the lounger beside her cooing out a song about unicorns and elephants – *Wait, what?* –while the hot neighbour from yesterday peeled his shirt off and dove into the gleaming water, revealing a set of abs so chiseled Michelangelo would have drooled.

The hottie from the lake surfaced right in front of her, slicked back his wet hair exposing arm muscles so defined she wondered if he was for real, and, smiling, asked her, "Do you wanna—?"

Spider's eyelids jerked open as the bed sheet pulled at her hair and slid toward her shoulder. Something sat on her feet, so she kicked toward it, hoping to dislodge whichever animal was making a nuisance of himself now.

And she'd been having such a delicious dream, too.

"Abbott!" She flung the sheets away from her, sat up, and glanced at the foot of the bed.

No cat. No dogs.

She blinked as she stared toward the door, which was still shut.

"Guys?" she whispered, and glanced around.

Something or someone had just tried to tug the sheets off her – right? She patted the bedding to make certain she was alone. Totally alone.

Hmmm. Dream? That kind of didn't make sense though. About as much sense as Elton John belting out a song about unicorns and elephants. Then again… She snickered and shook her head.

Sighing, she pushed the hair away from her face and decided she might as well get up. It was almost nine. Time to get up anyway.

She was wiggling her feet out from under the covers when the sheet she still held in her right hand ripped free of her grasp and landed in a heap at the end of the bed. Ripped. Right. Out. Of. Her. Hand.

And then she saw—

Holy crap!

Heartbeat racing to a near explosion, Spider screamed and bolted for the door, throwing it open and darting for the living room. Charlie and Costello started barking and nearly tripped her in the hallway as they ran like maniacs toward the room she'd just deserted. Abbott sprang to his feet and disappeared into one of the rooms in the opposite end of the house.

Spider pounced onto the sofa, grabbed the phone and hugged a pillow to her chest as she stared in the direction from which she'd come.

The dogs were barking like a pack of wild things.

"Be careful!" she called out to them from where she huddled at the edge of the couch.

She punched in 9 and 1 to her phone, then hesitated. Dang it all, what if she was overreacting?

In what seemed like minutes but was probably only seconds, the two dogs quieted to a few huffs and came trotting down the hallway. Costello poked his head around the corner and looked at her as if he was thinking, "Exactly why were you screaming again?" Charlie sprinted toward her, leapt onto the couch, and began slathering her face with yucky dog kisses.

The pillow made a great shield against yucky dog kisses. "Was someone in there or what?"

Probably not, since no one had tried to kill her yet.

Costello jumped on the couch beside Charlie and panted hot, stinky breath in her face in reply. She pushed his nuzzle away.

Oh yeah. She was so not a dog person.

"You're right." She petted both dogs as she glanced wide-eyed down the hallway. Had she seen what she'd thought she'd seen? "I was probably dreaming or something."

Probably.

*Bam. Bam. Bam.*

She squealed and both dogs went berserk, jumping off the couch and charging towards the source of the noise – the front door. Her rib-cage almost broke from how hard her heart slammed against it. Heaven help her, she was going to have a heart attack before this day was finished. Hand to her chest, she followed the animals, nudging them aside so she could see who on earth had just bypassed the doorbell and banged on the door so darn early … and with such force. Was it The Hulk? Sheesh.

No, not the Hulk.

Hello! Hottie neighbour alert.

After hurriedly punching in the alarm's deactivation code, she jerked open the door and flung herself at Noah. "Thank goodness you're here!"

Charlie whizzed past, but Noah reached down with one hand, grabbed his collar and pushed him back into the house before he could get far. She seriously needed to remember that dog did that. Realizing her arms were still twined around the man's waist, she pulled back.

"I would have come sooner if I'd known I'd get that kind of a greeting." Bent over now, Noah scratched the dog behind his ears and didn't seem to mind in the least when Charlie slipped him some tongue.

Eww. Just eww.

"Would you please come in and check the bedroom for me?" She nudged Costello back with her foot and gestured down the hall. "I think someone might be in there."

"What?" Noah straightened and stepped inside, pushing the door shut behind him. "Where?"

She led him part of the way and then pointed out the room. "There."

"Stay here." He disappeared through the doorway, both dogs trotting after him. He finally reappeared, hands held out. "I don't see anyone." He checked the other rooms before declaring, "Nope. I don't see anyone else in the house."

She released her breath in a rush.

He stopped a few feet away from her, so close the scent of soap teased her nostrils. "What happened?"

With Noah so close, she was aware of how her nightshirt clung to her free breasts and even more aware she'd been having an inappropriate dream about him less than fifteen minutes ago. She crossed her arms, not that he hadn't already seen her in her pajamas, and shrugged. "I thought someone pulled the sheet off me while I was sleeping. I guess I was dreaming."

"Maybe." His forehead creased as he glanced back toward the bedroom. "It could have been one of the pets."

"No. They were shut out of the room." She shook her head. "Anyway, I'm sorry. Did you need something?"

His gaze fell to her chest before flicking back up to meet hers. Heat engulfed her face. Her tank top's statement "Gamers do it all night" probably seemed a little provocative. Yeah. She really should go put on some more clothes.

"I wanted to ask you about the woman you saw in my house last night."

"Oh." She lifted a hand and played with the end of her hair. "What about her?"

"Did you get a good look at her?"

"Why?" She smiled. Was he harboring a criminal or something? Trying to decide whether Spider had seen too much?

Her smile slid off her face. Or he could be one of those crazy men who kidnapped women and kept them chained in the attic. She took a step back.

"This is going to sound strange, but there shouldn't have been anyone in my house last night. Are you sure you saw someone?" He watched her carefully, drawing her attention to the vibrant green of his eyes, shadowed by dark lines underneath. Even darker hair fell in shaggy waves that framed his face. He had that McDreamy Patrick Dempsey haircut going on. Stubble highlighted a strong jawline and luscious mouth.

He looked hot, but edgy. Kind of dangerous.

Serial killer dangerous? The way her luck was going, probably.

"I could have been mistaken." But she wasn't. She remembered everything about the woman she'd seen. Young – college age, probably. Long, dark hair and a pretty face. She'd been wearing a jean jacket over a white shirt. Something Spider wished she was wearing right about now. "Um, do you mind if I go throw some clothes on?"

"Go ahead."

She glanced at the dogs and wondered how exactly her boss Zach communicated with them – apparently he could, being a pet psychic and all. Costello lifted his beady little eyes towards her, and she tried sending him the thought: *Attack him if he follows me. Good boy.*

Costello opened his mouth and grinned.

She held up her finger and managed a smile for their guest. "Give me one minute."

Hurrying into the guest room, she shut the door behind her. Abbott was sprawled on the bed. Wait – she could have sworn the cat had disappeared into the office on the other side of the house.

"How did you get in here?" She shook her head. "Never mind.

Safety in numbers. Don't move."

She yanked a pair of jeans and a *Captain America* t-shirt out of her suitcase and tugged them on as fast as she could manage. In case she got kidnapped, her cell phone was turned on for tracking purposes. The small pocket tools her dad insisted she keep with her made their way into her other pocket, just in case. He'd also given her a little stun gun to attach to her keychain—not that she had done it. What the heck had she done with it? No time to search. On the way out, she risked a glance in the mirror and paused. One side of her head boasted a tangled poof while the other looked as though she'd stuck her finger in a socket. Oh, geez. Had she really opened the door to someone with her hair looking like that? She ran a brush through it real quick, scooped the cat up and paced down the hall.

"If he tries anything, claw his eyes out," she whispered to Abbott, who growled back a response she hoped meant *"Consider it done."*

Noah glanced around the house he'd only been inside once, when he came over to introduce himself to his new neighbours, and whistled. For a guy who'd grown up in a trailer park, this sure seemed a nice place for a couple with no kids.

He'd found its previous sale listing online and memorized some of its stats during his initial research into Collins. Single-level updated traditional ranch with a little over three-thousand-square-feet, four bedrooms, three baths, a side-garage, and a sizable fenced backyard. That was on paper. In person, the home seemed even grander with its 10-foot ceilings, open floor plan, modern appliances and warm decor.

He'd been amazed to see a home across the street up for rent at a shockingly affordable price. The Buckhead community of Atlanta was where the wealthy lived, and Noah certainly wasn't wealthy enough to afford even this neighbourhood, which was on the lower end of the pricey scale. But he'd grasped the opportunity and had considered staying in the two-storey fixer-upper after his assignment was done because he'd gotten such a great deal on it.

But maybe not, considering the crap he'd been dealing with since he moved in and the probable reality that his neighbours were going to hate his guts when they returned home. He picked up a framed photo of Zachary Collins and his bride posing with their wedding party. Their perky house sitter stood in a blue dress beside a smoking-hot blonde and attractive black woman on the other side of Hannah. His gaze skirted over the other women and stopped on the young redhead.

Anything wedding-related always gave him the creeps, but looking at this picture stirred an unfamiliar feeling in his chest. Was it guilt? Or envy? Sleep deprivation must be making him crazier than he'd realized.

"I had that picture framed as a surprise for when they get back," Emma said, catching *him* by surprise.

Some of the tension left his shoulders after seeing she'd covered up. She was even more distracting today than he remembered – and he'd remembered a lot. Hell if he knew why, but she'd been on his mind more than seemed reasonable for someone he'd just met. On second thought, her impressive chest pushed against a *Captain America* shield now. The woman was blessed. Maybe that's why he couldn't stop thinking about her. The West men had always had a weakness for well-endowed women.

Feline grumbling came from the black and white cat she held, giving him a good excuse to look at something other than her. The creature eyed him with an unnerving stare. How many animals did Zachary and Hannah Collins own?

"This is Abbott," she said. "I can't remember if I introduced you to the dogs, but that chubby little guy is Costello and the one who keeps trying to escape is Charlie."

He glanced at the stout mutt. "That one is a boy? I thought he was a she."

"People always think that because he's so pretty."

"Are any of them yours?"

"Nope. Just pet-sitting." She stroked the top of the cat's head. "So… have you called the cops?"

His heart skipped a beat. "About what?"

"The mystery woman inside your house last night."

Oh. Right. He shrugged. "Nothing was taken. They probably wouldn't believe me."

He'd used the so-called mystery woman as an excuse to come over and break the ice with her. Find out more about her and her relationship to Zachary and Hannah Collins.

Find out more about *her*.

Noah's gaze strayed down the hall toward the bedroom she'd directed him to earlier. Her descriptions had been a little… spooky. That had been almost a play-by-play of what he'd experienced a couple of weeks ago when things had started happening at his new house.

He cleared his throat. "And you're sure you didn't see anyone earlier?"

She fidgeted with the squirming cat. "Well, I thought I saw—" She stopped herself. Shook her head. "No, I didn't."

"What did you think you saw?"

She reluctantly lowered the cat to the floor. "When the sheet was wafting through the air, I thought it was covering a person. You know, like I saw the form of a person underneath the sheet? But I was probably dreaming. It was only a second or two."

The walls seemed to shift and move around him as he struggled to remain steady on his feet. Exact same thing had happened to him a week ago. "Did you have your house alarm on?"

"Yep."

She probably had been dreaming, but…

Damn. What were the chances?

He noticed the laptop on the coffee table. "What time do you get off work?" Her eyes widened, so he clarified, "So, I can keep an eye out, make sure you get into the house okay."

"I'm actually working from home while I'm here. I doubt I'll be in and out very much." Her eyes widened again. "Except, you know, my boyfriend comes over a lot. Yeah. And friends. I'm hardly ever here alone. Lots of people would miss me."

"Miss you?" Hell, she had a boyfriend. That blew.

She flicked her hand and laughed. "You know. If I weren't here."

"And how long will you be house-sitting?"

"Why?"

"So I can keep an eye out. Maybe check in every so often and make sure everything is okay. I'm sure you were dreaming, but you can never be too careful these days." He pushed back the urge to ask about her boyfriend and if it was the guy he'd seen stop by last night. He knew when to keep his cards close to his chest.

"Well, Zach and Hannah are taking a long honeymoon. Three weeks. That's how long I'll be here." She winced and murmured "You idiot" so soft he almost didn't catch it.

Interesting. She didn't want him to know. Why?

"Three-week honeymoon? Must be nice." He forced a smile. Three weeks was going to make his job very difficult. "You must be really good friends with them for them to trust you with their house and pets that long."

"Zach is my boss, so he knows I'm dependable, I think."

Her boss.

Noah tried not to grin. Maybe he had a legitimate excuse to get to know Emma better.

"I didn't ask what Zach did for a living." Of course he already knew, but she didn't know that.

"Private security." She gestured to her laptop. "My specialty is cyber security. Easy enough to do from home."

"Sounds exciting." He had dossiers on all of Collins' employees, but he didn't remember hers. Either he was getting rusty, or there hadn't been anything in her file to interest him.

He was definitely interested now.

She shrugged and crossed her arms. "So what do you do, Noah?"

"Photography." He pulled out his wallet and retrieved one of his new business cards. "I'm starting a job teaching part-time at the art institute for the summer semester. That's why I moved here. Figure I can freelance from home, maybe set up a studio downstairs, teach at night."

It was all true, and he was glad not to have to lie to her about it. He was beginning a new chapter of his life, one that wouldn't involve shadowing people who faked disabilities to cash in on insurance companies. It hadn't been fully explained to him why the attorney of a man who'd been rejected a worker's compensation claim wanted so badly to prove Collins was a fraud, and quite frankly, Noah could care less. He couldn't wrap up this investigation into Emma's boss soon enough. It was his last case, and one he'd only taken after a great deal of coaxing.

His original plans after turning in his resignation had been to spend a month in Arizona trekking through the Grand Canyon and shooting landscapes to pad his portfolio. Instead, he was being paid a lot of money to spy on two so-called psychic detectives.

Resentment threatened to sour his mood again.

Glancing at Emma as she examined the card he'd given her, he reminded himself this job might not end up being so bad. Not if he played his cards right.

"A professor." She stared at his business card and gnawed at her lip. "Cool. Thanks."

"Guess I'd better run." He edged toward the door. "My cell phone number is on there. Feel free to call if you need anything, Emma."

"Spider."

"Oh, right. I thought I heard that officer call you Emma."

"Emma is my real name, but I prefer for people to call me Spider."

"Why?" He preferred Emma. It was a pretty name. Feminine. He liked it.

She scrunched her face. "Because it's an awesome nickname. Come on now."

Stepping through the doorway, he processed what he'd learned about her. Cyber security. Internet. The web.

Spider. He got it.

"Emma suits you better." Winking, he pulled the door shut behind him.

# Chapter 4

Spider waited for the Internet to connect and realized she'd been tapping her foot for – who knew how long?

"It hasn't taken this long before. What the frack?"

Costello's response was a cross between a whine and a grumble. The dog always insisted on lying as close to her feet as possible. Sooner or later, she was gonna step on him and then hello animal emergency room visit.

"And it'll be your fault, you silly dog." She nudged him with the toe of her Converse hi-tops as she rebooted the machine.

The plush sofa cushions tried to coax her into taking a nap, but her nerves were too on edge to cooperate. Her stomach churned with an urgent desire to find out more about Noah West. Even though her smart phone didn't have the juice she needed to do a thorough Internet search, she tried it anyway while she waited for her laptop to restart.

She scrolled through the recommended websites a simple search returned, frowning. "This is useless."

Tossing her phone aside, she hopped to her feet, sidestepped the dog, and began pacing. Noah could be everything he claimed to be, but serious doubt nibbled at that idea. Few people were all they claimed, and she still had the emotional scars to prove it.

*Don't think about the a-hole. He's ancient history now.*

Too late. Her mind reeled back to her ex and how horribly their relationship had ended.

After her mother had died when Spider was in the tenth grade, she'd relied upon her best friend Paul to be her rock, and he had been – that is, until he'd changed from her kind and supportive boyfriend into a cruel and domineering fiancé. She became so meek and shy, letting him dictate her every decision. He'd all but forced her to drop out of college because he wanted to take care of her. No job, he'd said, because she would be too busy being his wife and mother to the three kids he wanted. A proper little lady who wore dresses and never spoke out of turn. Practically a cardboard cutout.

One day she'd taken a look at the hot-pink-haired leather-clad female avatar she'd created in a game – which, let's be honest, had been her escape to keep her sanity intact, not to mention her one act of rebellion, since video games were not at all lady-like – and wondered why she couldn't become more like her avatar in real life. Strong. Independent. Unique. Maybe even a little bit snarky. The desire to become those things had grown and swelled until, one day, she impulsively dyed her hair purple and ditched her closet full of dresses for a wardrobe heavy on jeans, combat boots, and skin-tight t-shirts.

And she ditched Paul, too.

Both he and her father had accused her of having an early quarter-life crisis, but she hadn't cared. She'd felt more herself than she had in her entire life.

She enrolled in computer programming classes, because she'd always had a knack for computers. Afterwards, she got the job at Zach's agency. And she was almost two years into her five-year plan to save money, get her own house and finally enjoy her fought-for independence.

Patience was all she needed, and not to get mixed up with any serial killer types in the meantime. Because dying before she could get her own place would really, really suck.

Before she could change her mind, she snatched up her phone and punched in the non-emergency number for the Atlanta Police Department. When an officer she didn't recognize answered, she said, "I'm trying to reach Officer Jack Lanier. He's been working in Zone 2."

"He's on patrol and unavailable at the moment. Would you like to leave a message?"

"Sure. This is Spider, er, I mean Emma. Emma Fisher and—"

"The chief's daughter?"

Her shoulders sank on a sigh. "Yeah."

"No kidding. What'cha been up to, kiddo? Haven't seen you around here in a long time."

*Yeah, well, for one, I'm not a kiddo anymore.* "You know. I'm working now." She cleared her throat. "I'm sorry. I didn't catch your name."

"Pruitt. I come over to your house every now and then for games."

"Oh, right. Pruitt." She had no idea which officer was Pruitt. The parade of new and old uniforms that came through her house was never ending. "How have you been?"

"Good. Hold on. I'll patch you through to Lanier's cell phone. Take care, you hear?"

"Uh. Okay. Thanks." She blew out a breath, hoping word wouldn't get back to her father that she'd called into the station. Maybe this hadn't been the smartest idea she'd had.

"Lanier," a gruff voice growled.

"Hey, Jack, it's Emma Fisher."

"Hey, kiddo, what's up?"

Enough with the kiddo stuff. Geez. "I have a question. Remember the guy who was here?"

"Yeah, yeah. The neighbour. West. Looked like he'd been on a bender. Why? He been bothering you?"

"No." Sweet mercy, how did she say this without sounding like a paranoid recluse who spied on her neighbours? She swallowed.

"Did you run a check on him or anything?"

"Yeah, standard check. Came back clean."

"So, no priors or anything?" She drew out her words slowly.

"What's this about, Emma?"

Drawing in a deep breath, she plopped down onto the sofa again. Here goes. "It's just that, well, you know how you always hear after police catch someone for doing something awful, that people will say, 'I saw something suspicious, but I never called the cops'? And you wonder, why didn't they call the cops? They could have caught the creep already. Know what I mean?"

There were a few seconds of silence. "You saw this guy do something suspicious?"

"I don't know." She sank back onto the cushions. As precisely as possible, she described everything that had happened. "I know I saw a woman in that window, but he claims there was no one in the house. I have this weird feeling I need to tell someone about it."

"Probably worth checking out. Tell you what, I'll stop by there in a little while, take a look around. It's probably nothing, but you did the right thing telling me, Emma."

Her face felt warm to the touch as she covered it with her hand. Sometimes meek old Emma reared her head and filled Spider with self-doubt. Was she actually doing this? "I appreciate it, Jack; but do me a favour? Please be discreet in case I'm wrong. Please don't mention this to my father either."

Last thing she wanted was a visit from her overprotective old man during her vacation from him. There was a point at stake here: the point that she could very well take care of herself without needing him or anyone else to look after her.

They ended the call on Jack's promise to keep it their secret, and Spider's chest tightened. What if Noah West had already gotten rid of any evidence because of what she'd said? What if this made him so angry he came after her next?

Grimacing, she rushed to the window and looked at the house across the street. No car in the driveway. How long would it take the cop to get here?

Something wet and warm touched the back of her arm, and she screamed. Charlie shrank back and cowered away from where he'd licked her.

"Charlie! You scared me to death!" Hand over her heart, she reached out to pet the dog, even as she glanced at her laptop. She'd forgotten about her computer problems.

Focus on work. Don't fret over the possible serial killer next door coming to murder you.

Biting her fingernails, she tried to connect to the Internet again and… nothing.

After she double-checked her laptop's settings, she got up to reset the router. If that didn't work, she'd call and check to see if there was an outage in the area. Could be a good excuse to hit up the closest Starbucks and avoid a possible confrontation with Noah.

The computer pinged once, twice, three times. What?

The screen was black except for fast scrolling green characters. It shouldn't be doing that. Not at all.

She sat down and reached to hit the ESC key when she noticed what those green characters said.

HELP!

DANGER#

HELP!

DANGER#

HELP!

Shrieking, Spider scrambled up onto the couch cushions and clutched a pillow to her chest. Looking around, she only saw the cat stretched out in the bay window and the two dogs curled up on the floor, each staring at her as if she were a lunatic.

Heart pounding loud in her ears, she pointed at the screen. "That is not normal!"

She chanced a lean forward and watched the words continue to fly up the screen. The hair on her nape and arms lifted as a chill settled along her spine.

Enough of that. It was freaking her the heck out.

Her fingers trembled as she held the power button, forcing the computer to shut down. She waited ten seconds and rebooted the machine.

Don't overreact. There's a logical explanation for this.

Could be a virus. Some a-hole probably infected her machine and set the creepy message to display upon startup. Shaky laughter bubbled in her chest as she pressed her palms to her eyes. Of course. That had to be what it was. Not anything irrational, like a ghost or demon or anything. Only a virus.

She sagged against the cushions.

Well, crap. That could take a couple of days to clean up. She had work to do, not to mention she wanted to cyber-stalk Noah West. Photographer. Maybe professor. Possible serial killer.

The familiar chime and login screen popped up.

She input the information and everything came up normal, including the Wi-Fi this time.

"Weird."

A virus scan should have been her first order of business, but she shook her head instead, pulled up the Internet browser, and searched for *Noah West, Atlanta, GA* to see what hits it returned.

Absolutely nothing of any worth.

Facebook. Couldn't find him. Not on Twitter either. She ran through every social media site she could think of. Seemed kind of odd that a professional photographer couldn't be found on Instagram.

"Hmm. Should I be bad?" she asked the dog at her feet.

Costello lifted his head and looked at her. Charlie's doggy eyebrows shifted in concern as he released a long drawn-out sigh. He probably knew she was going to do it regardless of their opinions.

"You're right. I should totally do it, just this once. He could be a serial killer, after all."

Still, she hesitated before putting her fingers to work. Hacking without permission was plain wrong, and Spider didn't take that lightly.

But hello, possible serial killer!

"I'll only check the database we use at work," she told the dogs. "Promise."

Her hands flew over the keyboard, tapping for several minutes until she had accessed the professional database the firm subscribed to for access to public records, telephone information, social network hits and other useful goodies. She located a handful of people named Noah West in the agency's database. Noah's sinfully handsome picture stood out amongst the others.

Crystal green eyes stared back at her, and his handsome smile added a charming and intelligent character to those eyes she didn't see very often in the guys she knew. They drew her in, sending a thrill of excitement racing through her veins.

He had great eyes.

So what? Ted Bundy was handsome.

She shook herself and tried to remain objective.

Seriously. What human looked that good in his driver's license picture? That alone was suspect. She noted his age. Twenty-nine. Four years older than her. Huh. She would have put him in his mid-thirties.

She trusted Jack about Noah's lack of a criminal record, but you could learn a lot about a person from their public records. If they had any outstanding fines. Whether or not they paid their property taxes on time. Previous addresses.

So much information was out there.

Noah's address had changed about a month ago. Prior to that, he'd lived in Savannah. Actually, the guy seemed to move a lot. Six different addresses in the past five years.

A series of high-pitched beeps from her phone reminded Spider of the time. She closed out of all of the browser windows and pulled up the video chat on her computer.

Her boss and his new wife were honeymooning in Europe, and

Hannah had insisted on checking in on her animals once a day, usually around noon Atlanta time.

Hannah, being the overprotective pet mom she was, insisted on seeing the animals, too.

Spider initiated the chat, angled the camera toward Charlie, who was snoring away, and went in search of her feline charge.

Abbott was curled up on the pillow Spider had been using at night – seriously, cat? – and hissed when she scooped him up.

When she re-entered the room, she heard Hannah's voice cooing to Charlie. Costello had lumbered over to the coffee table and lifted himself to stand at the edge of the computer, his fluffy tail wagging.

"We're here," Spider called out. "I had to get the cat."

Hannah Collins' pretty face filled the screen. Her long, dark hair was pulled back and she was wearing a sage-green dress. "How are things going, Spider? Everything okay there?"

"Everything's great. We're fine." *Except for the dog escaping.* "How's your trip?"

"I love it here! London is amazing."

Spider didn't have many female friends… scratch that. She didn't have many friends, period. Not since she'd ditched her Emma persona. But she and Hannah had gotten along like comrades on the *Starship Enterprise* from the moment they'd met. She was still a little awed the woman trusted her enough to invite her to stay here for almost a month. Spider sagged against the cushions and listened to her friend share a few stories as unexpected tears welled behind her eyes. She didn't even know why. It just happened.

For some strange reason, Noah's question about why she preferred for people to call her Spider came to mind. It was because most people hated it. Most times, the nickname creeped them out because they were afraid of arachnids or they thought it was stupid. Either way, it kept them at a distance, kept them from asking questions about Emma, kept her from having to explain about Paul, which is how she liked it.

But some people like Hannah had tiptoed around the barrier and found her anyway. She *did* have friends, good friends, and they didn't care that she sometimes had blue hair and spouted sarcasm like a second language.

"Spider, are you okay?" Hannah asked.

Blinking and sitting forward, she used the excuse of having the cat in her lap. "Allergies, I think."

Hannah tilted her head and smiled. "I hate to run, but we've got reservations for dinner and I don't want to be late." Hannah made kissy sounds at Abbott, Costello and Charlie.

"Hannah, quick question."

"Sure."

"How well do you know your neighbour? Um, the guy across the street."

"You mean the hunk who just moved in?" Hannah wiggled her eyebrows. "I only met him once. Things have just been too crazy to welcome him properly. Why?"

Spider shook her head. "Just curious."

"I was surprised when he moved in," Hannah continued as she adjusted her earrings. "That house has been vacant for a long time. You know, all of the neighbourhood kids say it's haunted."

Spider sat forward. "Haunted?"

"I doubt it is. You know how stories get started. I'm sure Alexandra would have mentioned it if it was." Made sense, since Alexandra saw dead people.

"Yeah, you're probably right."

"Remember. You can text us if there's an emergency. Thanks again, Spider. Take care of my boys."

Spider logged out of the chat, but her mind was stuck on the information she'd attained. It funneled through the conversation she'd had with Noah, about the woman in the window, his claim no one should have been in the house, and what she'd experienced that morning in bed.

Holy corndogs.

Had she seen a *ghost*?

"Shut the front door!" Spider's fingers flew over the keyboard, this time typing in the address for Hannah's house. It took her only a few seconds using satellite maps to figure out the house number for Noah's place, and then—

Dozens of hits returned on that address, many from a ghost-hunting forum connected to an Atlanta-area paranormal group. The topics posted under the address sent ice-cold chills racing down her spine.

*GeorgiaHunter414: Snuck into abandoned house at this address one night. Saw some freaky stuff.*

*MysticMerlin: Got some creepy EVPs here. This place is truly HAUNTED!!*

A curse word she never used slipped out of Spider's mouth. Noah wasn't a maniac who chained up young women in his attic. He was being haunted!

***

Noah dropped his satchel in the doorway and threw his hands up in a gesture of resignation. His morning had been a waste. After the electrician had stolen a wad of money to tell him his house's wiring was absolutely normal, he'd followed Alexandra King to the airport, watched her board a plane to Colorado and tried to figure out what the hell he was going to do now that his second best source of information had left the city.

His eyes stung with exhaustion as he sank into the recliner in front of the TV. A few hours of sleep would be so damn nice right about now. Help him clear his head.

*Bam. Bam. Bam.*

Every muscle in his body clenched tight until he realized the banging sound wasn't coming from upstairs or the kitchen. Someone was at the front door. He really needed to get that doorbell fixed.

He swore and waddled to his feet.

A peek through the peephole gave him the back of a ginger-haired woman. He yanked open the door.

"Emma? Everything okay?"

She turned around, holding a tray full of cookies. The sight and smell of melted chocolate triggered his mouth to start watering. He swallowed.

"Oh, boy. You're gonna keep calling me Emma, aren't you? Fabulous." Her tone was as resigned as it was dry. She shook her head a little before lifting the tray and smiling. "I made you some cookies as a thank you for checking on me. I mean, they're only the kind out of a box that you stick in the oven for like, 10 minutes, but hey – cookies!" She lifted them higher.

"Come on in, and we'll eat a few." He opened the door wider and gestured her inside. His gaze skated toward the room he'd been using as an office and verified the door was closed. "I take it there haven't been any more scares today."

"Scares?" Her eyes widened.

"Yeah, remember this morning? You thought someone was in your room."

"Oh, right. No. No scares." Her gaze strayed toward the stairs. "This is an interesting house. Do you like it?"

It needed a paint job and lots of repairs, but he supposed it was all right. "I've lived in worse places." He couldn't remember if he'd left any revealing papers in the living room, so he touched her arm and guided her toward the kitchen. "I bought some milk yesterday. It'll go great with those cookies. Want some?"

"Sure." She followed him into the one room he barely used. "Look, Noah, I wanted to explain that—"

*Bam. Bam. Bam. Bam.*

They both froze. Noah's heart did a quick step around his chest until he realized it was again coming from the front door.

"Sorry. Be right back."

"Um, Noah—" She opened and closed her mouth.

"Give me a minute."

He peeked out and saw the same uniformed officer from yesterday standing on his doorstep. Pushing a hand through his hair, he opened the door. "Officer. What can I do for you?"

"Mr. West, I was wondering if I could take a look around."

"Oh?" He crossed his arms. "Mind if I ask why?"

"I told him about the woman I saw in your window."

Noah turned at Emma's rushed voice behind him.

"I'm sorry," she hurried to add. "I think I might have overreacted."

Noah clenched his jaw to keep from swearing. This was the last thing he needed. If he refused the officer's search, it would seem suspicious. If he allowed the man to look around, he'd expose his surveillance from the past month, the photos of the Collins and King pinned to a corkboard, which would look damn suspicious indeed.

He stepped aside. "Come on in, officer. Do whatever you need to do."

"I'm sorry," Emma said again, red-faced. She took a step forward. "Jack, you don't have to look around. I, um, tried to call and tell you not to worry about it."

Noah watched the older man consider the young woman, his right hand not far from the weapon holstered at his side. "I don't see what the harm is in checking things out. Do you, Mr. West?"

He shrugged and leaned against the wall. "Like I said, do what you need to."

The officer's gaze lifted toward the stairs. "I'll start upstairs."

"Help yourself."

A grimace tightened Emma's features as the officer walked past her. Her eyes pleaded an apology as she turned and followed the other man up the stairs.

Noah swore softly and ducked into the office, hiding the corkboard and moving his camera away from the window. He left the room's door open and hurried to find them. He couldn't remember if he'd left any documents or photos lying about upstairs.

The officer was thorough, opening closets, inspecting every room, even lowering the overhead attic door and climbing up to look around. When he came downstairs, he glanced into the office and went into the living room, and Noah hurried to distract them from the pile of documents on the table.

"As you can see, there's no one here." A cold sweat trickled down the back of his stiff neck. Emma stood beside the folder he'd left open on the end table last night, so he shifted to stand closer to her, to block the folder with his body. One of his business cards almost screamed "Noah West, Insurance Claims Investigator" in bold print on top of it. His investigation could be jeopardized if she – if anyone – saw it.

The officer grunted an agreement. "No signs of intrusion either. If anyone was in here last night, it's not because they broke in."

"I did see someone," Emma insisted. "She had long dark hair, was wearing a white t-shirt and a jean jacket. She looked my age, maybe younger."

Lanier frowned. "You know anyone like that, Mr. West?"

Noah shook his head, losing his balance under the movement. He sagged into the recliner behind him. A week ago, he'd dreamt about a woman matching that description exactly. He found it difficult to breathe as memories from the dream overwhelmed him. The dark-haired girl walking alongside the road, carrying a backpack. An old truck pulling up alongside her. A man's voice muffled as he asked, "Need a ride?"

"Noah, are you okay?" Emma touched his forearm, calming a tide of dizziness and bringing him back to the present.

"Fine. Just tired. I haven't been sleeping much." He rolled his shoulders in an unsuccessful attempt to relieve the tension gathered there. "I appreciate you taking time out to come check my house, officer." He stood and held out his hand.

The cop's narrow-eyed gaze raked over him, dismissing the gesture. Noah sucked in his breath until the cop nodded. "Emma, can I have a word alone?"

"Sure." She followed the officer onto the front porch, and Noah could only catch a few snippets here and there as he hurried to cover up the papers on the table. The officer murmured something about her being careful and that Noah seemed strung out of his mind. Her whispered reply was too soft to make out.

A few seconds later, the creak of the door opening again signaled her return. She slowly entered the room. "Hi."

He clenched his jaw and met her gaze.

"The reason I came over was to warn you about that." She hitched a thumb over her shoulder. Her words spilled out in a rush. "I'm really sorry. I tried to call him, but I couldn't reach him again and I thought you were, well, never mind what I thought." She took a deep breath. "Do you hate me?"

He forced a smile. "No, Emma, I don't hate you. I'm glad you called him."

"You are?"

He nodded and gave up on sliding the manila folder underneath some magazines. He wasn't happy she'd called the cops on him, but he'd managed to avoid a messy scene and that was all that mattered. "Shows you're more cautious than I first thought. Maybe I won't have to keep an eye on you after all."

"I don't mind if you do." Their gazes locked, and a slow simmer of lust stirred an arousal in his jeans. She looked away. "I guess I'd better be going."

*Stay*. The thought caught him off guard. Asking her to stay would only lead to a complication he didn't need right now.

Grabbing the base of his neck, Noah frowned. "Maybe you should." She turned to leave, and he called out, "Emma?"

She lifted wide eyes to gaze at him. "What?"

"Just be careful. I meant what I said. If you need anything, give me a call."

"Okay." A few seconds later, the screen door banged shut behind her. Noah glanced around as unease settled in his gut.

Hell if he knew why.

# Chapter 5

Sweaty palm tightening around the strap of her messenger bag, Spider sucked in a deep breath and pressed the doorbell. When a minute passed, she knocked on the door before she lost her nerve. She had no idea what kind of reception she'd get, but she knew that she could do this. Three espressos, a pep talk in the mirror, and enough remorse bottled inside her chest to induce groveling were the perfect recipe for courage.

Then the door opened, and she wished she'd had something stronger than three espressos.

Noah stared back at her from beneath hooded eyes, and he was dressed... well, actually, he *wasn't* dressed. That was the problem. Her gaze immediately fell to his naked chest and lower, to the towel draped below his glistening rock-hard abs, to the trail of hair that led down. Eyes up, girlfriend! Jerking her head up, she focused on his face. The hair on his head hung in wet curls around his perfectly chiseled features, and he had the clearest, most enticing green eyes she'd ever seen.

"Everything okay?" he asked.

"Fine," she squeaked. Tightening her grip on the shoulder strap again, she cleared her throat. "I didn't mean to catch you at a bad time. I can come back later."

The little courage she'd mustered vanished at the sight of his half-naked body. She turned to make a run for it, but his strong grip on her arm prevented her from getting very far.

"Give me a minute to pull on some clothes."

"I can come back later," she said again.

"No need." One side of his mouth quirked up. "Do you want to wait here, or would you rather come inside?"

She steeled her spine and walked past him into the foyer, glancing around to keep from looking at his sculpted body. And it was fine, too. She half tripped on his hallway rug and tried to pretend that she'd meant to lean into the staircase rather than using it to catch herself.

"Make yourself at home," he told her.

His heavy footsteps climbing the old staircase signaled it was safe to untangle herself from the railing, and she sank into the comfy-looking chair inside the doorway to the living room. Peeling, faded wallpaper decorated the walls, but the oatmeal-coloured carpet seemed new and most of the furniture, too. The floor above her head creaked with movement, conjuring images of her hottie neighbour stripping the towel away and—

Shaking herself, she reached for her bag and pulled out some of the pages she'd printed before coming over. She spread them on the coffee table in front of her and waited, wondering how best to start the conversation.

*Hi Noah, I think your house is seriously haunted and you should probably move.*

That would likely get her tossed out faster than reminding him that she'd called the cops on him yesterday.

Right. New plan. Blowing out a breath, she considered what to say as his footsteps grew louder and evaporated all cohesive thoughts in her brain.

Noah's voice was strong as he spoke from the middle of the stairs. "I'm surprised to see you."

Moving to her feet, she turned and managed a smile. Not only was he barefoot with his wet hair still curling around his face, but he was also wearing a pair of snug jeans and had left a dark shirt hanging open over his muscular chest. A very nice, smooth muscular chest. The kind you usually saw on underwear models.

Down girl.

"I'm kind of surprised you let me in," she countered.

He walked past, shot her a grin, and began buttoning up his shirt. Thank goodness. "I told you I wasn't mad. What's up?"

Following his lead, she sat down and began fiddling with the papers she'd laid out for him. "You're gonna think I'm really strange when you hear what I have to say, but…" She chewed at her bottom lip and leaned forward. "Can I ask you something?"

"Go for it." He leaned forward too, so close the scent of soap teased her nostrils and threatened to scatter her thoughts again.

She pushed back, needing to clear herself of the distraction. "Have you … noticed anything odd about this house since you moved in?"

"Define odd."

"Things moving on their own. Unnatural sounds or smells. Weird feelings you get in certain rooms. That kind of thing."

Some of the twinkle dimmed in his eyes and his smile fell just enough to be noticeable. Ah ha! He *had* experienced weird stuff. Excitement sizzled through her veins, and she continued before he could answer.

"Have you seen anything, like a ghost? You have, haven't you? I knew it!"

"Whoa. Hold on." He shook his head. "I haven't seen a ghost. I don't believe in ghosts."

"But—"

He held up his hand. "Maybe you should explain why you're asking."

Sucking in a deep breath, she tapped her finger on the stack of papers. "You should Google your house, man. It's listed on a haunted places index, and you would not believe some of the messages people have posted on forums about it."

His forehead crinkled as he considered the printouts. "You're telling me this house is listed on a website, encouraging people to snoop around because they think it's haunted?"

"Well … yeah." Actually, she hadn't thought about trespassers. "What did the realtor tell you when you bought the place?"

"I didn't buy it." Frowning, he picked up the paper sitting on top of the others. "I'm renting it, and the realtor didn't say a damn thing about any of this."

Oops.

"Have you caught anyone snooping around since you moved in?"

The dark circles under his eyes seemed more pronounced as he skimmed the story: the one about a group of teens who believed the house was haunted by two ghosts, one good, one evil, after their friend was thrown down the stairs during a ghost-hunting expedition. The front door had been locked, trapping them inside, until a gentle voice had whispered, "Hurry. The back door. It's unlocked."

A chill caused Spider to tremble, remembering the tale.

"No." His voice was gruff now. "I've only been here a month. I don't know, maybe it only happens around Hallowe'en."

The calendar had just flipped over to April, so maybe he was right. "I'm sure people stay away if someone's living here."

His gaze lifted, amusement again in its depths. He set the papers back on the table. "So you think I'm haunted?"

It was an effort not to roll her eyes. She gestured upstairs. "The lady in your window, remember her? I saw her as clear as day, and ever since I saw her—"

Wait. She hadn't meant to mention the strange things that had been happening to her since the night she'd glanced up and seen Miss Pretty Ghost in his window.

"What, Emma?"

He probably already thought she was cuckoo for cocoa puffs. Might as well tell him the rest. "First there were the sheets being ripped off me in bed. Then there was a weird message on my computer. The words *help* and *danger* kept scrolling across for absolutely no reason. No reason!" She sucked in a deep breath. "Last night, I ended up huddling with the boys in bed after—"

His brow lifted. "The boys?"

She flicked a dismissive hand. "The dogs and cat. Anyway, the TV in the living room kept turning off and on while I was trying to watch it, and after I changed into my jammies and went to bed—"

"Jammies?" He chuckled.

She ignored him. "A loud noise from the kitchen spooked the animals and then the bedroom door started opening and closing on its own, Noah. Opening. And closing. On. Its. Own! All of us were scared to death. It's like the animals kept staring at something I couldn't see and whining. I didn't sleep a wink!"

She'd almost packed up her car and driven home, but she knew she'd be in for a round of twenty questions if she came dragging three animals into her house in the middle of the night. The only thing scarier than a ghost was her father intent on an inquisition.

The humour had fled Noah's eyes, replaced by a brooding but otherwise unreadable expression. She pointed a finger at him. "You know what I'm talking about because a similar thing has happened to you, hasn't it?"

*Bam. Bam. Bam.*

The loud knocking startled Spider so badly, she sprang to her feet and stared at the ceiling where it had seemed to originate while she considered making a run for the door. Noah's eyes were wide as they locked with hers. Without saying a word, he darted for the stairs. She was right behind him.

The echo of their footsteps on the uncarpeted landing was the only sound in the otherwise silent house. Noah stopped outside the only room with an open door. His chest rose and fell with deep, heavy breaths.

She pushed to her tiptoes to look over his shoulder and glimpsed the edge of a messy bed.

*Clunk.*

The new sound drew Noah into the room. He flung open the closet door while Spider entered more cautiously, darting her gaze around every nook and cranny and seeing no one. A weight settled in her lungs that felt … unnatural, as if she'd suddenly walked into a sauna, only the temperature was rather cold up here.

She edged closer and spotted nothing unusual in the walk-in closet. "What was that, Noah?"

"I don't know."

She took a step closer and—

"Aieee!" The jab of something in the middle of her back shoved her forwards and into Noah. They tumbled into the closet together in a mash of tangled limbs, Noah's weight cushioning her fall from beneath.

The door slammed shut behind them, flooding the room with near-darkness.

"Noah!"

"Are you okay?"

"Someone pushed me!"

"Are you hurt?" he demanded in a firm, but panicked voice.

She shook her head.

"Emma?" He practically shouted.

"I'm fine. You?"

"Fine."

He pushed up and against her, and it took serious effort to uncurl her hands from his hard biceps to let him go. Fear clawed at her insides as he shoved her away and frantically rattled the doorknob. She reached a hand around and massaged her back. What had shoved her so hard that she still felt the sting there?

Noah swore so harshly that Emma felt her face warm. She scrambled to her feet as he kicked at the door and then stepped back when he threw his shoulder against it. She wasn't thrilled to be in here in the near-dark either, but geez.

Um, why wasn't the door opening?

Her voice was a squeak. "We're locked in? How are we locked in?"

The door burst open and Noah rushed out, grabbing the edge of the bed to steady himself from falling. When he glanced back towards her, his eyes were alive with something wild and dangerous. The white of his knuckles as he gripped the bedpost betrayed his terror.

"Noah, are you okay?"

"Claustrophobic. Give me a minute." His breathing was as labored as if he'd just climbed a mountain. She reached out a tentative hand to comfort him, but drew it back when he looked away.

"Sorry," he managed. "Closets and I don't get along, especially when I'm locked inside one."

"No arguments here." Something about the tone of his voice triggered her curiosity. "You've been locked in one before?"

"Few times."

Well, that sounded awful. She shifted on her feet, uncertain what to do next. She was dying to ask him why he'd been locked in a closet a few times, but that probably wasn't polite. Turning, she realized the door was hanging at an angle, torn from one of its hinges. Dang. Noah, one – closet, zero.

She risked a step closer and another, until she was back inside the small space. The air didn't feel as heavy in her lungs as it had a few minutes before. She spun around, taking in the contents, mostly clothes and boxes, and noticed a small hole in the wall near the floor. Kneeling, she reached out and poked her finger in it. Coarse fabric scraped her fingertips.

"Noah, I think I found something."

"What?"

A shadow fell over her as he moved into the doorway. Dry plaster crumbled in her hand, expanding the opening. "Do you mind if I see what's behind here?"

He reached into his jeans and retrieved a pocketknife. Passing it over, he said, "Be careful. There could be wires in there."

Carefully, she jabbed the hard metal into the surface until the rotted area collapsed into dust. Not wires, but some kind of box covered in rough cloth. Sticking her hand into the enlarged hole, she retrieved a small black box caked in white powder.

"What is that?" he asked, lowering to his haunches beside her.

She lifted the lid and gasped. A gorgeous diamond ring sparkled in the stream of sunlight pouring into the closet. Arching an eyebrow, Spider lifted the piece of jewelry for him to see.

"I'd bet my entire Marvel collection someone tossed us in here because they wanted us to find *this*."

* * *

This was insane.

When Emma had pried the wall away with the knife, the loud scrape of metal against dry wood had sickened him. He'd attributed the gut-wrenching feeling to his hatred of small spaces and the traumatic feeling of getting trapped inside one again. But as the smooth, cold metal of the ring touched his skin, dizziness sent the walls spinning around him.

Memories of his father's voice mocking him through the closet door sent a rush of anger and fear coursing through his mind.

No!

Pushing to his feet, he escaped the cursed closet. Maybe he couldn't stop the panic, but he could shove it aside, or, better yet, hide it. He turned to see that she'd followed him, and his spine straightened. "None of this proves the house is haunted." Even to his ears, the statement sounded weak.

"Noah, don't pretend something weird didn't just happen." She pressed closer and snatched the ring from his grasp. "We were pushed into that closet. I think your ghost wanted us to find this for some reason."

"Why?"

"I don't know." She paced to the window, held the ring up to the light and examined it closer. "But I know people who can help. My friend, Alexandra – she's psychic. She'll know what to do. She deals with this stuff all the time."

His first inclination was to argue, but the mention of King stopped him cold. This could be the opportunity he'd been looking for to get closer to the supposed psychic detective.

Emma looked at him, moved closer. "You wouldn't hesitate if you didn't want help." Her fingers clasped his upper arm, and some of the tension eating away at him seeped slowly through his pores. It was strange, the calming effect this young woman had on him. "Let me call her. She'll probably come right away. We can rid ourselves of this pesky ghost by evening. What do you say?"

Did that mean King was back in town already? Or did Emma not know her co-worker had left? Either way, it was worth finding out.

"All right." He leaned closer. "But I'm only doing this because of the experiences you've been having."

One of her brows lifted. "Yeah, right." A beautiful smile erupted all over her face. "This is going to be awesome. I've always wanted to see her do this up close. My phone! Where's my phone?" She spun around and hurried down the stairs.

Sighing and wiping a hand over his tired eyes, Noah glanced around the room. Something damn strange *had* happened in here. This could be an ideal opportunity to see King work her magic, figure out how she conned people. He could be packed up and ready to move on in a few days if whatever was happening here escalated.

The distant sound of Emma's voice captured his attention and sent an unexpected pang of guilt piercing through his chest. It was a shitty thing to do, using her like this. He liked her, didn't want to hurt her.

His father's genes kicked in and reminded him that it was also an opportunity to spend more time with *her*, get to know her better and find out if she was willing to act upon their mutual attraction. Oh, yeah. He could tell she was interested. She hadn't been able to hide her appreciation earlier.

*Don't even think about it, West.* There's no telling how innocent she might be. Not to mention, the police chief's daughter. That was a whole mess of complication he didn't need.

He was the son of a convict: an abusive asshole, womanizer and alcoholic. Those things had a tendency to rub off, one way or another. Even if he was the type of man who believed in fairy tales, this young woman deserved better than him.

She'd also claimed to have a boyfriend, and Noah wasn't the type to poach a woman, no matter how attractive he found her.

Strange thing was, he was still tempted. How long had it been since he'd been with someone? Six months, at least. He'd been tiring of the whole dating scene, if that's what you wanted to call it. His longest relationship had only ever lasted a week. It had never bothered him until recently. Loath as he was to admit it, coming home to this empty house every day was damn lonely. The feeling had been amplified the more he'd observed Zachary Collins and his fiancée interacting. The friendship between them had been as obvious as their sexual chemistry. Such a weird thing to witness. All he usually saw were couples fighting. What would it be like to enjoy a woman's company so much you wanted to spend time with her out of bed as much as in?

With heavy limbs, he slipped on some socks and shoes before heading downstairs to see what Emma's plan was. He caught the tail end of her conversation. Didn't sound promising.

"So you don't know when you'll be back?" Emma dropped into the chair, frowning as she listened to the response. "Well, any ideas on what we can do in the meantime? I'm serious, Alexandra. I was terrified last night." She twirled a finger around her ginger locks and then sighed. "Okay. Thanks. I really appreciate it. And I'm sorry about your brother's marriage. I hope you can help him get things worked out."

Noah wandered over to the glass of whiskey he'd abandoned last night – another failed sleep aid – and downed the contents in a gulp. He'd found a half-empty bottle of the stuff in the cabinet and taken advantage, something he rarely allowed himself to do. She ended her call and sighed loudly.

"Sorry. She won't be able to help right now. She's out of town with a family emergency and doesn't know when she'll be back."

He leaned against the wall and crossed his arms. "Shame."

"Yeah. Her brother's in the military and his wife just filed for divorce. Since her brother's overseas, Alexandra went to try to find out what's going on. She's always trying to help people like that."

Interesting. "Except you."

She shot him a look of disapproval. "She's going to call a friend, some guy she knows who's psychic like her. Anyway, she's going to see if he'll stop by and help us figure this thing out. She actually seemed worried when I explained some of the things that had happened."

"So what do we do in the meantime?"

Excitement danced in her eyes. Wow. She really believed in this stuff. "I was thinking about it." She reached for her bag and pulled a laptop out. "I think the ghost is trying to tell us something. I think she wants help. If we can find out who used to live here and why they hid this ring in the closet, maybe we'll find some answers."

He moved closer to see what she was doing. "How do we do that?"

"We can check property records. Probably easier just to ask your landlord what he knows. Maybe it's something to do with him or his family. I'll do another search of the newspaper archives online to see if this address returns anything while you go call him."

Bossy, too. He liked that. "Yes, ma'am." Smiling, he found himself doing as suggested. It only took him a few minutes to come up short. "We've got a problem. He's not available now. His secretary scheduled me in for a meeting this afternoon. What are you doing for lunch?"

The clacking of computer keys stopped as she glanced up at him and shrugged. "No plans."

"We'll stop and grab something on the way. My treat."

"Really? I can come?" Her expression was bursting with delight now.

"You seem to know a helluva lot more about this stuff than I do."

"Oh, this is going to be awesome!" Setting her computer aside, she hopped to her feet and hugged him, so quickly he barely felt it. Gripping his biceps, she grew serious as she stared up at him. "Don't worry, Noah. You're not alone in this. Everything's going to be okay."

Coming from anyone else, he might have laughed. Something about the sincerity in her voice, the concern in her eyes soothed something inside of him.

He managed a smile. "Thanks."

Strange thing was, he meant it.

# Chapter 6

Why, oh why had she chosen her favourite deli as their lunch spot?

Spider and Noah had barely had time to sit at a table with their food when a familiar face pushed through the crowd toward them, his intent to make a nuisance of himself obvious in the tense lines of the man's all-too-familiar features. From across the room, her ex's sky-blue gaze had pinned her in her seat.

"Fudge," she whispered, angling her head down and hiding her face with one hand.

"What?" Noah asked.

"Nothing." She forced a smile and scooted her chair closer to the wall. Did she have time to make a run for the bathroom? Or maybe, the exit?

"Emma?"

Reluctantly, she looked up. "Paul. Um, hey."

Paul was dressed in his uniform, so hopefully he'd get a call from dispatch and leave. Soon. His thumbs hooked around his belt close to his pockets and his gun as his gaze raked over Noah. Frowning, he focused on her again.

She gestured to Noah. "Paul, this is—"

"Your hair's not blue anymore." His tone managed to sound both condescending and complimentary all at once.

Her face caught fire as she brushed the soft locks away from her brows. She'd managed to avoid him for about two months now, which was a real accomplishment considering how often he dropped by her house under the pretense of seeing her father. "I went natural for a friend's wedding. Didn't want to ruin her photos."

Not that Hannah would have minded having a blue-haired bridesmaid, or else she would have never asked Spider to participate. Spider had figured going natural for a few weeks was the polite thing to do. Besides, she'd been planning to go pink soon anyway.

Crossing her arms, she looked at the man sitting across from her to gauge his reaction. Noah's brows furrowed as he leaned back. Maybe he wasn't a fan of anime hair. She couldn't tell.

Paul ignored Noah. Smiling, he put his hand on the back of her chair and leaned closer, lowering his voice. "I told you not to dye it to begin with. This suits you so much better." His fingers toyed with the ends of her hair. "You should leave it."

Once upon a time, the gesture might have been intimate, pleasant even, but now his proximity made her stomach roll. She was a bit ashamed to remember all the times she'd allowed his possessive posturing, but, then again, Paul hadn't always been overbearing. Not until he'd gone through the police academy and decided he liked being a douchebag.

He leaned closer. "I miss you, Emma. It'd be nice if we could go out, talk, clear the air. It's time you snapped out of this phase you're going through."

He was pouring on the charm because they were in public, but *phase*? That was a passive aggressive insult if ever she'd heard one. She gritted her teeth to keep from causing a scene, which is pretty much what she'd always done with Paul after a point. That thought irked her so much, she lifted her eyes and glared at him.

The new her – Spider – wasn't nearly as timid.

She was about to open her mouth and shoot a stinger his way when she caught Noah's gaze on her. There was no judgment in his eyes. Only curiosity. Lord only knew what he must have been thinking.

His voice was loud over the scraping of his chair across the floor as he pushed back, stood, and told Paul, "We haven't met. I'm Noah West. Emma's date."

Spider slumped lower in her seat as Paul straightened and stared at Noah's outstretched hand without taking it. Bless Noah's heart for trying to save her, but oh, boy. This was not going to end well.

The young cop frowned as he looked at her again. "I don't remember your dad mentioning you had a new boyfriend."

"Does her father know everything about you?" Noah inserted with a skeptical I-don't-think-so look in Paul's direction. "Not to be rude, but we were in the middle of something."

"Not to be rude, but so was I." Paul's hand moved to cover his holster. "Emma, let's go."

Yeah, right. He was out of his freaking mind if he thought she'd even consider leaving here with him.

The radio at Paul's hip squawked out a call for assistance. Disorderly conduct a few streets from where they were, which was good, since there was about to be disorderly conduct in this restaurant if one of them didn't leave soon. His jaw muscles twitching, Paul lifted his handset and responded.

To Spider, he said, "I'll call you later."

*And I won't answer.*

The menacing way he and Noah continued to stare at each other reminded her of a couple of male lions she'd watched on the National Geographic Channel. They'd been fighting over a herd of lionesses, and it had gotten downright nasty.

Sheesh. Noah was one heck of a good actor here.

He watched Paul leave before he sat down again. "Old boyfriend?"

She bit her lip and sighed. "Ex-fiancé."

"Really?" He drew out the syllables, sounding surprised, in an almost insulting manner. Did he think she couldn't land someone in Paul's league? In the hottie department, Paul might not be in the same category as Noah, but he wasn't a dog either. Lots of women found her ex attractive. She'd heard he'd been quite the ladies' man since their split almost two years ago – which oddly didn't make her the least bit jealous. Just relieved.

It would make her feel even better if he started seeing someone regularly and stopped … what? Stalking her? Spider shifted in her seat, uncomfortable with that label. Paul hadn't done anything threatening to her in a very long time. Sure, he dropped by her house when she was home far too much for her liking, but the man was still a friend of her father.

Odd, though, that he'd been here today. He'd always claimed he hated the food whenever she'd wanted to eat at this deli.

Shaking his head and snapping her attention back to him, Noah reached for his sandwich. "I just can't picture a sweet girl like you with a creep like that."

Oh. That was a compliment, wasn't it? Maybe she'd misunderstood his reaction.

"What makes you think he's a creep?" She'd thought Paul had been on fairly good behaviour. A bit rude, but heaps better than when they were alone.

He half smiled at her. "The way he was crowding you, for one. The way he ignored me. For all he knew, I could have been your brother or boss or someone important."

Smiling wryly, Spider took a bite of a potato chip. "He wasn't always a creep."

"Maybe he was, and you just didn't notice."

She shook her head, feeling sad at the rush of memories she'd fought hard to forget. "We grew up together. I've known him forever. Trust me, he wasn't always like that."

It hurt to remember the boy Paul had been, knowing her friend was gone. Their fathers had been buddies on the force together, so they'd gotten paired a lot as kids. Memories of their childhood escapades still brought a smile to her face.

Paul had also been the first boy she'd ever kissed. Her first everything. They'd just graduated high school when he'd proposed, and since he'd helped her through the most hellacious period of her life, she'd felt obligated to accept. What an idiot she'd been. Sure, she'd loved him, but even then, she'd longed for something … more. Something to set her heart racing. Someone to inflame her passion. The Eric to her Sookie. The Edward to her Bella.

"Emma?"

Blinking, she realized Noah was watching her closely, as if waiting for a response.

"Huh?"

"I asked if you were okay?"

"Of course."

He opened his mouth and looked ready to ask more questions she didn't want to answer, so she sat up straight, leaned forward and cleared her throat. "What's your favourite colour?"

"Mine?"

She nodded. "Favourite colour. Go."

"Blue."

"Been there. Done that. I've been thinking pink. Maybe platinum-blonde."

"Are we talking about your hair?"

"What else would we be talking about?" She twirled her locks around her finger. "So far I've done purple, green, and blue. Is that weird?"

She might as well fly her freak flag now and get it out of the way. She was actually curious about his reaction to her unorthodox appearance. Not that it mattered, but it was a big turn off when guys treated her differently because of it.

"Can I be honest?" He leaned closer, a smile playing at the edges of his delicious-looking mouth. "I don't care what colour your hair is. It's your hair, not mine. Besides, you're a pretty woman. I doubt your hair colour changes that."

Whoa. He was *good*.

And she wasn't buying it.

"I read an article online the other day that said it was a huge turn-off for guys when a woman dyed her hair 'Rainbow Brite' colours, as they put it, but thank you for being nice."

"Maybe the surveyor asked the wrong guys." His smile stretched. He had a killer smile. "You are full of surprises, Emma Fisher."

She clenched her teeth to keep from reminding him she preferred to be called Spider.

*Wait.*

"I didn't tell you my name was Emma Fisher."

He didn't flinch. "You're also not the only person who knows how to do a search for somebody online."

"But—"

"You told me you worked for Zachary Collins, so I looked up his agency's website, found your full name, and did a little investigating of my own." His brow arched. "Not that there's much to find."

"A girl has to cover her tracks." She took a bite of her sandwich. "So, what *did* you find?"

"According to your Facebook page, you're one hundred two years old, your profile picture is a skeleton wearing a tutu and a tiara – nice touch, by the way – and you have a wicked sense of humour."

"I'm twenty-five." She threw that out there to make sure he knew they were compatible age-wise. "Find anything else?"

"I did get a hit on a picture of the chief of police at some ceremony a few years ago, and I'm pretty sure that's you standing beside him in a pretty little navy dress."

Crap.

"He's my dad."

"So I gathered." He leaned back, looking relaxed. Take away the five o'clock shadow and dark circles under his eyes, and he almost looked happy. "Can I ask you a personal question?"

No. No freaking way. She didn't do personal questions.

She gritted her teeth. "I suppose."

She didn't want to be rude.

"Do you actually believe your boss is psychic?" His tone implied he didn't.

She narrowed her eyes. "We don't advertise that on the website."

"I remember his TV show. *The Psychic Detective.*"

"Oh." That made sense. "Yes, I do. I've seen him do … things that aren't easy to explain. Alexandra, too. First day I met her, she told me things about me only my mom could have known."

He frowned. "Your mom is…?"

She swallowed the lump that always formed in her throat when she remembered her mother. "She died when I was fifteen."

"Sorry."

She shrugged. Until Alexandra had helped her get some closure, she'd never been able to say more than three words about her mom without falling apart. Now, it was easier to push them out. "I was lucky to have her that long, and now I know she's at peace."

"And you also believe in ghosts."

After what she'd experienced the past two nights? Abso-freaking-lutely. "You're the one living in a haunted house."

He shook his head. "I believe in logic. There's some explanation for all of this."

She tilted her head and considered him. "No offense, but you look like a crack-house reject right now. You obviously haven't been sleeping much and—"

"Insomnia." He rubbed at his eyes. "I've been stressed since I moved."

"Uh-hmm." She wasn't buying it. Something had been keeping him awake. "You must believe a little. Otherwise, what are we doing here?"

Noah took a deep breath and tried not to look cornered by the question. It wouldn't do him any favours to suggest he was humouring her, or the truth, that he was using her.

"We're here because you're experiencing something, and that has me worried."

She rolled her eyes and pushed the last of her sandwich into her mouth. She said nothing while she chewed, simply considered him, as if he were a puzzle that she was trying to piece together.

She was turning out to be quite the mystery herself. Obviously, she wasn't as innocent as he'd originally suspected – not if she'd had a fiancé. Why the hell did that thought irritate him so much? He had to enforce serious self-restraint to keep from pushing Robocop's teeth down his throat when he'd crowded her in her seat. At least she hadn't encouraged the behaviour, leaning away from the other man and not responding in kind to his not-so-subtle come-ons.

Noah wasn't the jealous type; and, hell, he barely knew this woman. Sleep-deprivation was effing with his mind.

"What about your boyfriend?" The words left a sour taste in his mouth.

"Boyfriend?"

"You said you had one." He'd also seen a man stop by the other night. "Did you tell him what happened? Is he going to stay with you tonight?"

Red crept across her face. "I'm not actually seeing anyone at the moment. When I said boyfriend I meant that I have a friend who's a boy. I mean, man. I have a man-friend. Several, actually. Totally platonic."

Some knots in his shoulder loosened, and he drew a deep, grateful breath through his nose.

He thought back to the dossier he'd compiled on her before he'd known who she was. There had been surprisingly little to discover about Emma Fisher considering she held such an important position in Collins' firm. Here was his chance to fill in the blanks.

"I'm curious, Emma. How did you get to be a computer expert? College?"

He knew she'd dropped out of Georgia State University as a junior, and she hadn't gone back to earn her degree until last year. There had been a gap in her schooling that had intrigued him.

She licked some stray mayo off her lips and swallowed, eyeing him cautiously. After a brief hesitation, she shrugged. "I started tinkering with web design in middle school. Realized I had a knack for it. Once you understand how a website is coded, it's not a big leap to figure out how to compromise one." She pushed her tray away. "I eventually got a degree in programming, but I already knew most of what they were teaching. My professor thought I was quite gifted. I even taught him a few things."

"Impressive." He leaned forward. "With skills like that, you could probably get a job working for the government or a bigger corporation. Why work for Collins?"

Something defensive sparked in her eyes. "Because he was the first person to give me a chance. He's a good guy. Fair. He didn't care that my hair was purple or that I wanted him to call me Spider. Speaking of the bossman, are you ready to go?" She glanced at her phone. "I've got to let the dogs out in an hour or so."

Half a sandwich still littered his plate, but he couldn't bring himself to force it down. He shoved the uneaten food onto the tray with hers and stood. "Ready as I'll ever be."

***

Noah had only met the gray-haired attorney who'd rented him the house once, when he'd signed the lease and picked up the keys. Looking around his landlord's office now, he figured the guy didn't need the extra income. Rich part of town. Full waiting room. Expensive décor. The guy's business was thriving.

"Mr. West, what can I do for you?" Lionel Carpenter greeted them both with a handshake. "I trust everything at the house is to your liking."

"Everything's great."

An elbow to his side was an unnecessary reminder about why they were here. While he hesitated, Emma cleared her throat and bumped him again.

She sure could be a bossy little thing.

"I had some questions I wanted to ask about the place." He

rubbed at the back of his neck. "Have any of your former tenants mentioned anything … odd happening at the house?"

The older man heaved a sigh as he sank into his chair. "Let me guess. You want to know if the place is haunted."

"Excuse me?"

"Ah ha! See. I told you!" Emma moved forward and braced her hands on the edge of Carpenter's desk. "Tell us what you know. Have you ever had the house exorcised? Investigated?"

Seeing the attorney's startled expression, Noah grabbed her shoulder and pulled her back. "Excuse my friend; she's a little excitable."

"I am not!" She shoved his hand away. She straightened the lapels of her leather jacket and arched a brow at him. "I am simply curious, thank you very much."

Carpenter continued to look at Emma as if alarmed. Eyes wide, he stared at her for longer than Noah appreciated. "Look, I told you in an email there were some issues with the house. I even disclosed those material facts in the lease."

Noah hadn't read every detail, just the important stuff. Had he missed something?

"What's a material fact?" he asked. He thought he knew, but he wanted clarification.

Frowning, Carpenter finally tore his gaze away from Emma. "Leaks. Structural issues. Past incidents at the home."

"He means murders, suicides, those kinds of incidents. Right?" Emma demanded. Crossing her arms, she moved closer to the desk again. "Have there been any deaths at that house?"

"Not to my knowledge. That house has been in my family for decades." The attorney gestured to a framed photo on the bookshelf beside his desk. "My great aunt and uncle left my father the house, and he left it to me. My great uncle built the house himself. Believe me, I'd know if there had been any deaths there."

Noah took a deep breath. He knew this had been a pointless meeting. "I'm sorry we bothered you, Mr. Carpenter." He reached for Emma.

"Wait." Emma held out a hand to push him away. She turned to the attorney again. "You knew we came here to ask you if the house was haunted. That means other people have asked. What have they told you?"

Shaking his head, Carpenter leaned forward, his glance straying toward the bookshelf again. "The last tenant claimed he experienced strange things while living there. Objects moving. Lights turning on and off." He narrowed his eyes as his gaze skimmed her figure again. "I'm sorry. Have we ever met?"

"Don't think so." She shrugged. "How long ago was your last tenant?"

"That house has been empty for three years."

"Empty?" Noah asked, moving toward the bookshelf. The other man kept looking between it and Emma. "Why?"

"The house has gained a bit of a reputation, it seems. Trespassers have vandalized it so many times, it's been a devil to keep up."

"Why not sell it?" Noah asked, scanning the framed photos on the shelf.

"My great uncle and his wife were very much in love, and they poured their love into that home. It was written into their will that it could never leave the family."

Noah skimmed the photos. A couple of blond-haired boys with a woman. Probably Carpenter's family. An older picture of a man who resembled Carpenter enough to be his father. One by one, Noah studied the pictures on the shelf until he came to one hidden in the back, behind them all. It was an old photo, black and white, of a man and woman standing close together in front of an old model car. His heart stilled long enough to stop his breath. He grabbed the photo and pulled it forward for closer inspection.

"Who's this?"

Carpenter stood and moved closer. So did Emma. "My great aunt and uncle. Melinda and Harold Carpenter."

Eyes wide, Noah glanced between the woman in the photo

and Emma.

They could have been sisters; their likeness was uncanny.

For once, Emma was speechless too.

***

Holy crackerjacks. Was she a long-lost relative of Melinda and Harold Carpenter, or what?

Sitting in the car beside Noah, who was broodingly silent as he drove, she tried to remember her family tree as best she could and realized she had very little knowledge of it. When her mom had died unexpectedly of a heart attack at age forty-one, Emma had tried looking into her mother's ancestry, worried sick that heart disease ran in the family. If there was a branch of her family tree labeled Carpenter, she sure as heck hadn't found it then.

That left only one logical answer.

"Oh my gosh. I'm the reincarnation of Melinda Carpenter!"

"Don't be insane."

"How else do you explain that picture, Noah? Or the fact that I found my way to that house after all these years. I don't believe in coincidences. Everything happens for a reason." This was just like an episode of The X-Files. Only minus Mulder and Scully, which was a darn shame. Mulder would know what to do next.

Noah took his gaze off the road long enough to frown at her. "Sometimes things just happen."

"And sometimes they don't."

When he pulled into Zach and Hannah's driveway, she crossed her arms. "I think I should go back to your house. I bet Harold has been trying to communicate with me because he thinks I'm her. Oh my gosh! I bet that's it!"

"Calm down. You're not coming back to my house."

"Why not?"

"Because I'm not encouraging this."

"How else are we supposed to figure out what's really going on?"

70

"Emma, thank you for lunch." His voice was firm. "I'll see you later, alright?"

Men! They could be so frustrating.

With a groan, she pushed out of the car and marched up the driveway. She needed to let the animals out, anyway.

Pushing inside, she slammed the door shut behind her and punched in the security code to disarm the alarm. She was immediately swarmed by eager-to-pee dogs dancing around her legs.

Tossing her stuff onto the sofa, she went out back with her charges, trying to think about her next move as she watched them prance around the fenced back yard. She should do research into the Carpenters, find out more about them. She supposed she should talk to her dad and find out if he knew anything about them, too.

Whistling, she called the boys back inside and went in search of her computer. The cat was lying on it and her bag and didn't seem in a hurry to abandon his newly made bed anytime soon.

"Abbott, I need my computer. Get. Off!"

The cat didn't budge, so she tried pulling the bag out from under him. He slid off to the side along with half the items in her satchel.

"You had one job, cat. One job, to get off the bag. Look what you did."

She spotted the small box underneath his front paw and realized she'd put the ring they'd found earlier in with her stuff. Oops. She should probably go return it to him.

"Ha! Now I have a legit reason to go back over there. Good job, cat."

Abbott's nonchalant feline expression told her she was still an idiot, but whatever.

The doorbell rang, sending her heart into her mouth and the dogs into a wild barking frenzy. She moved to the window, peeked out, and didn't see a car in the driveway.

*Ding dong.*

The boys were all over the place barking now.

"Alright. I'm coming."

She glanced out the peephole and saw no one standing on the doorstep.

*Ding dong. Ding dong.*

She was still looking through the peephole. No. One. Was. There.

Slowly backing away from the door, Spider took a deep breath. Stay calm. It probably wants to communicate with you. Don't panic.

"Harold, is that you?" Her voice was loud in the quiet space.

The dogs stopped barking and looked at her. Charlie immediately sat as though awaiting a command, and Costello shuffled closer before sitting on her feet. It was the cat's reaction that really caught her attention. Abbott arched his back and growled before slowly backing off the sofa and running toward another room.

Uh-oh. That couldn't be good.

"I found the ring." She held the item high in the air. "Did you want us to find the ring?"

Silence.

*Ding dong.*

Spider nearly wet her pants at the sound of the doorbell again. Rushing to the door, she flung it open, yelling, "If you want to communicate with me, stop pressing the darn doorbell!"

The man who stood on the porch blinked at her. "I wasn't expecting that reaction, but okay. I'll go with it."

Awkward.

Before she could blink, Charlie shot through the door, but the stranger grabbed his collar before he could get far. "Whoa. He likes to do that, doesn't he?"

She looked him up and down, not recognizing him from Adam. He was dressed in a black leather jacket, had short sandy hair, young, maybe her age, maybe a little older. Cute. Definitely cute.

"Who are you?"

"Connor Manning. Alexandra asked me to stop by and see if I could help with your—" He glanced around and pushed past her into the room. "—little problem."

# Chapter 7

Slipping the ring into her pocket, Spider deactivated the alarm before it went off. She was so taken aback, she couldn't find the willpower to do anything after that but stand in the doorway and gape. The stranger moved around the living room, eyeing the place as if he was taking stock of all the items he could steal later.

Charlie pranced around him in greeting until the guy reached down and petted him. Nice going, watchdog. Not to be outdone, Costello waddled over to the man, jumped up and began humping his leg. Well, at least that was slightly better than offering a tail-wag to someone you didn't know.

"Dude, you're humping me." The guy wagged his finger and sent a disapproving look at Costello. "Not cool." With a toothy grin, Costello sank back on his haunches and stared up at the man.

"Um, he does that." Keeping a safe distance, Spider crossed her arms and frowned at the two dogs, then at the man. "Who are you again?"

"Connor."

"A friend of Alexandra's?" Alexandra had mentioned she'd be sending someone over later to help. Spider had expected later to mean *later*. "Let me give her a call real quick. No offense, but – well, no offense."

She ducked into the kitchen and called the other woman, who

quickly reassured her Connor Manning could help her figure out this ghost problem.

She looked across at him sitting bent over on the sofa, petting Costello, and wondered how Alexandra had met the guy. Some kind of tattoo covered his neck, and he was dressed head to toe in black.

"He looks kind of…" She lowered her voice. "…dangerous."

Alexandra's soft laugh carried down the line. "Trust me. He's good at what he does. You're totally safe with him. Promise. Remember the guy who helped Dylan and Zach save my life? This is him."

"Really?" Spider peeked over her shoulder to get a better look at the man. She'd heard all about the – "scrawny" if you believed Dylan and "kickass" if you believed Alexandra – demon hunter who'd rescued Alexandra from possession last year. As in, full-on demonic possession. "This is *that* guy?"

"Yep."

Ending the call, Spider took a deep breath and hurried to greet him properly. She stuck out her hand. "Sorry about that. I'm Spider."

His lopsided smile softened his features tremendously. As he stood and accepted her hand, his grip was strong and warm. "I know." Something akin to disappointment flittered across his features as he looked her up and down.

"Right. Cause you're psychic." She put her hands on her hips and returned his full-body appraisal. What had he been expecting when he met her? A nerdy little desk-jockey? A spiky-haired guy? Some The-Girl-With-a-Dragon-Tattoo type? Yeah, she got those a lot.

His eyes sparked to life with amusement. "Alexandra told me Spider was a pretty redhead and not to be fooled by the name. You're the only pretty redhead here, aren'tcha?"

"Oh." That right there just earned him brownie points. She might end up liking this guy. "Well, thanks for coming on such short notice."

"I was in town to see Alexandra. Didn't have anything better to do." He looked around the room, narrowed his eyes at something behind her, and muttered, "Hmm."

She turned and saw Abbott sauntering into the room. The cat stopped and sat on his haunches right next to her feet. With a bored expression, he watched their guest from across the room.

"That cat's not very nice."

"Excuse me?" Spider scooped Abbott up and gave him a good petting. "He's a sweetheart." Sometimes.

"He thinks you're an idiot for letting me in. He thinks I'm a thug. Oh wait. Scratch that. He thinks we're both idiots."

Yep, that sounded about right.

She sat the squirming cat down again. "Not that I intend to sound ungrateful or anything, but I thought Alexandra said you could, you know, see dead people, not talk to animals." Neat gift and all, but it probably wouldn't do her or Noah much good right now.

"Oh, don't worry. I can see dead people. In fact, there was one here when I came in, but I have no idea where she went."

Her heart did a lap around her chest at the confirmation. Holy mackerel. She'd been right. The ghosts were real.

"She?" Spider had felt certain the ghost pestering them was Carpenter's great uncle. Maybe it was the great aunt instead. "Okay, this might sound crazy, but did she look anything like me?"

Connor's brow furrowed. "Not that I noticed. Why?"

She brought him up to speed on everything that had happened so far. "I don't know what's going on, but I suspect it has something to do with this ring." She dug it out of her pocket.

His frown had darkened the more she spoke. "Let me get this straight. You were shoved into a closet – physically shoved, with force?"

"That's what I said."

"And this neighbour—" He gestured toward the door. "You said he's been having trouble sleeping and looks like he's nursing a hangover every day?"

"I mean, I don't think he's actually nursing a hangover every day." Maybe she should start filtering her thoughts before she spoke.

"This is worse than I thought."

"What do you mean?"

He skimmed his gaze over her figure again. "How much do you know about ghosts?"

She shrugged. "Just that they can be really, really scary in a not-so-fun way."

"Oh, boy." Rubbing a hand over his face, he shook his head. "Okay. Here's the abridged version. Ghosts, especially young ghosts, shouldn't have the ability to move things or harm people. The longer dead people stay in this realm, the stronger they become, and that's not usually a good thing."

"It's not?"

"It's not natural for them to be here, and the longer they're here, the more warped they become until they—" His jaw muscles clenched as he fell silent.

"Until they what? Geez Louise, man, you can't leave me hanging on that!"

"They turn into demons, and demons are nasty little things you don't ever want to encounter. Trust me."

"Don't worry. You had me at demon." A chill sent an uncomfortable tickle dancing along her arms. She rubbed at them and tried to comprehend exactly what he was implying. "You think there's a demon in Noah's house?"

He shook his head. "I think there's at least one ghost well on his or her way to becoming one. Come on." Smiling again, he rubbed his hands together. "Let's go talk to this ghost of his, shall we?"

***

Noah finished typing the brief email and sat back to read it before hitting send.

*Collins Security Firm is legit. Can't find any evidence to the contrary. I'm done here. Expect a report in the mail in a week.*

His cursor hovered over the SEND button for so long, he finally swore and exited out of the program without sending anything. Rubbing at the sand gathered in his eyes, he marched upstairs. Smart thing would be to send the email and get the hell out of here. Then again, he was being paid a lot of money to do a thorough investigation, and out of the hundred or so cases he'd worked, he could count on one hand the number that had ended with a "Can't Prove Fraud" stamp on it. He'd been distracted, unfocused, and too damn tired to give this case his usual attention. As he entered the bathroom, he had to admit he wasn't ready to call it quits. Calling it quits meant saying goodbye to Emma, and that wasn't something he was prepared to do yet.

Hell if he knew why.

*Woosh. Woosh. Woosh.*

The rushing of blood in his ears, or maybe it was his heartbeat, accompanied an intense ache behind his left eye. Noah splashed water on his face and looked in the mirror. Grimacing, he hardly recognized himself anymore. He felt too damn bad at the moment to care, so he wiped the moisture from his chin with a cloth and tossed the rag on the floor. Sleep. If he could just get a few hours of consecutive sleep—

A crescendo of knocks downstairs caused the pain in his head to intensify with each bang on wood, even as his stomach tightened and rolled.

The idea that it might be Emma both excited and unnerved him. Turning her away had been hard. Much harder than it should have been. Hurrying to discover whether the source of the noise was a visitor or something else, Noah didn't even bother to look out the peephole to see who was on his doorstep.

Pulling open the door, he came up short at the unfamiliar man standing on the other side. Dressed head to toe in black, some kind of tattoo on his neck, the stranger looked like he'd wandered in from the gang-infested streets of Central Atlanta.

"Can I help you?"

"Noah, right?" The younger man nodded in greeting. "Wassup?"

The stranger jostled forward, and Emma's face peeked out from around the guy's left side. "Hey Noah. So remember the psychic my friend was sending over to help us out? Yeah, well, this is him. Connor, this is Noah. Noah, Connor."

"Don't worry, man." Connor slapped him on the back of the shoulder as he pushed his way inside. "I'm here to help."

Emma was more cautious about entering, biting her lip as she slowly followed him across the threshold. "I didn't know he would be able to come today, but that's good, right?"

Noah frowned, looking between his two guests.

Tugging her closer, he demanded, "How well do you know this guy?"

"Ow!" She pulled her arm away from his grip. Damn. He hadn't meant to hurt her. "I don't, but Alexandra trusts him and that's good enough for me." She rubbed her arm and glared at him. "What's wrong with you? Don't you want help?"

More than she knew.

"I'm sorry." He ran a hand through his hair and glanced toward the man now standing in front of the stairs, looking up. "Do you really think he can help?"

"No idea, but it's the best plan I have right now. Why not give him a chance?"

*Because I don't believe this guy can talk to ghosts. Because ghosts aren't real. Because I didn't like how close you were standing to him.*

Even as the thoughts raced through his mind, he recognized how weak his resolve was becoming on the former. The things he'd seen, the events he'd recorded. How could he explain them?

His behaviour was starting to scare him too. His unnatural attachment to this woman after only a few days was … odd.

"Okay." He waved her into the foyer. "What do you need me to do?"

Connor turned and shook his head. "Nothing. I can already see what your problem is."

"What?" Emma demanded before he had a chance. "Demon or ghost?"

"Ghosts. As in multiple."

"Really?" Her face lit up with excitement. "How many?"

"Two, for certain. More, I think. I think at least one more is hiding from me."

"Why would it be hiding from you?" Noah asked skeptically.

"Good question." Connor moved into the living room, glancing around. "Usually when dead people realize I can see them, they swarm me. You've got one who's a little shy for some reason."

"How do you know there's another one?" Emma rushed to get in front of Connor, demanding his attention. Noah had to resist the urge to yank her away. "What about the other two?"

Connor nodded toward the chair in the corner. "There's a lady sitting over there, and damn, she looks a lot like you. Now I know why you asked." His eyes narrowed as he glanced between Emma and the chair. "There's a guy in my face, demanding I leave and take all of you with me. He doesn't like us being here." He frowned and turned away from her. "This is his house, he's saying. He doesn't want anyone here but family."

"Oh my gosh. That's the Carpenters!" Emma covered her mouth and glanced at Noah. "I knew it!"

Noah couldn't help but wonder how much she'd told the supposed psychic before bringing him over here. "Are they giving you their names?"

Connor stared at the chair and shrugged. "Funny thing about ghosts. They don't place importance on the names they had when they were alive. I'm not even sure they remember them. Some do. Most don't."

Noah struggled to keep the sarcasm out of his smile. "How convenient."

Spearing him with a look that could freeze hell, the other man met his gaze. "Spider, would you mind giving me and Noah some privacy?" He glanced at her and his face softened again. "Please?"

She put her hands on her hips. "Why?"

"Because I need privacy to do what needs to be done."

Pursing her lips in disappointment, she crossed her arms, hesitated, and looked at Noah for encouragement. He nodded. He wanted her as far away from this clown as possible. He couldn't stand the way the guy kept looking at her. "It's okay."

She reached into her pocket, looked at her phone, and murmured, "I do need to check in with Hannah." Heaving a sigh, she moved over to where he leaned against the arched doorway to the room. "I'll give you fifteen minutes, twenty tops, then I'm coming back over here."

"Sounds great. Thank you, Spider." Connor waved her off before turning around again and inspecting the room.

Once the outside door had closed behind her, Noah pushed away from the doorjamb. "She's gone. Why don't we cut the BS and get real for a few minutes?"

"Good plan." When Connor turned around, all pretense of his friendly demeanour was gone. "So, Noah – if that's really your name – why don't you explain to me why you've been spying on that sweet young lady who just left. Taking pictures. Watching her house. Is that real enough for you?"

His unexpected words had the impact of a punch to the gut, and Noah almost stumbled backward in a rush of dizziness. "What did you say?"

"You heard me." Connor stepped close, eye-to-eye. "The lady in that chair over there has grown very fond of Spider because of their resemblance, kind of thinks of her as the daughter she was never able to have, and she's telling me all sorts of interesting things about you. Keeps showing me pictures, pinned up somewhere in this house, of my friend Alexandra, and I'm pretty sure the guy in the photos is Zachary Collins. Care to explain that?"

Noah struggled to calm his breathing. How the hell had this

quack known any of that? Had he left the door to his office open? He glanced over his shoulder to verify. No, he hadn't.

"Because I'm psychic, you moron." Connor turned away, putting some space between them. "Yeah, I can read your thoughts too. Convinced I'm the real deal yet?"

"No. That's not possible."

"I can keep at this all day if you want. Lucky for you, I'm good. Good enough to sense you're not some psycho stalker Spider needs protecting from. Otherwise, you'd be flat on your ass and the cops would be on their way."

Noah swallowed, struggling to regain his equilibrium. "I think you should leave."

"I'm not going anywhere." Connor shook his head and grimaced, holding his hand out to his side. "Yeah, and I'll deal with you later. Get out of my face."

Noah got the feeling Connor wasn't talking to him anymore. Feeling disoriented, he reached for the chair beside him and caught himself before sinking down into it. Supposedly, there was a ghost already sitting there. A woman.

Hell. Was he buying this?

He moved instead to the sofa, sank back into the lumpy cushions and felt himself hyperventilating. His chest heaved with ragged breaths. Fire spread through his lungs.

Spinning round to look at him, Connor's face paled. "Whoa." He rushed forward, pushing Noah's shoulders toward his knees. "Take deep breaths. Stay calm, man. Close your eyes and try to relax."

Some of the tension seeped out of his shoulder where Connor's hand pressed against it. Slowly, he felt the dizziness pass. The tightness in his chest released.

"Ease back now," Connor told him, guiding him into a sitting position. Skimming his face for … something, Connor took a deep breath and then backhanded his chest. "Good job. Yeah, this is worse than I thought."

Noah rubbed at his shoulder. Tiny tingling sparks still shot in every direction. "How did you do that?"

"You're looking at a walking, talking smorgasbord of psychic abilities. Psychic medium. Empath. Healer. Telekinetic. Precognitive. I can do it all. Not all of it well, but it is what it is."

"That's not possible."

"You need another demonstration?"

"Who *are* you?"

"Sweet Odin, give me strength." Connor shook his head and glanced around. "I hate dealing with the stubborn ones." He moved to the window, glanced out the curtain. "Here's the thing. You've got two angry dead people – angry because you moved into their home. They're especially angry because you brought an attachment with you. Another ghost, pardon the term. They might've been fine with you being here, but this other ghost being here is really pissing them off. Add to that, the resident female ghost is protective of Spider and doesn't like that you're using her. Follow me so far? I'm using layman's terms here." He dropped the curtain back into place.

"Yeah, but—"

Connor moved to the other window, followed the edges with his eyes and kept talking. "Add to all of that, there's some residual energy here. This couple was very much in love. That's affecting you, and it's not helping that Spider looks so much like the lady who lived here. It's screwing with your mind, pulling you toward her, making you possessive. Still with me?"

"How did you—?"

"You're a real brainiac, aren't you? Where do you keep your spices? Kitchen?" Not waiting for an answer, Connor moved into the other room.

Noah rose and followed. It took effort, but he finally managed to push the words out. "So how do we stop this? How do we get rid of these ghosts?"

Murmuring to himself, Connor opened cabinets, inspected bottles – not that Noah had many – of spices, and then answered,

"It ain't gonna be easy, I'll tell you that. Right now, my concern is you. Your mind is one step away from a full-fledged takeover, and we need to nip that in the bud." Connor grabbed a few bottles of spices, set them aside, and glanced around. "Cup?"

Noah handed him one and watched as he poured a mixture into the glass before sticking it under the faucet and filling it with water.

"Spoon? Something to stir with?"

Noah gestured to the drawer to his right. "What are you going to do with that?"

"Not me. You. Here, drink it. Drink it all." He pushed the cup into Noah's grip. "It'll make you stronger, push out the residue. Downside is you're gonna feel like hell for the next twenty-four hours. Think of it as a detox program. Or the flu. Same difference."

Noah took a whiff of the mixture and jerked his head away. Nasty. He glanced at the bottles more closely. Sage. Cayenne pepper. Garlic. Olive oil. A couple of others he couldn't see. "Then what?"

"While you're feeling like hell, I'll be doing my best to convince the ghosts who live here to cross over. Trust me. It's in their best interests as well. What worries me is your tag-along. Why is she hiding? What does she want from you? We need her to cross over, too."

He was almost resigned to believe everything, except that part. "How could I have had a dead person attached to me, and I never knew it before?"

"Lots of reasons. She probably wasn't old or strong enough to communicate with you. Maybe she still isn't. Maybe she's learned a thing or two after seeing the ghosts here interact with you." Connor gestured to the cup. "You gonna drink that or am I gonna have to force it down your throat?"

Noah took a deep breath and gulped back the liquid. He could barely keep the stuff down. He rushed to the sink, filled the glass with more water, and drank like a starving sailor. Wiping the back of his mouth with his wrist, he glared at Connor. "This had better not be a joke."

"Eh. I admit I put the pepper in there because you've been an asshole, but trust me. The rest will help." Connor began putting the spices away. "Tell me. You ever lost anyone close? Your mom? Sister? Aunt?"

"Thank God, no."

"Close family friends? Any woman who was attached to you in life?"

Noah couldn't think of any woman being that stupid. "None."

"Awesome. I love it when my job is beyond difficult."

Noah sat the glass in the sink. "Why are you doing this?"

"You mean, why aren't I calling the cops on you and telling Spider what you're really doing here?" Connor shook his head. "Not my business. I'll tell you one thing though. You hurt her, and you'll wish you'd never been born. She's got a whole army of people in her corner who will swoop in and kick your ass."

"Don't worry. I plan to stay away from her." She deserved better. He knew that.

Connor chuckled. "Sorry, dude. Not gonna happen."

A frantic knock on the door was followed by a thud and Emma's voice calling out, "Guys? You still alive in there? I finished early."

A wave of dizziness and nausea so strong it weakened every limb in his body passed over him, forcing him to grip the edge of the sink to keep from passing out. Seconds later, he was heaving out the contents of his stomach into the stainless steel container.

"Good sign." Connor pushed a towel at his face, put a hand on his shoulder and began whispering something that sounded awfully close to a prayer.

Eager as always, Emma appeared in the doorway, her eyes widening when she saw him. He opened his mouth to speak, but the words came out slurred. "What are you—?" His vision blurred as he felt himself sinking to the floor.

"Noah!" Emma screamed.

That was the last sound he heard.

# Chapter 8

"Costello, *please* stop humping people! Especially sick ones! Gah!"

Shoving the dog away from Noah, who had one leg hanging off the bed – an easy target, she had to admit – Spider rolled her eyes and made sure the door was closed to any and all curious animals before turning back to her patient.

Florence Nightingale had nothing on her. She had an assortment of cold and flu medicines at the ready on the bedside table. Chicken broth sat steaming and ready to be pushed down his throat as soon as he woke up. Possibly sooner, if he didn't wake up within the next five minutes. She'd been exchanging a cold washcloth for a fresh one every half hour or so. All she had to do was lay it on his forehead, right? That's what they did in the movies. No idea why, but she was giving it a try. He sure did look cute with it on, anyway.

All cute and vulnerable. Like a little boy.

Noah was sprawled across the bed and tangled in the sheets in one of the guest bedrooms and, poor baby, he'd been dead to the world for the past nine hours or so. She and Connor had all but dragged Noah across the street to Zach's house so she could keep an eye on him. Connor had muttered something about needing to get Noah out of his house, so the residual energy or some such thing could leave his body without interference. Meanwhile,

Connor was camping out at Noah's place, trying to do his mojo-jojo on the dead people there.

Seriously, though, Spider felt a little cheated. What if he was doing something cool like they did on TV? Chanting and stuff? Or holding a séance. That would be so cool to watch.

A groan from the man in her care forced her attention back to him. Okay, so having Noah in her bed was a pretty good consolation prize. She might as well enjoy it while it lasted.

"Mmmm. No." Thrashing his head so the rag fell away from his forehead, Noah groaned in his sleep, grimacing. "Don't."

Sitting on the side of the bed, Spider nudged his shoulder. "Noah? You okay?"

Geesh. He was hot to the touch. Burning up. Maybe she should call a doctor or something.

Blinking his eyes open, he looked at her as if he had no idea who she was. "Emma?"

She sighed. "The one and only."

Smiling, he reached for the rag now settled across his neck and glanced around. "Where am I?"

"My place. Well, sort of."

"Why am I here?"

Shushing him, she explained everything, from his epic kitchen flail to the reason Connor had demanded he stay here. "He's cleansing your house while I take care of you."

"You shouldn't have to take care of me. I can go." He tried to sit up, wobbled like a Weeble and sank back down. "Or maybe not. Damn, I feel like crap."

"You've been sleeping though. That's good, right?"

Rubbing his eyes, he nodded. "I do feel more rested. I need to take care of some business. Bathroom?"

"In the hall."

Pushing up again, he hesitated before taking more than a step. He was still unsteady, so Spider hopped up and slid her arm around his waist.

"I don't need help."

"Yes, you do. Stop acting macho and come on." She urged him forward, trying not to swoon at his warm side pressed into hers. "It's easier to keep you standing than to pick you up. Trust me on this."

He grimaced but let her lead. "Sorry about passing out earlier. I don't understand what happened."

She got him to the bathroom door before untangling herself from him. "This is as far as I go." She pointed a thumb down the hall. "I'll go see if I can find some sweats or something of Zach's to loan you. Sleeping in those jeans can't be comfortable."

She didn't wait on a response. She hurried into the main bedroom before having a what-the-heck-did-I-just-do moment. Her face grew warm. It felt kind of skeevy to be searching through her boss's stuff. She did it anyway, quickly finding a white t-shirt and pair of black sweatpants in a drawer. She hurried back down the hall and knocked on the bathroom door. "I'll sit these outside the door, okay?"

Costello and Charlie had wandered up to inspect the situation so she made a quick dash to the kitchen, grabbed rawhide treats for both dogs to keep them distracted for a while, made sure Abbott was staying out of trouble, then met Noah back in the hallway.

"Hope you don't mind. I opened the new toothbrush in there."

"Fine."

Even with his hair sticking up funnily, droopy-eyed, barefoot and wrinkled, he looked good standing there. Oh yeah. She had it bad.

He was steadier on his feet now, but she could tell by the way his shoulders sagged and his feet dragged that he was still weak.

Trying not to stare as he climbed back into the bed, she reached beside her for the soup. "You need to try and eat this. My very thorough Internet search assured me that it will help you feel better. Plus, Gina always gives me some when I feel under the weather. It's pretty yummy." And thankfully, still warm.

"Gina?"

She shrugged and pushed a spoonful of the broth toward his mouth. "Our neighbour. She was my mom's best friend. She checks in on me and my dad every now and then."

"You still live with him?"

"Uh huh."

"Why?"

It was strange because that was the question she always expected that no one ever asked. Finally hearing it out loud jarred her. Her hand trembled as she pushed another spoonful between his lips. "It's complicated."

"I'm a captive audience. Enlighten me."

He probably already thought she was beyond weird. And pathetic. Might as well add some more logs to that fire. "Main reason is I'm saving up money." She scooped up more broth and fed it to him. "I want a house of my own. Not an apartment either. A house. I don't see the point of throwing money away on rent when I can own something." She considered her words before she spoke them. "Plus, my dad doesn't take care of himself very well. He's so busy trying to take care of the city that he neglects things at home. I do his laundry, keep the house somewhat in order, make sure he takes his medicines when he's supposed to, make sure the bills get paid on time. That kind of thing."

"Is he sick?"

She shook her head. "He has high blood pressure. High cholesterol. He assures me it's all normal in his line of work, but still."

"He has a tough job."

She shrugged, shovelled more soup into him. "On the other hand, he argues that he doesn't need medicine, which is always fun. I have no privacy. My dad expects me to tell him where I am *all* the time. He was hoping I'd meet a nice young man, get married, and stay barefoot and pregnant for the rest of my life. You should have seen how ballistic he went when I broke up with Paul and then took the job for Zach. It's frustrating. If he didn't need me, and if I weren't so determined to save a twenty percent down payment, I'd—" She snapped her mouth shut.

He pushed the spoon away. "Maybe he doesn't need you as much as you think. After all, he does run the police department for a major city."

"He *does* need me." She forced the spoon past his lips to shut him up more than anything. Glancing down, she realized the bowl was now empty. "Why am I feeding you, anyway?"

His boyish smile grew bigger. "I was wondering the same thing."

She sat the bowl back onto the nightstand. "Sorry, I was having a Florence Nightingale moment."

"No complaints here. Thank you for taking care of me."

"You're welcome. It's nice to have someone who lets me take care of them." She pursed her lips. "Wait. Did that sound weird? Cause I just had a flashback to the movie 'Misery,' and I promise I'm no Kathy Bates. I don't want to break your legs or anything."

"No, it's not weird. Well, that last part was. Kind of." His hand reached out from under the sheets and covered hers. His fingers were still too hot to the touch as they squeezed hers. His eyes also had that glazed sheen of sickness that told her he wasn't completely well yet, but he did look better. Not as edgy as he'd been looking the past couple of days. "I get it." His smile faded. "Is that why it bothers you that I don't call you Spider?"

"Wait, what?"

He smiled again. "Because calling yourself that is part of your independence. I'm guessing your dad hates the name. And he hated the blue hair, didn't he?"

She thought about how much she was comfortable admitting. "I might have decided to experiment with certain things in an effort to remind certain people that I'm my own person." Ultimately, she'd been trying to remind herself of that more than anyone.

He opened his mouth, as if he wanted to say something, but shook his head instead.

"What?" She poked him in the chest. "Out with it."

"Why wait so long? The hair, the nickname, your clothes – that can all be summed up as normal teenage rebelliousness. You're twenty-five."

Grinding her teeth, she started to leave, but no way would she let him know how much those words needled her. Paul had once said a similar thing. "Is there an age limit on finding yourself? Cause I missed that memo."

He shifted so he could look at her, his gaze raking over her face as if inspecting every freckle, every pore. Several seconds passed, but she refused to show how uncomfortable his perusal was making her. "You were with Paul when you were a teenager, you lost your mom and you probably felt the need to cling onto your father after that."

He was good. Too good – or was she so obvious? She leaned back against the headrest, slid her legs up beside his on top of the covers. "Don't psychoanalyze me, Noah. This isn't some phase I'm going through. For the record, I like having funky hair and a cool nickname. And my clothes?" She tugged at her t-shirt that read "People HATE when sentences do not end the way they potato" and glared at him. "My clothes are awesome!"

"I didn't mean to imply anything negative, Spider. I'm sorry." His eyes gleamed with sincerity. "I want to understand you better."

Her temper waned, hearing him call her by the nickname she'd fought hard to own. Were they having an honest-to-God breakthrough? Shouldn't she be happier that he'd finally honoured her request to call her Spider?

Picking at some dog fur that clung to the bed, she shrugged. "I don't mind that you call me Emma."

It was the truth, even if she was just now realizing it. Hearing her given name in his voice sent an unexpected thrill of pleasure coursing through her veins. It seemed somehow intimate.

"Good. Cause it suits you. A pretty name for a pretty woman."

She squirmed. "Please. I'm no model."

"Why would you want to be?" He scrunched his face. "They're

too skinny. A bunch of sticks, all of 'em."

She giggled. "Wait. Should I be offended?" She feigned a look of horror. "Did you just imply that I'm fat?"

"Voluptuous. Hardly fat."

Voluptuous. Grrrrr. Paul had used to call her that after he went through the Tool Academy, but she'd never gotten the impression it was a compliment. *You're too voluptuous, Emma. For God's sake, put a sweater on when we're around other people.* Her jaw stung with pain from how hard she bit down to keep her mouth shut. Glancing down, she realized their fingers were now linked. When had that happened? "I have big boobs. Too big."

"A woman's boobs can never be too big. Trust me on this."

"You're such a guy."

"Glad you noticed."

Smiling, she slid down lower, so low they were practically face-to-face. "What about your family? Are you close to them?"

His smile fell, but he didn't let go of her hand. "I have two little sisters who have me wrapped around their fingers and they know it, an older brother who's a pain in the ass, and my mom is…" His lips tugged up again. "She's great. She got remarried a couple of years ago. Nice guy. I suppose she could have done worse."

"Oh. Is your dad alive?"

He nodded. "Unfortunately."

Spider's brow rose in surprise, and shock. Not too many people said stuff like that about their parents without a reason. "That's heavy."

He pulled his hand away and reached for the nightstand beside him. "What time is it, anyway? Where's my phone?"

Disappointment chased the shock from her thoughts. "Um, I don't know." She considered him carefully. "Do you need it?"

He sank back against the pillows and blinked up at her through half-closed eyes. "I always need my phone." The words were slightly slurred.

"So what's the beef with your dad?"

"Complicated." The word escaped his lips on a deep breath. His eyelids had sunk shut.

"Noah?"

Snoring softly, his head rolled to the side, away from her. He was out again. And they'd been having such a nice conversation too, up until the last bit.

She needed to go walk the boys, make sure her computer script was still running and send an email to the office with her report. Instead, she cozied up to his side and pretended they did this often. It had been a long time since she'd been so close to a man. When he didn't push her away, she lowered her head to his chest and listened to his heartbeat, thumping steadily and strong beneath her ear.

"Noah?" she whispered.

A slight rumble beneath her ear was her only response.

Pushing up on her elbow, she skimmed his features. Still asleep. She liked looking at him while he slept. Against her better judgment, she reached and traced the area where his worry lines usually showed. They were gone now, helping him look his age. When he didn't react to her touch, she drew a line from his cheekbone to his lovely sculpted mouth, her fingertips barely skimming his skin. So warm. Rough. Tiny pricks grazed her hand, verifying he was in desperate need of a shave. A sexy image of slathering him in shaving cream and giving him one stirred something naughty inside her.

"Noah?"

He didn't budge, nor did she expect him to.

Leaning over, she gently pressed her lips to his, lingering longer than was probably decent. Her heart was thumping like a jackhammer. What was it about this man that made him so irresistible to her? She'd made a vow after Paul not to get emotionally involved with anyone again until she was ready. Was she ready? She didn't think so. Surely this was only a classic textbook case of lust. Pulling away, she made sure he was covered before slipping out of the room. She didn't trust herself to stay. Her fingers traced the contours of her own mouth. Have mercy. Had she actually kissed him? Heat engulfed her face. Thank goodness he was asleep!

She hurried into the living room and checked the progress on her work. Satisfied the computer was still doing as needed, she glanced at the clock. It was late. Almost midnight.

The robotic voice of her ringtone announcing "You have a call. Answer it now or prepare to be terminated!" scared the bejesus out of her. Squealing, she grabbed her chest and stared wide-eyed at the screen. An unknown number flashed across the caller ID.

Fumbling, she answered, "Hello?"

"Get over here. Now."

"Connor?"

When she heard nothing but silence, she looked and saw the call had ended. What the devil was that about?

Grabbing Noah's keys, she whistled for the dogs and put their leashes on. It was freaking midnight, and she wasn't going into that house alone.

The boys did their business, and she pulled them toward Noah's place with more than a little trepidation weighing down her limbs. Neither one put up much of a fight when she dragged them onto the front porch, opened the front door and went inside. Hopefully, that was a good sign whatever Connor had been doing had worked.

"Connor?" she called.

"In here."

She followed his voice to the main room downstairs, the clicking of Charlie and Costello's toenails on the hardwood floor echoing eerily throughout the quiet house. He stood leaning against the wall, arms crossed, all brooding and dark.

"Hey. Where's the fire?" she asked.

"What have you been doing?" He spoke slowly, and his voice held a hint of accusation in it that confused her.

Oh dear. He was psychic. Had he seen her practically molesting Noah, kissing him? How mortifying. She let go of the dogs' leashes, hoping they'd divert his attention.

*Costello, you have my permission to hump him. Go, boy. Go!*

Costello turned and shambled in the opposite direction, sniffing the carpet as if following an invisible trail. Unreliable mutt.

She glanced up and saw that Connor was still watching her, one side of his mouth twitching just enough to be noticed.

"Me? What have I been doing?" She brushed her hair behind her ear. "Taking care of Noah. Stuff for work. Why?" She narrowed her eyes. "What have *you* been doing, mister?"

"So you didn't do a search for my name online, and you didn't try to hack a certain website an hour ago? You sure that wasn't you?"

Oh. That.

She shifted on her feet, glancing around. "I didn't *find* anything."

And she hadn't. Not one single hit on his name that could have possibly matched this guy, not even in the database they employed for the agency. No driver's license. Nothing.

Suspecting Connor Manning wasn't his real name, she'd remembered the tattoo on his neck. Resembling a boomerang, it was more angular, like the pointer on an arrow. She'd drawn it into her phone and sent it through an image search. Browsing the results, she'd realized it was a rune, specifically, the rune Kenaz. Searching Kenaz tattoos had led her to a bunch of hits on something called the Bellator de Lux. Best she could tell, it was some kind of cult or secret society. Some claimed it was sanctioned by the Vatican. Others thought it was a shadow agency of the U.S. government. Everyone agreed its members showed up when something bad was going down. Terrorist attacks. Mass shootings. Hauntings. You name it. She had traced the cyber footsteps of one particular, frequent commenter to the portal for a members-only website, but no matter how hard she'd tried, she hadn't gotten past its second firewall.

Shaking his head, Connor pushed away from the wall and moved toward her. "Do you realize you're the first person to ever get past the first firewall? It only took you nine minutes."

"Sure, but—" She jerked her gaze back to his. "How do you know that? How do you know any of that?"

"Spider, you need to drop it. I mean it."

Well, now. He didn't know her very well. "What's the Bellator de Lux?"

"I said drop it."

"You're a member, aren't you?" She took a step toward him. "I've done some reading on psychics and psychic abilities, and it seems really unusual that you can do everything you claim you can do. You're part of some kind of weird government experiment, aren't you?"

He turned away, reaching down to pet Charlie, who'd come trotting back into the room after inspecting whatever he'd been inspecting. To the dog, he said, "Your handler is a stubborn one, isn't she? Huh, boy?"

Charlie barked and leapt up against his leg.

Connor chuckled and rubbed the dog's ears. "He says yes, which makes it all the more fun to play tricks on you. Something about leading you in a chase around the neighbourhood?"

She was going to kill that dog. "Lies. All lies. Stop changing the subject."

Connor's chest heaved on a deep sigh. His gaze searched her features, the hint of a smile on his lips. "Why couldn't you have been her?"

"Who?"

He shook his head and turned away. "Don't you want to know what I've been doing tonight?"

She crossed her arms. "Yes. I believe that was my first question, one of many, thank you very much."

"Helping Mr. and Mrs. Carpenter cross over. They're gone now."

"Really? That's great!"

"Remember the ring you found? The guy was building this house before he even proposed to his wife. Somewhere in the process, he lost her ring. Never was able to find it. That ring had belonged to his mother, so it had great sentimental value to him. That's the whole reason he didn't cross over when he died. Crazy, huh?"

"Was that what they wanted from us? For us to find the ring?"

"Yes, and for it to stay in their family. How exactly did you find it?"

She shrugged. "After we were pushed in the closet, I assumed there was some reason they wanted us in there. Guess you could say I was following a hunch."

"Mrs. Carpenter said she guided you to it. She has no idea why you look so much like her either. Personally, I think there's some kind of family connection here. Maybe on your father's side of the family. You were meant to find that ring, Spider. I'd check into it."

"Really?" She would add researching it to her to-do list. "What about the other ghost? Did you help her cross over, too?"

"No sign of her." He moved to the sofa and picked up his jacket. "I suspect she's been with you and Noah tonight. As much as I'd like to stay until she shows herself to me, I've got a situation to deal with, thanks to you."

"What? No. You can't leave." But he already was, striding toward the door as if he hadn't heard her. Hurrying after him, she grabbed his bicep and stopped him. "What if this other one is really … dangerous?"

"You'll have to figure that one out on your own."

"But—"

"Look. Figure out what she wants, who she is. Then give me a call. I'll see what I can do."

"How are we supposed to do that? When will you be back?"

"Listen to her. She's probably been communicating with Noah for a while. Maybe you too. Ask him if he's been having any strange dreams. That's a great place to start."

"But—" He turned and walked away. "Connor!"

He showed her the back of his hand in dismissal as he walked across Noah's lawn toward the black Dodge Charger sitting at the curb.

Doggone it! She stomped her foot and growled out her frustration before turning around. Her heart jumped into her throat when she realized he'd left her alone in the house. A haunted house. Possibly former haunted house, but still.

*You should get Noah's phone while you're here. How hard can that be?*

Looking toward the stairs, she wasn't sure she could go up to his bedroom. That's probably where he left his phone. Oh well. Not happening. She turned and realized she was standing beside a closed room. Hadn't Noah said it was his office? Made sense that his phone might be in there.

Spider pushed open the door and searched for the light switch with her hand. Brilliant light flooded the room a second later. Blinking, she glanced around and stilled.

A picture of Zach hung on a corkboard. Her boss was climbing into his car.

"What the frack?"

The picture drew her closer to the board, which was actually covered in dozens of pictures. Of Zach. Of Alexandra. Of her.

She reached for the printout of her standing in front of Noah's house. She remembered this – the night she'd seen the woman in his window.

"That rat!"

She hurriedly flipped through all the papers on his desk, finding papers with every member of the firm's information. Background checks. A business card peeked out from a dossier of Zach.

Noah West. Insurance Claims Investigator.

Nausea nosedived like a bomb into her gut, and she stumbled backward, falling into the desk chair, grasping her stomach and trying to squelch back the sensation. How could he do this to her? She'd trusted him. She'd more than trusted him.

She must have hit his computer keyboard when she stumbled because the monitor suddenly blinked on. Staring blankly at the screen, she took a deep breath.

Okay.

There was no denying the obvious. Noah West was using her.

What case could he be investigating? Her mind searched for answers, but she was too scatter-brained.

Speaking of scattered, his desktop was littered with documents just sitting there for anyone to open. Scooting forward, she took the keyboard.

Noah wanted to play games?

Game on.

# Chapter 9

The woman standing at the curb had long, dark hair and wore a white shirt underneath a denim jacket.

Something nibbled at Noah's consciousness about that description, but his mind couldn't connect it with anything. His body felt light, too light, and the scene unfolding around him didn't seem to involve him. The slow swish-swish of windshield wipers was loud inside the car.

He watched from the back seat as the pretty dark-haired woman slid into the passenger seat, reaching to pull the heavy door closed. A dark-haired man sat at the wheel.

"Thanks for the ride. I was afraid I was going to get drenched out there."

"Glad to help. Where are you headed?" The driver's voice was deep, raspy.

"Buckhead Village."

"Waitressing at Wally's tonight?"

"Yeah."

"Ah, Kate, you got to stop working so much. Have some fun. You're too young to be working two jobs and going to school."

Pushing her hair behind one ear with a trembling hand, the young woman snuck a glance at the man beside her, her nose wrinkling. "No choice." She glanced over her shoulder and seemed not to see Noah sitting there. A couple of empty beer cans littered the back seat beside him. "Have you been drinking, J.D.?"

"Maybe had a few."

Familiar landmarks were whizzing past, only they looked different somehow. Strange.

"Um, this isn't the way to Buckhead Village," the young woman said, sitting forward and glancing both directions in front of her.

The man said nothing as he directed the car left.

"I can get out here and walk the rest of the way." Face pale, eyes widening, Kate reached for the door handle the same second a click and thump reverberated around the car.

Noah jolted awake, blinking the fog and haze from his mind as he realized he'd been dreaming again. He rubbed at his chest. His heart was thumping like a sonofabitch. Glancing around, it took a few seconds to recognize his surroundings.

Zachary Collins' house.

He sat and massaged his forehead. There was no ache there anymore. No dizziness. No more sand in his eyes. He felt … normal. Actually, better than normal. Pushing off the bed, he noticed daylight was streaming through the curtains. How long had he been out? His clothes sat neatly piled in the chair beside the window, his phone and a note on top.

*Grabbed these from your place. Washed your others. They're in the bag. Feel free to shower. – S*

She'd been in his house.

Wandering toward the bathroom he distantly remembered using, he glanced down the hall. Where was Emma? The two dogs came running at him, so he bent and petted them both, even the chubby blond one who hadn't seemed to like him before.

Satisfied by the quick stroke, the animals turned and went trotting back the way they came. The clacking of computer keys echoed down the hall. His chest lifted and fell on a sigh of relief. For a second, he'd been worried she'd found him out, left another note somewhere telling him to get the hell out of her life.

Shaking his head, he ducked into the bathroom and took care of necessities.

When he emerged, his head felt clearer than it had in weeks.

"Emma?"

He followed the sound of her hammering the keyboard and then paused at the sight of her sitting on the sofa, socked feet propped on the edge of the coffee table, computer in her lap.

Hadn't Connor said his obsession with her would go away after … whatever the hell he'd done to him?

Not quite. A zing of happiness at the sight of her almost stole his damn breath. It was an odd and unfamiliar feeling, one he'd never felt before, not toward any woman.

"Hey," he said.

"Hey back." She didn't look up from her typing.

The mouth-watering aroma of bacon lured him to notice a plate of food sitting on the counter.

"Figured you might be hungry." She finally stopped typing long enough to gesture toward the kitchen. "Bacon and scrambled eggs are about the best I'm capable of. Eat at your own risk."

"Thanks." He pulled out a chair and sat at the breakfast bar, facing her. He was starving. "What are you working on?"

"Work."

Pushing a piece of bacon into his mouth, he took two bites and had to fight the urge to spit it out again. Freaking thing was spicy hot. What had she done? Sprinkled chili pepper all over it or something? He liked pepper but … damn.

"Something wrong?" She peeked over the laptop.

"No." He swallowed the meat and chased it with a gulp of water from the glass sitting beside the plate. Bitter, sour foulness assaulted the tip of his tongue.

Eyes watering, he spit the vile liquid back into the cup.

"What's wrong?"

"This … isn't water." His mouth was really on fire now. He rushed over to the faucet, leaned down, and began lapping up the heavenly liquid to chase the revolting taste from his mouth.

"What do you mean it's not water? I grabbed a water bottle from the pantry."

Switching the faucet off, he straightened and wiped the moisture from his chin. "Vinegar." He barely managed to get the word out. He grabbed a hand towel and began wiping up the mess he'd made.

She slapped a hand over her mouth. "Oh no! I must have mistaken a bottle of the white kind for water. Shoot. I'm so sorry! I didn't even read the label before I poured it."

Clearing his throat, he pushed his chair under the counter. Funny thing was, she didn't sound sorry. Her tone was more on the side of sarcastic. "Honest mistake. Don't worry about it." Patting his stomach, he pushed the plate away. No telling what else she'd done to sabotage it. "You know, I'm not all that hungry."

His stomach betrayed the words by rumbling a long, loud growl.

"Suit yourself." She shrugged and went back to typing.

Pushing a hand through his hair, he glanced down at the two dogs that'd been shadowing his every move. Had he said something in his sleep? Maybe Connor had ratted him out. Either way, something had pissed her off.

Grabbing his bag of clothes, he moved toward the door. "I think I'm going to head back to my place, check on things."

"You do that."

He took a few steps, stopped. "Is your friend still over there?"

"He left last night. Oh, but he got rid of the Carpenters. The house should feel different now. I thought so." Her gaze scanned him head to toe. "How about you? Are you feeling better?"

"Yeah, I am." Or, he had been. Now he didn't know what the hell to think.

"Good." Her cold smile did nothing to relieve the tension that had been creeping back into his body. Maybe she was fine, just too into her project to pay him much attention. She waved him off without another word.

"See you later," he agreed and hurried out the front door.

No. She must know, or at least know something. Either Connor had told her or she'd gone snooping. His heart jumped into his throat, fearing either scenario.

Walking into his house, he went straight to his office. The door was still shut; nothing looked out of order. He checked the bedroom, living room and kitchen. Everything was as he'd left it.

"Why was she so upset?" He took slow steps down the stairs, mentally retracing all of his actions since yesterday. Emma Fisher had been nothing but kind to him since the day he'd met her. She'd even played nursemaid for the past however many hours he'd been down.

It was time he repaid her for that.

Heading back to his office, he sank into the computer chair and tapped the space bar on the keyboard. Hopefully, he still had that last email saved in his drafts folder. He'd send it and end his investigation here. Hell, he suspected her friends were exactly what they claimed. He didn't care for the guy all that much, but Connor had opened his mind to the possibility that he was too damn skeptical for his own good. It was time to own up.

He clicked on the email icon and froze.

The sound of liquid bubbling blasted through the speakers. The image on the screen began to melt down the background as maniacal laughter caused the desk to vibrate. Cursing, he reached to turn the speakers down using their manual knobs.

"What? What's happening?" He tapped the ESC button. "No. No. No!"

The screen went black. A small golden puppy ran across, stopped in the center, and hiked its leg, shooting virtual pee toward him. A message appeared in a cloud of smoke on the screen.

"F U A-HOLE."

Grabbing a fistful of hair, he sank back in his seat. "What the hell?"

He had documents, very important documents, pictures, videos, everything saved on there. Not all of it was backed up. All of his work—

"Eh hem!"

Spinning, he looked behind him. Emma stood in the doorway, arms crossed, tapping one foot to a silent, angry rhythm. "Piece of advice, creepface. Never mess with a computer nerd."

* * *

Spider held her ground, even as Noah sprang to his feet and took a step toward her. "What the hell did you do?"

"Oh, nothing much. Just destroyed all of the information you've been collecting on me, my friends, and my employer." Her voice grew louder as she spoke each word. Swallowing a breath, she reined in her temper … and failed. She couldn't resist shoving him in the chest. "You creepy stalker psycho!"

He clasped her wrist and held it still. "I can explain."

"Too bad you didn't do that when, oh, I don't know, you *met* me." She took a step back, forced herself to calm down. "I'm not stupid. I know what you've been doing here." She gestured toward the camera set up in the corner.

His eyes narrowed. "It was Connor. He told you."

Holding up her hands, she exploded again. "Connor knew about this?"

He flinched. "He figured it out pretty quickly. Emma, please—"

"Don't call me that!" She seriously wanted to punch him in the face. Her fist clenched and almost did its own bidding, so she growled and turned away. She didn't need an assault charge on her record. With her luck, Paul would be the responding officer. "What do you want? What insurance fraud case could involve us?"

"I don't know. I was hired freelance by an attorney. Emma—"

"I said not to call me that!" Crossing her arms, she demanded, "What did he or she hire you to do?"

"To prove Collins and King are frauds. Emma, look at me."

"To prove them frauds – why?" She continued pacing away from him into the living room. "They're very careful about the cases they take. Nothing they uncover using their abilities is admissible in a court of law. We state that in our contracts."

"It has to do with a worker's comp case. That's all I know."

That made no sense. Neither Zach nor Alexandra had worked a worker's compensation case that she was aware. "Are you incapable of telling the truth?"

He grabbed her arm and spun her to face him. "Emma, I'm sorry. I didn't mean to mislead you. I didn't expect…"

She glared at him when he didn't elaborate. "Expect what?"

"For us to become friends."

Tears welled in her eyes, which made no sense. What reasonable person wouldn't feel a stab of hurt that his words didn't reveal deeper feelings than friendship? She turned and dashed them away so he wouldn't see them. "That's stupid, Noah. We barely know each other."

"I know that you're funny and loyal." His voice was loud in her left ear; she realized he'd followed her. "I know you're a good person – better than I deserve."

She snorted. He knew the right things to say. She'd give him that, but she refused to let him know how much he'd wounded her.

Sure, she liked to look at and maybe even flirt with her hot co-workers, but that was because they were safe. They were all married or had girlfriends for the most part, and they had become her friends. Noah had been the first man since Paul that she'd truly let herself wish for more with. That she'd actually *wanted* more with.

She was such an idiot. He'd probably laughed at how easy it had been to charm her into trusting him.

Turning, she met his gaze. His deceitful, beautiful, yummy green gaze. "Nice words, but I'm still waiting for you to tell me what you want from me. Why are you really here?"

"You really want to know what I want from you?"

"Yes!" She knew it wasn't attractive, but she stomped her foot anyway.

One second she was glowering at him from her spot near the chair. The next, her front was pressed against his, her head was yanked backwards, and his mouth was feasting on hers. He had one hand at her back and the other weaved in her hair, not that she noticed much. She was a little distracted by the swarm of bees that rumbled to life in her belly, zipping through her limbs and leaving tiny stings at each of her nerve endings, especially wherever he touched her. Moaning, she gasped in surprise, and he took advantage, forcing her lips further apart, dipping inside, teasing her tongue with his.

Heat spread like honey over all of those tingles, and she reached up to hold him closer. To better taste him.

She'd never been kissed like this. Not ever.

Wait.

Why was he kissing her?

Oh, fudge! She'd turned into one of those stupid, idiotic women who let her brain be ruled by sexual urges. He had to know the effect he had on her. He *had* to be manipulating her yet again. Pushing at his shoulders, she tore her mouth away and tried to calm her pounding heart.

"Noah, stop."

His mouth tasted hers again, and she moaned, liking it too much, struggling not to give in. Breathing roughly, she jerked her lips away, drove her knee into his groin and shoved him backwards.

Slapping her hand to her mouth, she stared wide-eyed as he fell into the chair and groaned in agony. "Why the hell did you do that?" His voice was rough, strained. "I would have stopped."

She reached toward him but yanked her hand back when he rolled away. "I'm sorry! I just … reacted." Combine all of that self-defence training she'd done with Alexandra with a bad temper, and bam! Man down. Whoa. She was dangerous. "Um, are you okay?"

His face was twisted in pain. "I think you should go now."

"What can I do?"

"Leave!"

"Ice-pack?"

He pointed toward the door. "Go!"

Halfway toward the exit, she turned and pointed at him. "By the way, you deserved that!"

She slammed the door behind her, too, the smack of wood so loud it echoed around the neighbourhood.

Her anger was still simmering her blood to a boil as she sank onto Zach's lush, comfy sofa. The nerve of the man! To kiss her and try to use her obvious feelings for him. Jerk.

"You okay?"

She jumped at Kellan's question.

She'd almost forgotten her sexy co-worker was here waiting for her to return. *She had* also forgotten that he'd been virtually hiding in Zach's office and could see everything, thanks to the hidden cameras he'd installed in Noah's house this morning.

"I'm peachy."

He sat on the cushion beside her. "I was fixing to come over and kick his ass after he grabbed you, but you did it before I had the chance." One side of his mouth curled up. He was staring at her as if he'd never really seen her before. "Remind me never to piss you off."

"From your mouth to God's ears."

A niggle of guilt wormed its way into her conscience. Calling Kellan for help before she gave Noah a chance to defend himself might have been a bit impulsive, but she'd figured Zach's business was at stake. Her job. She could've tried to thwart Noah's devious, deceptive, creep-tastic movements on her own, but she was smart enough to know when she needed backup.

"Maybe I should have waited to call you." She glanced toward the window. Was Noah still writhing in pain? Was he really hurt? Heat warmed her face and she buried it between her hands. She might have kneed him harder than was decent. "Oh, gosh. I'm such a horrible person."

"Hey." Kellan's hand squeezed her shoulder. "You did the right thing."

He was right. She knew that. Being a badass wasn't supposed to feel this way.

She searched his face for confirmation. "You didn't tell anyone else? Promise?"

"Promise. I've got your back, Spider, just like we've both got Zach's back. We're family. It's okay to call me when you need help."

Family.

He was right. These men and women were her family, the one she'd made on her own, the one that accepted her and her quirks, just as she accepted them and theirs.

A car door slammed and an engine roared to life outside. Pushing to her feet, Spider hurried to the window. Noah's jeep backed out of the driveway and tore off as if the devil himself was after him.

"He'll be back." Kellan stood beside her. "In the meantime, we've got the video feed from his house wired to Zach's computer here and my computer. You've got the backup of his hard drive?"

Nodding, she reached into her pocket for the small flash drive she'd stored everything on before wiping Noah's laptop. "Want a copy?"

"You go through it. If anything seems suspicious, call me. I'll see if I can't figure out what case he's been working and why." He grabbed the duffle bag he'd sat at the doorway. He reached for the doorknob and hesitated, looking back at her. "You did good, Spider."

She managed to summon a smile. "Thanks."

"Call me if you need me. Day or night."

Crossing her arms, she nodded and watched him leave. She almost forgot to punch in the alarm code too.

"Mrreow."

She turned. Abbott, Charlie, and Costello all sat in triangle formation staring at her. She glanced at the clock. Feeding time.

"Sorry, guys." She took a deep breath to quell the tears that threatened to escape and moved toward the kitchen. "I think we deserve a treat. Ice cream for me. Tuna for you, cat. Whatever those bone things are for you, dogs. Whaddaya say?"

Charlie began spinning in a circle. Costello hopped up on his back legs and danced backward. Abbott brushed between her legs, tail sticking straight up and twitching.

She took that to mean, *heck, yes!* This. This was why animals were awesome to be around.

They'd pig out together, watch some *Battlestar Galactica*, and not one of them would mention Noah West's name again. That lying, scheming, full-of-himself a-hole.

If he thought a few kisses would stop her, he didn't know a darn thing about her.

The spider always ate her prey.

# Chapter 10

"What's eatin' you, bro?"

Noah spared a look at his older brother, who was doing the same thing he was – leaning back in his recliner, nursing a cold one and watching the boring-ass Braves game on TV. Fifteen hits, one walk, four runs scored. Couldn't someone at least try to steal a base?

"Nothing. Bored, that's all."

John lowered the volume on his big-screen. Oh, hell. Here it came. John brushed his shaggy brown hair back on his forehead. "You've been here two days. Not that I mind the company, but you've been about as pleasant as a sewer breeze since you got here. You gonna tell me why or what?"

"No." He nodded at the beer in his brother's hand. "You're not turning into dad, are you? Is that your fourth or fifth one?"

"See that right there? That's what I'm talkin' about." Scowling, John snapped his footrest down and shoved to his feet. He thrust a finger at Noah. "I'm fixin' to beat you if you keep it up." Instead, he headed for the kitchen, probably to grab another beer.

Noah grimaced, knowing he'd crossed a line. All it took to get on his or John's bad side was any comparison to their deadbeat father. Derek West had been quite the role model, if you considered womanizing alcoholic abusers good enough to emulate.

As much as possible, Noah had always been determined to prove himself to be different, but he'd only succeeded on a few counts. He only allowed himself one beer a day, although he usually didn't even indulge in that many. He'd gone to college, dropped his heavy Southern accent, focused on his goals, and made a decent career for himself. So decent, he'd been regarded as one of the best insurance investigators in the state, highly sought after even after he'd turned in his resignation six months ago.

It had felt wrong. Spying on people all the time. Digging up dirt to give someone else an advantage.

Emma's hurt face forced itself to the forefront of his thoughts again, but he pushed the image back into that corner of his mind labelled *don't go there.*

Worst part was, both he and John *did* take after their father in various ways, not the least of which were their dark features that attracted women like shoe sale signs. Noah had given up a long time ago trying to deny his philandering nature. Only ten years older than Noah, John was three times divorced and always seeing someone new. At least Noah knew better than to trade vows he couldn't keep.

"Sorry. Forget I said that. You're nothing like him." The brand-new house that his brother had built with his own hands through his successful construction company, with his own money, was proof of that.

His brother propped himself against the wall, watched the game, a fresh water bottle in his hand now. "Is that what this is all about?"

"What?"

John shifted his weight. "The old man." He scratched at his neck. "Did he, uh, say anything to you?"

A laugh void of humour escaped him before he could stop it. "Haven't talked to him since before he went in this last time." Their father was currently serving a five-year sentence for his fourth DUI after killing someone's grandfather.

"Good." John blew the answer out on a rush of breath.

Something about his careful tone piqued Noah's interest. "Why?

What are you afraid he told me?”

“Nothing, man. Just askin’.”

Noah’s bullshit detector was blasting a loud alarm inside his brain, but he knew pursuing the subject would only lead to more talk about their father and he wasn’t in the mood.

“If this ain’t about the old man that leaves only one thing.” John pushed away from the wall and began pacing. “Women.”

Not women. One woman.

Emma was still on his mind despite the fact he’d put nearly one hundred miles and a couple of days between them. At first, he’d been pissed that she’d destroyed his computer and tried her best to neuter him. He preferred that slow boil of anger stirring his blood to the dreaded hopeless feeling that now left his chest feeling hollow.

Whatever Connor had done hadn’t cured Noah completely of his infatuation with the prickly woman. He thought about her day and night. The dreams were the worst. Shifting in his seat, he tried to ignore memories of those night-time visions, always lust-filled fantasies of Emma that segued into the dream about the dark-haired woman getting into the car. He always woke up when the driver locked her inside the vehicle.

“See there? I’m right.” John took a long gulp of water. “I knew you’d find a woman who’d tangle you up one day.”

Maybe he should talk to John about her. His brother was the only person likely to understand the hell he was going through.

Putting his drink aside, he wiped a hand over his face and tried to think of the best approach to what he had to say. One that wouldn’t have John encouraging his strange behaviour.

“Let me ask you a question. Do you believe in ghosts?”

John’s head jerked back. “You mean, like, *ghost* ghosts? Dead people?”

Noah nodded.

“I reckon I’d better sit down for this one.”

Once John was back in his chair and the TV volume was muted,

Noah told his brother everything. About the job he'd taken because the attorney he'd once worked with had been so insistent no one else could do it. About the house. Emma. Everything.

"Damn," was John's only comment.

"That's real helpful."

Something about his brother's expression had changed during the telling of the story, had become pensive, almost shocked. Rubbing a hand against the front of his shirt, he couldn't seem to meet Noah in the eyes.

"This guy, this psychic character, he wanted to know if a woman in your family had died?"

Noah pushed to his feet, feeling the need to pace, expend some energy. "Yeah."

"And these dreams you're having. You're sure the woman is named Kate?"

"Pretty sure."

"Hell." John stood, one hand finding his hip, the other crunching the plastic bottle in his grip so hard the crinkle was as loud as a garbage compactor. He turned back around, met Noah's gaze. "You believe any of it?"

His easy-go-lucky brother was acting damn strange all of sudden. Noah lifted one shoulder. "Don't know what I believe anymore."

"And this other woman, Emma, you still have feelings for her?"

Smiling bitterly, Noah shook his head and looked away. "You know it's not like that."

"What's it like then?"

"Lust. Attraction. That's all. That's all I'm capable of."

"This guy removed the lust spell that you were under, and you're still thinking about her. I'd say you're capable of more than you want to admit."

"I'm just like dad. So are you, only at least I don't fight it. I'm incapable of loving any woman. You know that."

"You love Jennifer and Kristina, don't ya? And mom?"

"That's different." Of course he loved his sisters and mother.

"No, it ain't. Not when you boil down to it." The bottle crackled again in his brother's clasp. "You think you have to be like dad, but you don't. It's a lifestyle choice, not some stupid disease."

"Whatever." Noah considered it more of a family curse than anything. He might be capable of loving someone, but he'd eventually do something to turn it all to shit. Better to avoid that unpleasantness altogether.

Tossing the empty bottle aside, John blew out his cheeks and slowly let out the air. He gestured to the recliner. "Maybe you should sit down."

"Why?"

"Sit. Down." John's voice boomed out the command. It wasn't a request.

Hands on his hips, Noah met his brother's gaze long enough to make it clear he was only sitting because he wanted to. John shifted on his feet in front of him.

"You know I love you, right?"

Grimacing, Noah moved to stand again, but John pushed him back.

"I mean it."

Noah looked around, wishing he'd never started this conversation. "Yeah. Same goes."

"I'm only telling you this because I think you really need to know it, and mom's halfway across the country right now. She told me once I could tell you if I ever felt you needed to know, if anything ever happened to her."

Noah stilled. "Tell me what?"

Cursing, John spun around and paced toward the outside wall. "Should I be doing this? Hell." Grabbing the thick curl of hair at his forehead, he faced Noah again. Took a deep breath. "We're not related by blood."

"What?"

"That didn't come out right." He swore. "Mom and dad adopted you when you were a baby. I remember the day they brought you home. Didn't think they could have any more kids, and dad was trying to make sure mom didn't leave him after she found out about one of his other women."

The room crumbled around Noah as his mind reared with the implications. "You're joking, right?"

"I wish I was."

Adopted. He was adopted? Nausea filled his gut, along with a healthy helping of denial. He pushed unsteadily to his feet. "You are. You're joking."

John's eyes held none of the mischief they usually boasted. They were dulled by the sheen of something close to sadness. "Thing is, I snuck around once and found your papers. Mom would have killed me if she knew, but the name of your real mother, the one listed on the papers? It was Katherine. Noah, your birth mother's name was probably Kate. I don't remember the last name, but I do remember that."

Shuffling back a step, or maybe two, Noah sank into the chair that hit against the back of his knees. It took him a few seconds to find his voice, which sounded shaky to his own ears.

"Tell me everything you know."

***

Stabbing her finger repeatedly against the down arrow on her keyboard, Spider stared blankly ahead at her laptop monitor, barely seeing the file names through which she scrolled.

"Meow." The familiar growl that accompanied this vibrated with menace. The chorus of whining that followed was downright pitiful.

Stilling, she looked over at the cat now perched beside her on the sofa. Abbott's bland expression probably mocked her own. Below him, Costello and Charlie stared at her with big eyes full of longing, their heads resting on the edge of the cushion. She glanced at the clock and abruptly erupted in surprise, nearly tossing her laptop to the floor as she jumped up.

"Fiddlesticks! I'm sorry, boys. I'm sorry!"

This time, she was almost a full half hour past the animals' feeding time. She was getting worse, not better. Doggone it!

Rather than mentally cursing Noah as she'd done the other times, she accepted that no one else was to blame but herself. The cat seemed to forgive her, if the way he weaved in and out of her legs was any indication. Charlie and Costello joined the kitchen circus with their nightly shenanigans, twirling and prancing around her legs. They gobbled up their food like a pack of hungry wolves when she scooped it into their bowls.

Squatting, she patted each of their heads as their frantic crunching filled the room. "Sorry, guys. I promise I will do better. Pinky swear. Er, paw swear. Or whatever."

So far, she was an epic failure in the pet-sitting department. Not her forte, apparently.

Since the incident with Noah, she'd fallen into a funk of self-pity unlike any she'd ever known, which she knew was stupid. Everything about her reaction to that man was stupid. Seriously, someone needed to slap her. She hadn't even been this messed up when she'd called off her engagement to Paul.

It ended now. No more feeling sorry for herself. No more scattered mind. She was over it.

Moving to her feet again, she stepped toward the sofa and paused. Her laptop was gone.

Shifting her eyes around the room, she sighed. "Funny, ghost. Ha ha. Where did you put it?"

This had been a nightly occurrence since she'd closed herself off to the outside world again, going out only for walks with the dogs. Things disappeared. Objects moved. She heard sounds.

At first, it had scared her near-to-death, but it was all getting a bit annoying.

A clank beside the couch was her first clue the laptop had been moved there. Peeking around the corner table, she saw it lying on the floor. She knew she hadn't put it there.

Picking it up and trying to decipher what the ghost was attempting to tell her now, her gaze zeroed in on the video file pulled up on the screen.

She'd spent the last few days scrolling through the contents of Noah's hard drive, not finding anything to explain what he'd been doing here. He deserved points though for keeping his files organized and easy to archive though. Bonus points.

She'd been saving the folder full of videos for last, simply because it had contained over twenty video files of boring stuff she had no desire to watch. The one she'd opened as an experiment had been of some guy doing yard work and had lasted for more than an hour.

Total snooze-a-palooza.

She looked at the date on the file that had been opened for her. Only a few days old. If that jerk had videotaped her doing something dumb, she'd chase him down and knee his groin again.

Tapping play, she fell back onto the couch.

The screen showed Noah entering his living room. Okay, that was not what she'd been expecting. He sank into the chair and sprawled his long limbs out, shifting to get comfortable. Why on earth had he recorded this? Unless…

Funny that he had forgotten to mention he had video evidence of his haunting. Imagine that. *Scumbag.*

She fast-forwarded the clip, stopping when he sprang out of the seat again. She rewound it a little, hearing the loud knocking that must have woken him up. The scene that unfolded was peculiar, to say the least. His TV turned on and off. It sounded like a marching band was roaming his house. And then, something else. A whisper?

Charlie jumped onto the sofa beside her, swiped the side of her face with a few licks, and settled in as if to watch the show with her, which was crazy since he was blind. She cranked it up to full volume and rewound the footage.

The dog tilted his head at the screen and made a sound that resembled, "Huh?"

She looked at him. "You heard that?"

Another swipe of tongue across the face. She'd take that to mean yes.

She played it again, but the whisper was so inaudible, she still had no idea what was said. Charlie again tilted his head and grumbled at the screen. Costello even shambled over to inspect it.

All right. Good clue. *Thanks, ghost.* This was progress.

It took her a few minutes to determine the best software for decoding EVPs – electronic voice phenomena – and less time to download and install it. She messed around with the settings, adjusted them, played the clip so many times she'd memorized every movement her jerkface of a neighbour made in it, and finally decoded five distinct words spoken in a soft, feminine voice.

"I was killed … near here."

Seconds later, her mobile screamed out in its robotic tone, "You have a call. Answer it now or prepare to be terminated."

Spider squealed and dumped her laptop on the floor.

Heart pounding – she was gonna have a heart attack if this didn't stop soon – she reached for her phone. "Hello?"

"Spider? I only have a few minutes to talk."

Connor's voice was curt, as if he was bothered to return the ten or so messages she'd left for him over the past couple of days.

"It's about darn time you called me back, you … you creep!"

There was a pause. "Why am I a creep?"

"Oh, I thought you were Mr. Psychic and knew everything."

"Spider." He drew her name out in a threatening manner.

"You knew about Noah and you didn't tell me? I'm sorry. I thought Alexandra sent you here to help me, not him."

"I thought I was helping *both* of you." He grumbled something incoherent. "Look. As far as Noah is concerned, there's a reason for everything. Remember that."

"O-kay. Could you be any more cryptic and vague?"

"Yes, but I won't." She could hear a smile in his voice now. He sucked in a breath. "Something happened there. Are you okay? You're scared. Nervous."

"Duh!" She described the EVP. "What am I supposed to do now?"

He sighed. "I can't leave here for a few days." He hesitated, and she picked up on voices in the background. Loud, angry voices.

"Where are you?"

"Not in Georgia." Again with the vague and cryptic. "I have to hurry. Have you been having any dreams or anything? Anything that would help you identify who she is?"

"I keep having a weird dream about—" She caught herself before mentioning Noah's name. "Elton John, singing a song about elephants and unicorns to me beside a lake. Weird, I know, but there it is."

"Recurring?"

"Yes."

"Before you go to sleep tonight, tell her out loud you welcome her to communicate with you through a dream as long as she doesn't try to harm you. Ask her to be clear about what the other dream means."

"That's it?"

"I have to go. Spider?"

"Yeah?"

"Be careful. I'll call you when I get back."

"But—"

He'd already hung up.

She heard a car door slam somewhere outside and moved to the window. Pushing back the curtain, she watched Noah grab his bag from the back seat, shut that door and turn to look towards her.

Excitement danced along her nerve endings when one side of his mouth kicked up in a half smile and he lifted a hand to wave at her.

Frowning, she dropped the curtain and moved away from the

window.

Blockhead. Who did he think he was?

She paced along the rug, gaze darting to the front door in anticipation of his inevitable visit. She wouldn't open it if he came over. No way. Not gonna do it. She crossed her arms and waited.

Minutes passed. Nothing happened. Her shoulders slumped in relief that he wasn't going to approach her tonight. Good.

"I was killed … near here."

Slapping a hand over her chest, Spider jumped at the sound playing from her computer.

Crap. She'd almost forgotten about that.

"A little warning would be nice." She addressed the ceiling, although she doubted any ghost worth her while was actually floating up there.

She scooped up her laptop and chewed her bottom lip. Maybe she should go play this for Noah? Obviously, the message had been meant for him.

Her brain drifted to the video setup Kellan had left in Zach's office. Hmmm. Should she be bad and go see what he was up to?

Pfft. He'd done it to her, hadn't he?

She ran to the monitor on her boss's desk. Flipping it on, she smiled in triumph, seeing four squares appear on the screen. Noah moved into the frame on the top right square. His bedroom. She had an eagle's eye view of the room, looking down on him. Clicking to maximize that screen on the display, she watched Noah toss his bag onto the bed, sit down and stare at the wall for several seconds.

Something about his slumped posture seemed … sad. Defeated. Like a little boy without a sled on a snowy day. Leaning closer to his image, Spider wished she could smooth away his worry lines, make him smile, give a hug. Something to bring back that sexy sparkle of interest always so evident in his eyes. Even if he was a creep, no one deserved to look so hopeless.

Wiping a hand over his face, he stood again, lifting his hands to unbutton his shirt.

"Oh. Well, maybe I shouldn't—" Jerking back, she looked around, as if anyone could see what she was doing and then chuckled at herself.

Who was she kidding? She should. She totally should watch him undress. Consider it his payment for being such an a-hole. Noah West still made delicious eye candy.

Leaning forward again, she watched him yank his shirt off and toss it toward the corner of the screen.

"Nice," she murmured to herself.

She'd tried not to stare at his muscular chest and biceps the day she'd caught him just out of the shower, but her gaze was glued to him now. Nice pecs. Great abdomen. Strong, muscular arms. His fingers were long, too. Wasn't that an indication of, um, other body parts?

She tugged at the collar of her shirt and shifted on the chair. A nice heat was beginning to spread from her belly outward, making her wet in places she hadn't been in … too long.

Then he reached down and popped the button on his jeans, revealing a pair of boxer briefs. She might have recognized the brand from advertisements, and, oh my, he looked so much better than most of those models she'd drooled over.

"Meow, mreow."

The slow drawl of the feline suspiciously resembled an accusatory, "What are you doing?"

She shoved with her foot at the black and white animal that crept around the desk. Noah was tugging off his jeans now. "Go away, cat. I'm busy."

Abbott leapt onto the stained wood and manoeuvred his fluffy body right in front of the monitor.

"Move, cat!" She brushed him away.

With a vicious protest, Abbott flopped onto his side, latched his claws onto her hand, and began bunny-kicking her wrist.

"Owwww!"

Growling, the cat leapt away and scattered off again. Clasping her throbbing hand against her stomach, Spider yelled after him, "I thought we'd gotten to be friends!"

That brat!

Glancing at the monitor, she realized Noah was no longer on the screen. She clicked out to look at the other rooms.

"Bathroom? Shower. Didn't Kellan put a camera there?"

Of course he hadn't.

Clicking the monitor off, Spider retreated to her own bathroom to put ointment on the wounds Abbott had left her with, no doubt in return for making him wait for his dinner. She supposed she deserved them. Watching Noah undress had been kind of a pervy thing to do.

She let the dogs out and changed into a fresh pair of pajamas since she'd been wearing her others all day. Gathering her laptop, she climbed into bed and reviewed the EVP footage again.

Should she share it with Noah?

No.

Maybe later, but not now.

She saved the audio of the file as a clip and considered her options. One, her father was the most obvious resource she had. He would know about any unsolved murders in the area, might even be able to point her toward a specific case file. Not that she knew anything to give him the specifics he'd need to do so.

Shoot!

Two, she could present her findings to Noah and let him have at it. Wipe her hands clean and be done with the whole mess. Get back to playing *Days of Adventure* with her online guild in peace and passing her time here without any interference whatsoever. The vacation she had wanted and deserved.

Three, she could handle this on her own. Prove she could handle an investigation without help from anyone.

Yeah, she quite liked option two, but she liked option three better.

She could do this.

Stretching her arms out in front of her, she cracked the joints in her hand, wiggled her fingers, and started with what she knew best. Internet research.

# Chapter 11

"Hey, kiddo. Haven't seen you in a long time. Is your dad in Zone 2 today?" Officer Van DeLorenzo leaned across the front desk, his large hand outstretched, fingers wiggling so that Spider felt obligated to smack palms with him in the private handshake they'd established years ago.

DeLorenzo, who usually ran the supply room, had often been saddled with babysitting her at the precinct whenever her dad was on duty, her mom was working late, and they hadn't been able to find a sitter. Nice guy. She liked him. Plus, he didn't seem very busy at the moment since the lobby was empty.

So far, so good.

Sitting her messenger bag on the counter, she leaned against it. "No. He's at command today, doing fun Chief-of-Policey stuff."

She put in the obligatory phone call each morning to let her dad know she was still alive, and to make sure he was too. This morning, he'd been on his way to some meeting to update department policies and regulations.

"I was hoping I could have access to some of Zone 2's public records." Spider pretended to pout. "My boss has me doing research on one of his cases, and I'm not having any luck on the computer."

He tapped the counter top. "You came to the right place. What case are you working?"

Smiling, she reached into her satchel and retrieved the list she'd made last night after searching the online archives of the Atlanta Journal Constitution for longer than she cared to admit. Her list contained five names of missing or murdered women from the Buckhead part of Atlanta over the past thirty years. All dark-haired women approximately 20 to 30 years old. One name was circled – Katherine Levine – because her grainy photograph had resembled the woman Spider had seen in the window more so than the other four.

"Can I see the police reports for these missing persons and homicide cases?" She handed him the list.

"Katherine Levine. I remember that one. Sad story from about, what? Thirty years ago? College kid. She had a little boy. Single mom trying to make good. You know?"

Spider leaned closer. "What happened?"

DeLorenzo skirted his gaze around, propped his arm on the counter. "One of her friends reported her missing. Her boy, ah, he was about one or two, I think. He got taken by the state. Wonder what happened to him?" He drummed the notepad against the counter. "He the one who hired your boss?"

Biting her lip, Spider shrugged. "Can't tell you that. Confidential." Maybe tracking down the woman's son would be one of the next things on her list. "Did you work that case?"

"Nah. Don't remember who did." An officer was walking past and DeLorenzo called out, "Lanier. Com'ere."

Oh, no. Spider sank a little lower, wishing the counter could shield her completely from view. She had hoped not to see Jack again anytime soon after that whole accusing-Noah-of-being-a-serial-killer fiasco.

A huge smile engulfed his wrinkled face when he saw her. "Emma! What brings you down here?"

DeLorenzo didn't give her time to answer. "You remember who worked the Katherine Levine case? College kid whose friend reported her missing. Worked at Wally's. Remember?"

Smile falling, Jack scratched the back of his neck. "Yeah, we never found a body."

"Who worked the case?" DeLorenzo asked again.

Jack's brow furrowed as he considered Spider more closely. "Can't remember. Why?" He arched one brow and pinned her with a half smile. "You're not still trying to play detective, are you? What is it this time? Another neighbour you suspect is a serial killer?" He chuckled.

So not funny.

His radio chose that moment to squawk a request, which he thankfully answered. He was talking into his handset as he disappeared down the hall, where the private exit was.

DeLorenzo slapped the counter to get her attention. "Come on. We'll see if we can find these records."

Thirty minutes later, Spider emerged with the spoils of her victory in hand. Photocopies of the police reports filed to report Katherine Levine missing, along with a handful of others for the other women. Sitting in her car, she dug Katherine's files out and glanced over them again. A photograph of the woman had been paper clipped to the file, and she'd copied that too. With crinkle lines from laughter around her eyes, the pretty, dark-haired woman smiled back at her with familiar features.

A tingling in her belly sent a shot of adrenaline through her veins. Call it a gut feeling, but she suspected she'd found the identity of her ghost. She skimmed the report from twenty-eight years ago. Katherine, or Kate, as she was known to friends, had never shown up for work one evening at the bar where she waitressed. One of her classmates had filed the report when she didn't return home either. That classmate, who'd been babysitting Kate's unidentified son, had assured the responding officers that it was out of character.

"Wonder if I can track down this friend." Pursing her lips, Spider entered the woman's name into her smartphone.

No-go. Plus, the woman probably had a different last name by now.

"Well, I wonder if anyone at Wally's remembers her." Turning the engine over, Spider directed her old car toward the bar that had recently been remodeled and renamed, but everyone on this side of town knew as Wally's.

An excited energy buzzed along her nerve endings now. Was this how her co-workers felt when out in the field? It was thrilling, addictive.

When she'd been a teenager, she and her dad had often stopped at Wally's for its out-of-this-world burgers. The décor had been tacky and dark, and the place didn't smell like anything a man should bring his daughter around, but that was her dad. Stepping into the bar now, she stopped in the entryway to take inventory of the sleek, new atmosphere. The update, in her opinion, was a nice change from what she remembered. Light-grey walls were painted with sports emblems and team logos. Gleaming silver chairs and tables had replaced the yucky booths and wood tables that had once greeted patrons.

Much brighter. Huge improvement.

"What can I get for you?" The middle-aged bartender asked when she stepped into the raised bar area.

Pushing her sunglasses to the top of her head, she waved her hand dismissively. "Sweet tea. Thanks."

The silver-haired man, who looked to be in his fifties at most, eyed her quizzically but moved to get it ready. "Never seen you around before."

She drummed her fingers against the counter, looking for any members of the staff over the age of forty. This guy seemed her best bet. "I'm trying to find someone. Maybe you can help?"

"I'll try." He slid the tea in front of her and winked.

"She used to work here about twenty-eight years ago?"

"Yeah? My uncle owned the place then. I used to wash dishes in the back. What was her name?"

"Kate Levine."

"Kate. Yeah, I knew Kate." He reached for a rag and began

wiping down the bar top. "If you're looking for her, you're not the only one. She went missing, long time ago. Who did you say you were again?"

"I didn't." She leaned forward. "Do you remember if there were any suspects in her disappearance?"

He shrugged, nonchalant. "Not that I remember. Everyone thought she ran off. She'd been seeing some guy, getting serious. I figure they went away together. He probably didn't want her kid, so…"

"What happened to her kid? Do you know?"

"Heard he got put in the system." He narrowed his gaze on her. "You and the guy who was just up here – you together? Cause it seems odd, two people in one day coming in to ask about Kate."

Excitement widened her eyes. "What guy?"

He nodded behind her. She turned. Noah was sitting at a table not far from where she stood, watching her. He lifted his glass, and smiled.

* * *

Noah had no idea what Emma was doing here, but it was embarrassing the way his palms had started sweating when he'd seen her walk in. Heart thumping out of beat, his breath had caught and held until his brain reminded his lungs to start breathing again. Discreetly wiping his hands on his knees under the table, he'd been grateful she didn't see him right away. Gave him a chance to pull himself together, watch her, figure out his next move.

Figure out what the hell she was doing here.

When she saw him, she looked about as affected as he had. Cheeks flushing with red, she opened her eyes wide and her mouth fell open in a way that might have been cute in any other circumstance. Then her eyes narrowed, her lips thinned and she glared at him.

Turning back to the bartender, she said something, grabbed her bag, and advanced in his direction.

Oh, hell.

He took in his fill of her, almost laughing aloud when he read the writing beside the cartoonish tyrannosaurus-rex on her pale-blue t-shirt: "If History Repeats Itself, I Am So Getting A Dinosaur!"

Damn, but he'd missed her.

She stepped up to his table and put her hands on her hips. "Are you following me?"

He leaned back. "Me? I was here first. Ask him." He nodded toward the bartender.

Her mouth made an 'O' as her gaze skittered around. "Well, what are you doing here?"

He lifted his mug of soda and looked at the half-eaten burger on his tray. "Eating. What are *you* doing here?"

She crossed her arms. "I dunno."

"You don't know what you're doing here?"

She half shrugged before spinning on her heel and walking away. Noah found his feet, tossed a few dollars onto the table and hurried after her, catching the door before it closed on him.

"Emma, wait!"

She kept walking. "Not talking to you."

He jogged to catch up to her. "Why won't you let me apologize?"

"Apology accepted. Buh-bye." She waved him away as if he was an annoying pest.

"Can't I explain?"

She stopped and looked at him. "Sure. Why were you really spying on us?"

"I told you. I was hired by an attorney. Worker's comp case or something."

Rolling her eyes, she started moving forward again.

"I'm not lying."

She stopped, rounded on him. "You are so full of it! How come you never mentioned you recorded a video of your haunting? Or do you consider omitting certain facts not to be a lie?"

His forehead tightened. "You saw that?"

She snorted. "Not only saw it, I decoded the message in it."

"What message?"

Her face crumpled into one of disgust as she looked at the sidewalk. "Dammit, I wasn't going to tell you that yet."

He grabbed her forearm. "Emma, what message?"

Frowning, her gaze searched his features. "A woman whispers something. I know what she says."

His hand fell away. "What does she say? Tell me."

He wasn't fully aboard the my-birth-mother-is-a-ghost train of thought yet, but if solving this mystery helped him reconcile his own past, he was in.

She glanced toward the Wally's entrance and shuffled her feet. Leaning close, she lowered her voice. "She says, 'I was killed near here.'"

Dizziness threatened to send him backwards. He reached out, clasped her arm to steady himself.

"Noah, are you okay?"

Deep breaths. In and out.

"Yeah." He held onto her because he liked the feel of her skin. Soft and warm. "How did you know about Wally's?"

She tugged her arm out of his grip. "What do you mean?"

He turned away, ran a hand through his hair, and wondered how much of this he should share. She was listening, so he might as well. "I keep having this dream about a woman. It's like a memory or something. She gets into a car with a man, mentions she's late for work—" He gestured to the sign. "—at Wally's. He locks her in the car, and I wake up. I know her name is Kate, but that's all."

Her mouth fell open again. "Oh. My. Gosh!" Reaching for her bag, she dug out some papers. "I knew she was the woman I saw in the window! I knew it!" She tapped a copy of a printout. It was an old article clipping, and a small, grainy photograph in the corner was labelled *Katherine Levine*.

Noah's legs threatened to give way.

The smiling, dark-haired woman pictured was the same Kate he'd been seeing in his dreams.

"She went missing twenty-eight years ago. Her body was never found. Noah, do you know what this means?"

His heart was racing, trying to spin out of his ribcage. He could barely breathe, let alone talk. "What?"

"She's your ghost! She wants us to find her killer!"

Her declaration was so loud, the couple passing them on the sidewalk turned and stared. Noah pushed Emma toward her car, sitting at the curb. "Too damn bad you destroyed my hard drive. I'd like to hear this message for myself." His hunch told him she'd have a backup somewhere.

She pulled away from him, thoughtful. "Yes, it is a shame, isn't it?" She dug her keys out of her bag. "Well, it's been fun. Gotta go." She hurried around to the driver's side door.

"Wait a second. I thought you said she wanted 'us' to find her killer. That implies we need to work together."

She feigned a look of innocence. "Sorry. This is your problem now. I've got other things to do."

"Like what?"

She waved, ducked into her car, and slammed the door shut behind her. A couple of seconds later, she pulled into traffic like a bat out of hell.

Noah stared after her, feeling a bit like he'd just been tossed up in a tornado.

Emma Fisher turned him into an awkward schoolboy again, and he didn't like that. If he was smart, he'd leave her alone – but how could he?

She knew too damn much. More than he did.

He glanced at his watch, wondering what time the library closed and how hard it would be to track down the article she'd found in the archives. He'd let her go, for now, but he wasn't done with her yet.

# Chapter 12

Excitement zinged through Spider's brain, sending tremors of anticipation down her arms and legs as she stepped up to the mahogany door and pressed the doorbell. She bit her lower lip and primly clasped her hands in front of her to keep from smiling inappropriately, or heaven forbid, doing a triumphant Snoopy dance on the front porch of this extravagant-looking home.

Jennifer Ritzer-Abercrombie.

Who had tracked down Kate Levine's friend all by her lonesome? *That would be me – cyber security specialist turned field investigator extraordinaire. Ha!*

Seriously, Zach might start using her to do legwork on cases if she ever revealed to him how good she was. A search through the public records database the agency employed had given her a probable lead, which she'd followed to this wealthy neighbourhood not too far from where Zach and Hannah lived.

The door opened, and a middle-aged blonde peeked her head around. "Yes?"

Recognizing the woman from her driver's license photo, Spider smiled. "Mrs. Abercrombie, I'm Spider Fisher with the Collins Security Firm." She held out a business card, and the woman opened the door wider to take it. "I'm investigating the disappearance of Kate Levine, and I wondered if you would have a few minutes to speak with me?"

"Kate?" Frowning, the woman glanced over her shoulder and back again, opening the door wider. "Yes, of course, but I'm not certain I can help you in any way that matters. That was a long time ago."

"I understand. I've been reviewing the old files and saw where you reported her missing, so I'd love to find out what you remember from that night."

"I'm curious enough to ask who hired you. Kate didn't have any family she was close to, only her son." Eyes widening, Mrs. Abercrombie lifted a hand to her chest. "Oh, dear, is he the one who hired you?"

"No, I'm afraid not. I can't actually say who—"

The slap of pounding footsteps grew louder, causing Spider to turn at the approaching noise. Her lower jaw dropped.

"I'm sorry I'm late!"

Noah jogged to her side, winking at her when she could only manage to gape at him. Sliding his hand around to her back in a far too familiar gesture, he held out his other hand to the petite woman. "Noah West. My apologies, but I got held up. I told my colleague here to go ahead and see if you were available to speak to us."

Mrs. Abercrombie blinked at him. "I was just about to invite her inside." She moved back and gestured into the entryway. "Won't you both come in?"

Smirking like the jackal she knew him to be, Noah swaggered inside without looking at her. The jerk! He must have followed her, and what could she do about it? Create a scene and lose the only opportunity she might have to question her as-of-now only witness?

Nails biting into her palms, Spider followed him, certain by the heat in her cheeks that her face was probably red and unbecoming. He was gonna be in so much trouble when they left here.

Mrs. Abercrombie offered them drinks, which they both

declined, and led them into a sitting room. Spider avoided getting too close to Noah – if he was sitting, she wasn't – until she had no choice but to dance around him to take a seat on the settee. A sigh of relief escaped her lips when he remained standing, moving behind the furniture and out of sight.

"As I said before, I can't imagine who would have hired you to find Kate after all these years." Taking the seat across from the settee, the older woman adjusted the burgundy-coloured wrap that fell over her white silk blouse. The silver bracelets at her wrist clinked together, and Spider couldn't help but wonder if she came from money or had married into it. "Not that I'm not glad someone is trying to find her. The police at the time didn't seem to care very much." Offering a smile that didn't reflect in her eyes, she looked at Noah. "What questions did you want to ask me?"

Ha! Noah probably had no idea who this woman was, let alone what to ask her. He surprised her though. "How did you know Kate?"

Reaching out to pour herself a cup of tea from the pot sitting on the table between them, she smiled fondly. "We met at school. I was failing history, and I hired her to be my tutor. We shared a love of Elton John and 'Remington Steele' and immediately became friends."

Spider jerked her gaze up. "Elton John?"

Holy moly. Was that why she kept having bizarre dreams about the singer? Because Kate had been communicating to her while she slept, like Connor had suggested? It had to be, but … why Elton John? What kind of clue was that?

Mrs. Abercrombie smiled, genuinely this time. "We were huge fans. In fact, I bought Kate a ticket to go see him with me when he was in concert about a month before she disappeared. She rarely got to go anywhere like that because of Billy."

"Billy?" Noah repeated.

"Her little boy. I was quite fond of him myself. I started looking after him for her in exchange for tutoring. Kate was working two jobs and attending classes so she could hardly afford to pay anyone to babysit."

"So she was a single mother?" Noah's voice sounded low but firm, and Spider resented the fact he was asking the questions she wanted to ask. She also hated that he was standing somewhere behind her. It made her uncomfortable. On edge.

"Yes. She never talked about Billy's father, but I know he abandoned her when he found out she was pregnant."

"What happened to Billy?" Spider asked, inserting a question before Noah had the chance.

"I always wondered that." Sipping from her cup, her expression became pensive. "I was so fond of him, I considered trying to adopt him myself, but … well, I was young and not confident enough to be a single mother. I'd seen how hard it was for Kate. I can only hope he found a good home."

Spider leaned forward, elbows on her knees. "Do you remember anything suspicious from the night she disappeared? Anything about what might have happened to her?"

Platinum-blonde curls bounced around her shoulders as she shook her head. "No. She was worried about catching the bus in the rain, so she left to try to catch it early before the storm rolled in. She usually got a ride home from one of her co-workers, but when she didn't get home at her usual time, I called and found out she had never showed up for work. That wasn't like her."

"Did she have any enemies?" Noah asked.

"No, I can't think of anyone."

"What about other friends?" he asked at the same time Spider questioned, "Did you know her boyfriend?"

Gritting her teeth, Spider repeated her question.

Mrs. Abercrombie leaned back and frowned. "She wasn't seeing anyone. She got asked out, yes, but Billy was her priority. She always said there'd be time for dating later." Her eyes darted toward the wall as she frowned. "Except for this one guy. He was pushy, so she did go out with him once. But he ended up being married, so she put an end to it real fast."

"Do you remember his name?" Spider asked.

"I'm sorry. I don't."

The creak of a door was followed by a deep voice calling, "Honey?" A dark-haired man appeared in the doorway. He was sharply dressed in a navy suit and tie and carried a briefcase. Undoing his tie, his gaze caught and held Spider's before moving past her. "You have visitors?"

"Yes, dear. These are investigators looking into Kate's disappearance."

"Kate?" He frowned and looked at Spider again. "After all this time?"

"Did you know Kate, too?" Noah asked, and he came around the settee, settling a hand on the top cushion just behind Spider's head.

"Barely. Jennifer and I started dating a few weeks before she disappeared."

Mrs. Abercrombie's eyes crinkled beneath a wry smile. "My husband asked her out first, but she turned him down. My good luck. I caught his attention instead."

Jerking his tie from around his neck, her husband wrapped it around one arm. "I hope you find her, or find out what happened to her." Looking at his wife, he added, "We have that dinner in an hour, remember? I need to go take a shower. Can I have a word in private real quick?"

He turned and left the room, and straightening, his wife excused herself to follow.

"Interesting," Noah whispered, and Spider glanced up to see him glaring toward where the couple had exited.

Biting her tongue, she refrained from launching into a scathing argument with the infuriating man. Her muscles still quivered from the restraint it took to hold herself in check. *Think about Kate and what you've learned instead.* Her mind sorted through the information and kept going back to Kate's fanaticism of Elton John.

What was the song he always sang in her dream? Did it have

any significance?

She struggled to recall the lyrics and found herself singing them softly in an attempt to remember more clearly. She'd have to do an Internet search to see if it returned any matches.

*"There was green alligators and long-necked geese, some humpty backed camels and some chimpanzees. Some cats and rats and elephants, but sure as you're born, the loveliest of all was the unicorn."*

Mrs. Abercrombie had re-entered the room and stopped, staring wide-eyed at Spider. Lifting a hand to her neck, she frowned. "I haven't heard that song in years."

Spider's pulse sped up. She hadn't realized she'd been singing out loud. "You recognize it? Wait. Does Elton John sing a song like that?"

The older woman chuckled and waved her hand. "Oh, no, dear. He doesn't sing that song."

Shoot. It had been a nice theory.

"It's odd, because I haven't heard that song since … since she went missing. Kate used to play and sing it to Billy. I wish I could remember the name of the band that made it famous. 'The Unicorn Song'. That's the name of the song."

Say what?

Spider wasn't sure what surprised her more: that the unfamiliar-to-her song was supposedly famous or that Kate had sang it to her son.

*Do do do do do do do do.* The theme song from "The Twilight Zone" whizzed through Spider's brain and sent shivers up and down her spine. This situation just got real.

***

Noah had to give Emma credit. She didn't explode on him after the Abercrombies showed them the door, and she didn't go ballistic while walking back to her car.

She sped up her steps to get away from him though.

"Emma—"

"You dirty scoundrel!" She rounded on him so quickly that he jerked back defensively, anticipating a slap or worse. Instead, she poked him hard in the chest. "You followed me!"

Guilty as charged.

In his defence, it had been a crime of opportunity, and one he'd do again if the chance occurred. He'd been returning home from doing his own research at the library when he'd spied her big ole Buick pulling out of the driveway. He hadn't been certain where she was going, but he'd assumed it involved Kate Levine.

"Don't get too angry, sweetheart. I tried playing fair, but you shut me down. Remember?"

"Fair? Ha! You have no idea how much self-control it's taking me not to kick you in the balls right now. Don't push your luck." Spinning around, she grappled with her keys, dropping them with a ting at her feet. She snatched them up in a huff and marched onward to her car. Noah couldn't help but grin as he followed from a distance. She sure was cute when she was in a tiff.

"Can we call a truce please?" He held out his hands. "I'm going to keep following you until you say yes."

That stopped her in her tracks. Turning, she wrinkled her nose at him. "Stalker, much?"

Uncomfortable with that accusation, he scrubbed his face with his hands. "Look, Emma. I have a feeling there are pieces of this puzzle that only you can solve, just as there are pieces only I can solve. If we work together, we can find what happened to Kate Levine and let her have some peace. Can't we put our differences aside long enough to do that?"

She muttered something beneath her breath and opened her car door. Turning, she looked him up and down. "How can I possibly trust you?"

He had no idea, but he'd like the opportunity to try and earn it. Whatever it took. Mow her grass. Walk those dogs. Grovel at her feet. He'd try anything.

Feeling a bit foolish at his thoughts – since when did he ever grovel? – he stiffened his spine. "All I'm asking is that you give me a chance to prove you can trust me."

"I'll think about it, but don't hold your breath." Ducking into her car, she eyed him warily. "If you follow me again, I'm calling the police." She pulled her door shut, pointed at him, and mouthed "*stalker*" through the window.

He watched her drive away, wondering if she meant it. Hell. Probably. Pacing back to where he'd parked, he glanced toward the grandiose estate they'd just left. Mr. Abercrombie – Noah needed to find out his first name, do some digging into his background, and figure out his involvement in this – stood in one of the upper windows, watching him.

Noah climbed into his car and replayed the conversation in his head.

Billy.

William was Noah's first name, but no one had ever really called him by it. He swore beneath his breath. All he had was a colourful story spun by his older brother. No corroborating paperwork. No supporting statement from his mother. Never mind that John wasn't the type to play cruel tricks or pranks – not like this. His father, on the other hand…

The memory of being shoved into a small, dark closet as a child flitted through his brain. Anytime he'd misbehaved by his father's standards, he'd been forced into the closet.

Sweat trickled down the back of his neck and his heart galloped around his chest just thinking about it.

If he had been adopted, Noah couldn't help but wonder what his life would have been like if someone like Jennifer Abercrombie had adopted him instead. Would he be more worthy of someone like Emma if he'd been raised differently?

*Stop it. You don't even know for a fact that you're Kate Levine's son.*

He pulled to a red light and slammed the palm of his fist against the steering wheel. How the hell was he supposed to prove or disprove who he was?

Finding Kate Levine, or her body, would allow for a DNA test. That was one way. Talking to his mother, the woman who raised him, was another. Reaching for his phone, he dialled his mother and waited for her answer. When she didn't pick up, he left a voice mail. She and Larry were travelling the Midwest in an RV right now. No telling when she'd get it.

Turning onto his street, he noticed Emma's car was parked in front of Zach and Hannah's house. Relief flooded through him that she wasn't off chasing more clues and getting into trouble.

If Kate Levine was dead, it was likely she'd been murdered by the man he'd been dreaming about. That man could still be out there, still be dangerous and still be killing. The thought of Emma in danger shot a pang of worry so intense through his body, his muscles bunched and stung from the pain.

His mind was made up.

He'd make such a nuisance of himself that Emma would either give up her investigation altogether or let him help her with it. For the next few days, he would seize every opportunity to spend time with her. Win her over. Keep her safe.

Whatever it took.

He would be the ideal man, catering to her every whim.

His mom had always said you could catch more flies with honey than vinegar. He supposed he was about to find out.

# Chapter 13

The last two days had been so peaceful that Spider was starting to grow a little bored with her isolation.

Bored if she weren't so miserable, that is.

Clipping the leashes on the dogs, she peeked out the window, searching for any sign of her tempting neighbour. He'd been showing up *everywhere* since their confrontation outside the Abercrombie house the other day. She went to check the mail, and wouldn't you know it, there he was, smiling and whistling and looking sexier than any rogue had a right. He'd sauntered over on both occasions, asked if she'd given any thought to his request to give him a second chance and quietly ambled away without a fuss when she'd informed him that hell hadn't frozen over yet.

Yesterday afternoon, a florist had delivered stargazer lilies and a stuffed teddy-bear with a single note attached that read *Forgive me? Please? – Noah.*

Okay, that one had been pretty good. No one had ever sent her flowers before, and the teddy-bear had been snugalicious. The protective shell she'd built to protect herself had started to crumble a little then.

When she'd taken the boys for their nightly walks, Noah had sat on his porch and watched them from a distance, his bare feet crossed over the railing while he sipped at a mug in his hand.

After they'd gone inside, he'd moved back into his house. Had he been watching to make sure they were safe? The silly idea warmed her insides and chipped at the shell some more. Not that she needed someone to watch over her, but the sentiment was nice.

She seriously should have learned her lesson with men though. Obviously, she had terrible instincts when it came to them. Anytime she started to crumble toward Noah, she simply reminded herself of Paul.

*Remember your five-year plan. Much easier to obtain if you're single anyway.*

She was swearing off men. Well, except for looking at them with their muscular chests and handsome faces and … wait. Looking was okay, right?

Geez, she was hopeless. Maybe she needed to find another job, working with a bunch of unattractive nerds. Or women. Maybe she should become a nun.

Wait. Were nuns allowed to use computers? Probably not. That was definitely out. It had only been half an hour since she'd checked her email and she was already going crazy, wondering if she'd missed any important ones.

Pulling her laptop close, her breath caught when she saw Noah's name in the sender field. Clicking on the message, she saw a simple question. "What's your favourite food?"

Okay. That was random.

How the devil did he have her email address anyway?

Still, she gave it serious thought, finally typing, "Not that it's any of your business … but I cannot pick only one type of food for my favourite. Who does that? I will, however, narrow it to three things: macaroni and cheese, lasagna, and potato chips. Don't judge." She hovered over the Send button before deciding to add, "Why are you asking?" Then she hit SEND.

It didn't take long for her to complete her work assignments for the day, so Spider returned to the personal investigation she'd been doing in her spare time to help take her mind off Noah, ghosts, and men with muscular chests … like Noah.

Her family tree was really taking shape, and as she spent a few hours inputting the details she'd found from searching obituaries, she couldn't help but have a surreal oh-my-gosh-that's-amazing moment. Melinda Carpenter was her father's great aunt. She totally was related to the woman who'd haunted Noah's house!

Was that weird, or what?

She went over to the curtains and looked at the home across the street, feeling a new attachment to the place. Her ancestor had lived there. Spider wondered what other items had been left behind, things that belonged to *her* family. If she'd been on better terms with Noah, she might have asked him if she could do a little exploring, but no. No way could she risk asking him for a favour. He might expect one in return.

She put on a movie, watched a little bit of it, and opened her email again.

He hadn't responded in the past five hours. Not that she'd been checking. Much.

"Come on, boys." Gathering Costello and Charlie close, Spider opened the front door, doing a double take when she spied the box sitting on the doorstep. Glancing around, she saw no one. No delivery truck. No Noah.

She met Costello's gaze. "Not even one little bark to let me know someone was out here? That's your job."

Costello opened his mouth, stuck out his tongue and grinned.

Pushing the curious dogs back inside, she considered ignoring the box, but she did need to move it so she could take the boys out for their walk. So she brought it inside. Abbott sprang onto the back of the sofa and stared at the present with lustful eyes.

"What do you think it is?"

The cat jumped onto the box, frolicked about, and spread his plump body on top of it in an obvious display of possession. Charlie had his front paws on the sofa, sniffing around the edges. Costello sniffed the bottom.

"Is it a bomb?"

Charlie began pawing, trying to get into the box.

"Whoa, whoa, whoa. Take it easy. If it were a bomb, we'd all be dead, thank you. Bunch of geniuses. Geez." She brushed them all away.

Opening it, she stole a look inside, warily. The aroma of something delicious and Italian triggered her mouth to start watering. Setting aside a bag of potato chips – yum – she pulled out a Tupperware container, peeled back the lid and almost had a food-gasm right then and there. Lasagna. Mmmm. It smelled delicious. Another container held macaroni and cheese. Had she died and gone to heaven? A card sat in the bottom beneath it all. She ripped it out of its envelope, eager to see the message this time. It was short and to the point. *How am I doing so far? This is me begging. – Noah.*

She chuckled at that. Allowing Abbott to have the box, to his purring kitty delight, she grabbed rawhide treats for the dogs, fetched a plate for herself, and pulled her laptop over to the break-fast bar so she could email Noah while she devoured this latest gift.

"I hope this isn't poisoned because I'll be dead in minutes. It's delicious, by the way. Homemade?" She clicked SEND.

A few minutes later, a click signaled a response. "No poison. I slaved over a hot stove for you. Surely that's worth something? Tell me. What are you wearing?"

She almost spit out her food. Typing, a chuckle escaped her. "Why, sir! Email sex. Really? So tacky, even for you." Send.

*Click.*

"Ah. Thank you for giving me an understanding of where your mind is. Shame on you. I simply enjoy your t-shirts. What does this one say?"

She glanced down. Her simple black babydoll t-shirt stated, "I see dead pixels" in a pixilated font. She shrugged and conveyed the message.

His response was fast. "Where do you find these things?"

"Duh. Internet. Sometimes the mall, although the mall scares me. Too many people. People in crowds scare me." Send.

*Click.*

"About this email sex…Does this mean I'm forgiven? If so, yes, please. Would love some email sex."

Rolling her eyes, she smiled, thrilled by the suggestion, absurd as it sounded. "In your dreams. Jerk."

She waited a beat before typing another message. "Closer to forgiven though. I have to take the dogs for a walk now. Thanks for the meal. Since you're in the mood, I could use a new car."

After hitting SEND, she wondered if she should've invited him over. He'd made dinner for her. She supposed he deserved to be invited over to eat it with her. She scrunched her face. On the other hand, she hadn't asked him to make her food, and it was mostly gone now.

She regretted nothing.

Grabbing the dog's leashes, she gathered them up and took them outside, keeping an eye on Noah's place as they passed it. Anticipation knotted in her chest, making her feel slightly nauseous at the thought of talking to him. Was she ready for that? She didn't think she was. Her shell had too many cracks now.

As they rounded the curve of the cul-de-sac on their return around the neighbourhood, she saw him, feet propped up on his railing, sipping from a mug, and watching them.

Communicating behind email was easy for her. Less pressure. Safe. Communicating in person, not so much. Cowardly? Yes, she totally owned it. She veered toward Zach's house, hurrying to get back inside in case Noah decided to be a pest.

She hurried in, shut the door, activated the alarm, and sank against the wall. Squealing, she pushed both dogs away when they slathered her face with doggy kisses. "Guys, that's so gross!" Pushing to her feet, she rubbed her face and shook her head. Actually, she was starting to get used to it. Go figure.

Grabbing her phone, she went into Zach's office, switched on the monitor to watch Noah, and dialled Kellan. He answered on the second ring. Good. He was her life raft, the last thing between her and drowning in the abyss of uncertainty. She needed him to remind her why she shouldn't trust Noah again because, doggone it, she was wavering.

"Spider, what's wrong?"

"Nothing." She sat back and twirled a lock of hair around her fingers and stared at the monitor. Noah was sitting in the recliner in his living room now, a laptop on his knees. "I was wondering if you'd found out anything about Noah West yet."

"Yeah. Been meaning to call you." There was a muffled sound in the background. A feminine giggle. What on earth had she interrupted? But Kellan's voice was normal when he continued, "Hate to admit it, but the guy's solid. A friend of mine worked with him. Said West was the best claims investigator he'd ever dealt with, fair and precise, but apparently, he quit the gig six months ago. Whatever case he's working now isn't through any specific agency."

"He said it was a freelance job."

"Must be. Kind of hard to hate the guy when he does the same thing we do, huh?"

She mumbled a sound that could be interpreted as agreement, or not. She'd leave that up to him. "What case could he be investigating us for? Have you figured it out?"

"Afraid not. Working on it though. You got anything new?"

"Nope." She cleared her throat. "Sorry I bothered you."

"You're never a bother, Spider. Call me anytime."

Oh, how she loved that man when he said things like that. Ending the call, she traipsed back to her computer and checked for more emails from Noah. There was only one.

"Sometimes I get lonely in this house. Do you, over there?"

Totally random. What was he trying to accomplish with such a question? Make her feel sorry for him or something?

The *Harry Potter* movie she'd been trying to enjoy to keep her mind occupied and off of Noah and pesky ghosts was paused, frozen on the big screen TV across from her. Hermione stood fiercely pointing her wand, her face dirty, hair mussed from battle. It was as if the badass heroine was making a statement straight to Spider.

*Be strong, girlfriend. Don't take any of his crap.*

She steeled her resolve.

The image of his face the night he'd returned, when he'd looked so lost and alone staring at the wall, pushed its way to the front of her mind. Perhaps this was a rare case of sincerity on his part. Pursing her lips, she typed, "No. I don't feel alone with the boys here to keep me company. It's nice. Maybe you should get a pet." She hesitated before hitting SEND. She tacked on a few more words. "Why have you been watching us?"

A few minutes passed before he responded. "You're a beautiful young woman, at night, alone. I watch to keep an eye on you … for safety's sake."

Putting away the happy thought of that to savour later, she smiled. "Thank you, although this neighbourhood appears to be quite non-threatening. Pretty sure I could have taken the grey-haired little lady we passed on our walk."

A mental image of the old lady swishing her cane through the air, anime style, and Costello jumping up to hump the old gal in defence made her giggle. She covered her mouth. Maybe Noah had slipped some silly powder into her food.

Minutes passed as she imagined him typing a rant to argue with her facetious remark. His response, when it came, surprised her.

"Experienced any more ghost stuff?"

She leaned back and glanced around the room. The dogs were either curled up or stretched out on the carpet, snoozing. Abbott was no doubt still blissfully napping inside his new box.

"No. Is she bothering you? It's been quiet here."

So many minutes passed, it seemed likely he wasn't going to reply.

*Click.*

"I have an appointment tomorrow to meet with the former owner of Wally's. Claims he knew Kate well. Want to come?"

Pinching herself to make certain she hadn't fallen asleep and was dreaming, she laughed. "What? I've been trying to get in touch with him!" She hesitated in typing her answer. Was this some kind of trick to get closer to her again?

Probably.

At least she knew that going in. "Yes, I want to come. When?"

She had a hair appointment in the morning she'd hate to reschedule, but this was more important. For the past two days, she'd essentially been stuck in the middle of a lake without a paddle. She waited for people to return her calls while she waded through old news reports, trying to detect a pattern between Kate's disappearance and any others. And trying not to mope. Keeping herself occupied so she didn't obsess over the handsome man across the street.

*Click.*

"1 p.m. I'll drive."

"We'll see." She hit SEND and waited for a reply. Disappointment weighed heavily in her chest when, after thirty minutes, she turned off her computer because he hadn't responded.

It hadn't gone unnoticed by her that he'd never answered her question about the ghost.

***

Noah blinked at the sunlight and slid a pair of sunglasses over his eyes before he locked up the house behind him.

He hadn't gotten much sleep – again – thanks to the persistent dreams no amount of sleeping pills or setting up his private studio could shake. Nightmares of Kate Levine and the menacing, unknown driver always segued into feverish dreams of a more passionate nature involving Emma. Undressing her. Hearing her breath catch in his ear as his fingers sank into her moist, tight warmth. Tasting her lips as she came apart against him.

Forget seducing Emma. They were friends only.

He'd almost convinced himself he could treat her like one of his sisters, a friend, anything else, without messing up her life, maybe even without messing up his own. But unless he could get these ridiculous urges under control, they were both screwed.

He winced at the poor choice of words.

Turning, he saw Emma making her way across the street toward him, hugging her messenger bag to her side, walking with a confident edge in her stride that told him she was still not suffering fools lightly. She'd gone somewhere this morning, the first time in two days, and he was tempted to ask where, but … not his concern.

"For the record, I'm still mad at you," she said in greeting, adjusting the strap of her bag, drawing attention to her hair. Long, ginger hair that was now streaked with blue. She tilted her head, probably to point out he was staring at it. "Also for the record, I wore this shirt for your benefit."

His gaze fell to the writing on the blue t-shirt that matched the streaks in her hair. White lettering stated "You read my shirt. That's enough social interaction for the day." A smile tugged at his mouth.

"I like that one."

He liked how the writing gave him an excuse to admire her chest.

She spun and headed for his jeep, giving every indication she wasn't impressed or didn't care. Only the way her hand shook before she gripped the handle of her bag betrayed otherwise.

He circled around to open the door for her. That earned him an arched eyebrow. "Seriously?"

"I'm trying to be a gentleman here."

Her shoulders relaxed. "Well, thanks." She hopped into the passenger seat and he shut the door behind her. His cell chirped out a ring, and seeing the caller ID, he answered it as he slid in beside her.

It was his new employer, wanting to discuss the class curriculum

Noah had submitted last night. He kept the call short, ending with, "Yes, sir. I'm looking forward to meeting my students. See you then."

He slid the phone back in his pocket and directed the car toward their destination.

"Wait a second. You're really some kind of teacher?" Emma sent him a sideways look, eyes narrowed in disbelief.

He nodded. "I told you. I'm teaching photography at the local art college next semester."

She snorted. "I didn't realize there was a major called Stalking 101."

He wasn't going to keep apologizing to her. It was done. No changing the past. He'd spent the past two days thinking about her, wishing he could be different, wanting to be that guy who could give her everything she wanted. His garage was now cleaned out and he'd framed his best prints to hang in his future studio. And still, he couldn't get this woman off his mind.

With a long sigh, she rubbed at her forehead. "I'm sorry. That was rude." She lifted her gaze, and he saw the thaw there. Finally. "I haven't been sleeping much."

"Bad dreams?"

She nodded and looked out the window. "I asked Kate to communicate with me while I slept. I kind of wish I hadn't. I still don't know what she's trying to tell me."

"What kind of dreams have you been having?"

"They start out strange. I'm running through a forest. I think I'm being chased, and I hear water nearby. I think I fall, and that's when I wake up. Does that make sense?"

He nodded, even though it didn't match any of the dreams he'd been having.

She shifted against the door and looked at him again. She must have decided to be pleasant because she asked, "Anyway. What kind of photography do you do?"

He felt himself relax. "I enjoy landscapes, mainly. I had a

showing at a gallery in Atlanta last September.  Got offered the teaching gig after that."

"That's cool."  She turned her profile away to look out the window, but her silence spoke volumes. He'd surprised her. Good. Gripping the steering wheel so hard it squeaked beneath his hands, he squashed the hope that thought conjured. "I had hoped to open a portrait studio in my house to supplement my income soon, but my computer got fried and caused me a bit of a setback. Impossible to be a photographer without a computer these days."

She shifted in her seat, crossed her arms, and refused to look at him. Guilting her into admitting she had a backup of his hard drive wouldn't be easy. He'd keep trying though. He'd like to get back to the spreadsheets he'd started to organize his new business.

"Why did you take the case to investigate us?" Her quiet words were firm, demanding. She finally turned her head to watch him answer. "I know you quit your job a few months ago."

Sucking in a deep breath before releasing it, slowly, he decided honesty was the best policy. "It paid well, and I needed extra funds for advertising. Simple as that."

Her shoulders relaxed enough to be noticeable, but she said nothing else until they reached the mall.

"What are we doing here?" She scooted out, glancing around the parking lot.

"This is where the guy wanted to meet. He insisted on a public place."

"That's kind of weird, don't you think?"

"The guy doesn't know us. Meeting in a public place seems pretty reasonable to me."

Hand at her back, he directed her inside the entrance and toward the food court at the centre of the mall. Satisfaction that she allowed him the small, intimate gesture made him reluctant to remove his hand once they were inside, but he did.

"How are we supposed to find him?"

Noah's gaze skittered across the late lunch crowd. "He said he'd be wearing a red bowtie."

"At the mall?" Smiling, Emma helped search the crowd. She hit his arm and pointed out an older man sitting alone in front of the pizza place. "That's got to be him. Come on."

Grabbing his hand, she tugged him along after her, and he was happy to let her. It was embarrassing how these simple intimacies pleased him and gave him hope that … no. He wouldn't go there.

He tugged his fingers free from hers and grabbed the back of the chair across from the heavy-set older man. Noah surveyed the man's features. Black hair peppered with gray. Skin so tough it resembled leather.

"Mr. Holcomb?"

"West?"

Noah nodded, and the man stood to extend a hand in greeting. "This is my … friend, Emma. She's helping me look into Kate's disappearance. I hope you don't mind that she joined me."

Holcomb waved a dismissive hand and grumbled, "It's fine." He folded the newspaper in front of him and reclaimed his seat. Noah and Emma sat down across from him.

"I was surprised to get your call. No one's asked about Kate in a long time."

Noah leaned forward so he wouldn't have to raise his voice above the chatter of the crowd. "What can you tell us about her disappearance?"

The man launched into a spiel, relaying all of the information they already knew from police reports and newspaper clippings.

When he finished, Noah reminded the man of their phone conversation. "You said you still had some things that belonged to her?"

Reaching down, Holcomb grunted an affirmative. He slung a plastic bag onto the table. "Found this stuff in one of the lockers I kept for employees. Offered it to the cops, but they didn't want it. It's a bunch of junk really. I don't know why I held onto it all these years. Guess I kinda figured her kid might want it someday, but who knows where he ended up."

Noah's gaze jerked up to his at the comment. Did Holcomb suspect he could be Kate's son? The man hadn't even asked. Not for the first time, Noah wondered if he favoured the woman. He reached for the bag and looked inside.

A folded magazine advertisement for a Teddy Ruxpin doll tugged at his chest for a reason Noah couldn't explain. A faded photograph showing Kate Levine standing behind a toddler, both smiling big for the camera, fell out of a spiral notebook filled with neat handwriting that described formulas and calculations.

That was all. Three simple things left behind to define a woman who might or might not be his mother.

Noah stared at the photograph, hand trembling slightly.

"Was she dating anyone that you knew about?" Emma asked. It wasn't the first time he'd heard her ask the question.

Holcomb's face wrinkled as he looked away, thinking. "She got asked out a lot. She was a pretty thing, but no, I don't remember her seeing anyone." He cleared his throat. "Wait a second. There was a guy who used to come in a lot and ask for her. I don't think they were dating. I think he was just sniffing around, you know what I mean?"

Noah shifted, uncomfortable. "Did the police consider him a suspect?"

"Yeah, right. If it hadn't been for that friend of hers contacting the paper and TV stations, I doubt the police would have looked for her at all, let alone narrowed down a suspect. Can't count on the cops for nothin'."

Noah could practically hear Emma grinding her teeth beside him. She leaned forward and stared daggers at the man. "Actually, the police serve quite a useful purpose. Unfortunately, they're as understaffed, overworked, and underpaid as the rest of America, not to mention—"

Noah interrupted her tirade by placing his fingers on her thigh beneath the table and squeezing gently. Heat radiated from her body and warmed his palm, which itched to lie there for longer than necessary.

She shifted beneath his grip, knocking his hand away. "Anyway, I'm sure the police only stopped looking for Kate because they ran out of leads."

Noah was eager to steer the conversation back to before she'd inserted her thoughts. "This guy who sniffed around. Do you remember his name?"

"Nah. That was a long time ago."

"What about a guess? Initials?"

Holcomb looked away. "Could have been Jay. Jay something."

"J.D.?" Noah asked, although he'd sworn not to ask any leading questions.

"J.D. Yeah, that's what she called him. Wiry-looking fellow. Used to come in a lot when Kate worked, but I don't know how well she knew him."

"Any idea who might know who he was?"

Holcomb shrugged, clearly not interested in helping any further. "It was a long time ago." He glanced at his watch and moved to his feet, looking around as if making sure no one was spying on them. "Like I said, I didn't think I'd be much help. You can keep her stuff. No one else has ever come looking for it."

When the man left, Noah barely noticed. He was too busy comparing the pictured woman's sharp, angular features to the child's and wondering if he shared any of those characteristics too.

Emma's hand reached for his, grounding him again. "Can I look?" She took the photograph and stared at it. Her voice dropped to a whisper, tinged with sadness. "You can tell how much she loved him." Her gaze returned to his, the hint of a smile playing at the edges of her lips, and she handed him the picture back. "How did you guess the name J.D.?" She leaned closer. "Are you still having dreams about her?"

Strawberries teased his nostrils, causing them to flare and luring him to lean even closer and take a better sniff of her hair. He held himself in check. "Yes. She calls the man in the car J.D."

Emma's slight gasp of surprise snapped him out of his pensive mood. Pushing to his feet, he grabbed the bag. "Let's get out of here."

She kept quiet, keeping pace beside him, climbing into the truck without protest. It was only once he was inside and had just kicked the engine over, that she turned and asked, "Noah, were you adopted?"

His hand froze on the gearshift. He met her gaze and admitted the truth. "Maybe."

# Chapter 14

*Ping. Ping. Ping.*

The incessant tap of rain against the window grated on Spider's nerves as she tossed and turned in the big, comfy bed, disrupting the cat, who insisted on lying on her feet, and the two dogs, who formed a force shield around her in the centre of the bed.

Pushing to her elbows, she glanced toward the rivulet of shadows streaming down the wall where light managed to sneak through the blinds.

Was Noah asleep, or was he awake and thinking about all that had happened since they met as well?

She looked around the room. "Kate? Are you here?"

If the ghost was, she didn't respond. It's not like she could have answered questions anyway. Sinking back against the mattress, Spider tugged the sheets up to her chin, remembering that little-boy-lost expression on Noah's face earlier when he'd explained what his brother had revealed a few days ago.

He was still partly in denial, unwilling to accept it as fact. That much had been obvious in his voice, in the defensive way that he'd argued that his mother hadn't confirmed anything yet.

Spider's instincts told her he was Kate's son.

It made sense, given all that they knew, and all that Connor had implied. She could understand why Noah had a hard time accepting it though. Who wouldn't?

After returning home, she'd left him alone, sensing his sombre mood and need for privacy. She'd thought she'd feel better uncovering that truth, but her chest ached for him. If she'd stuck around, she probably would have done something stupid, like wrap her arms around him and hold him until she'd chased that wounded look away from his eyes.

Her fingers found and played with the ends of her hair, drawing her gaze down to inspect the new colour. When she'd entered the salon this morning, she was determined to go pink for a change, but as she stared at herself in the mirror, Noah's assertion that blue was his favourite colour had wiggled through her brain.

She *had* liked the blue hair she'd previously sported.

She'd also grown a little bit fonder of her natural colour as well. She'd hated her orangish-red locks, suffered countless teasing in school because of them, but now she was grateful that she was a redhead. It linked her to her mother, who had shared her colouring.

Red, for her mother, and blue for Noah. One would always be ingrained in her DNA; and the other, perhaps a passing fancy...

Combining the two colours had been an impulsive decision, one her hair stylist had questioned skeptically before raving about the results. Spider quite liked it herself. What did Noah think of it though?

"Ugh!" Pushing herself to her elbows again she glanced at the shadows still dancing on her wall and froze.

The shape of a person formed against the wall now, shifting until it came to a standstill. The eerie unease of seeing it sent a knot of tension falling straight to her gut. Uncertain if her eyes were playing tricks on her, she reached a hand down and shook Charlie. "Hey!" Her voice was barely a whisper. "Do you see that?"

Charlie lifted his head, looking the opposite direction.

*Duh. Blind dog. Try the other one.*

Even as she roused Costello, Charlie turned his head, moved to his feet and aimed his snout toward the window. Huffing, he lowered his head into a classic hunting-dog poise. A bark finally ripped out of him, and Costello sprang to his feet and began barking, not to be excluded from any ruckus.

The shadow fell away, and Spider flung the bed sheets off, bouncing to her feet and racing for her phone. Her phone! Where had she left it?

She found it and punched in Noah's number before realizing she was even doing it. He answered on the first ring.

"Emma?"

"There's someone snooping around my window!"

"Did you call the police?"

"Not yet."

"Do it. Find somewhere and hide."

Ending the call, she punched in 9-1-1 and glanced around for a proper hiding spot. She explained what was happening to the operator while she searched out the best location. She shut herself in the bathroom, but … the animals.

Bursting back out of the room, she tried to round up two barking, excited dogs and one MIA cat. Tossing the cardboard box from the day before onto the floor, Spider stepped back. Abbott darted out from behind the chair and into it as if they'd been practicing a circus act together for years.

Scooping him up, she wrangled the dogs into the bathroom and shushed them, straining to hear movement beyond the door or outside the window.

Honestly though, they'd have all been killed already if this were a horror film.

The dispatcher held on the line, conveying encouraging words, and trying to keep her calm.

A beep signalled she had a text message. It was from Noah.

"Whoever was here is gone."

Releasing the breath she'd been holding, she opened the bathroom door and rushed to meet him as she read his second text.

"Footprints all over the place. Need to show you something."

Making sure her grip on the dogs' leashes was strong, she opened the front door and flung one arm around his neck, not noticing until he pressed her close that both his shirt and jeans were unbuttoned, his feet bare. Anywhere her skin was exposed felt hot and wet against his. She pulled away quickly, blinking.

"This was taped to the front door." He nodded to something he held in one hand. A piece of paper.

"What does it say?"

The dispatcher cut in, demanding to know what was happening. Spider thanked the woman, explained that a neighbour had come over, and then ended the call.

Lips thin, eyes dark and glittering with something dangerous, Noah only stared at her. Wet hair dripped a trickle of water down the side of his face.

"Noah, tell me." She reached for the paper.

"It says, 'Stop looking into Kate Levine's disappearance. I won't warn you again.'"

She stepped back and away from him, startled by the words. Police sirens approaching preceded the glow of blue lights falling on neighbouring houses. Spider looked past Noah and saw Jack climb out of his patrol car. Another patrol car pulled up behind him.

Of course, it would be Paul.

Groaning, she pushed past Noah and went to greet them, only a slight mist tickling her face and arms now.

"Emma, what's going on?" Jack's gaze skimmed over Noah's half-dressed figure beside her.

Crossing her arms to cover her own scanty attire, she took a step forward to meet him, ignoring Paul altogether. "Someone was at the window while I was sleeping. I called Noah, and he came over to make sure I was all right."

Her glance strayed to where Paul stood, frowning at Noah before aiming an intense look of displeasure in her direction. She couldn't help but wonder…

No. She wouldn't allow herself to believe Paul had been spying on her tonight. He'd have had no reason to leave such a note anyway. *But you've got to admit, he did get here awfully fast.*

Lifting his flashlight, Jack quickly rushed to inspect the premises, instructing Paul to take the other side of the house. Pressing into his side, Spider pushed at the paper in Noah's hand. "Don't let them see this. Please, Noah." She didn't want to worry her dad – or have to endure a lecture from him tomorrow.

Narrowing his eyes, he hesitated before tucking the paper into his back pocket.

"What the hell is going on, Emma?" Paul's voice demanded from behind her.

She spun, crossing her arms to cover herself, and raked her gaze over him. "Exactly what I told Jack."

He pointed his flashlight in Noah's face before blinding her with the beam. "You little slut! You're shacking up with this guy now?" He took a step toward them, ready to fight. She felt Noah press forward, so she flung out an arm, holding him back.

"So what if I am?" she countered. "It's none of your business, Paul."

He grabbed her arm and jerked her against him. "You're mine, goddammit! You've always been mine."

Her feet slipped in the wet grass as she struggled against him. Hard to knee his groin if she couldn't find her balance. "Let. Me. Go."

He never got the chance. She was ripped out of his grasp, and he was sent sprawling backwards as Noah's fist connected with his jaw. Noah shoved her behind him and growled, low and threatening, "Don't *ever* touch her again."

Paul scrambled to his feet, struggling to unholster his gun. Once it was free, he aimed the weapon at Noah. Spider lunged between them. "Stop it!"

Slushy footsteps came running up behind her as Jack's voice called out, "Put the gun down, Paul." Sidling up to them, hand held up in treaty, Jack placed himself as a barrier between them. "What the hell is going on here?"

Paul's face contorted as he snarled, "This asshole hit me. You're under arrest for assaulting a police officer. Go ahead. Handcuff him, Jack."

Jack glanced around, met Spider's eyes, and grimaced. He turned back to Paul. "Did you not hear me when I said to put your gun away?"

"But—"

"But nothing." Jack stepped forward and took Paul's gun straight out of his hands.

"I'm pressing charges. I said handcuff him!"

Jack shook his head, glancing back at Spider. "I didn't see him hit you. Emma, did you see anyone hit Paul?"

She shifted on her feet, uncertain. "N-no." Gaining courage, she straightened. "But Paul tried to assault me. Maybe I should be the one pressing charges."

Jack frowned, turning back to Paul. He shoved the younger officer toward his car. "What the hell is wrong with you? Huh? Don't you know better than to threaten a woman? Get the hell out of here before I punch your smug little face. Go cool off before you lose your badge."

Sputtering, face so red it looked close to exploding, Paul punched his car and ducked inside, putting it in gear and tearing away.

Scrubbing a hand over his eyes, Jack walked back toward them. "You do realize I'm about a year away from getting my pension, don'tcha? I don't need this kind of excitement." He patted his chest. "You two okay?"

Spider crossed her arms and nodded. Noah stepped closer and slid his arm around her shoulders. "Thank you, Jack."

Glancing around, the older man said, "Whoever was here is gone. Did you get a good look at the person?"

Rubbing away the chill in her arms, Spider shook her head.

"Probably someone trying to steal copper from the air conditioning unit. I noticed it was right outside one of the windows. Left side of the house?"

Spider swallowed the lump in her throat and lied. "That's where I was."

Shoulders relaxing, Jack nodded. "I hate to say this, but the person snooping around could have been Paul. He's not even supposed to be patrolling this area tonight, and he almost beat me here." Something twisted in her gut upon hearing those words, making her feel nauseous. Jack continued, "I'll need to take a statement from both of you for the report. I'll have someone patrol the area at night, keep an eye out. Don't worry. I'll make sure it's not Paul."

The mist was starting to pelt her skin with more force, so she led Jack inside. She retrieved a towel for Noah and tried not to stare when he rubbed the cloth across his damp, exposed chest.

They each told Jack their sides of the story, leaving out all mention of the note that had been taped to her door.

"I think you'll be safe, but if you want to go home, Emma, I'm happy to wait for you to get dressed and follow you," Jack told her when he finished taking notes.

She shook her head. "I'm fine."

Jack exchanged looks with Noah, shrugged, and pushed out the front door with the offer to call his cell phone if she got spooked again. Charlie shot forward, but Noah caught him before he could squeeze through the opening.

As she closed the door, Spider noticed someone peeking through the curtains of a neighbouring house.

"I've got to be the worst house-sitter in the history of anything." She covered her eyes and groaned. "Wait until Zach finds out about this. I'm. So. Fired."

Noah's arm curved around her shoulder and pressed her forward. "We need to talk."

Letting her hands fall away, she caved into his warmth for a fraction of a minute.

"Emma."

She pulled away, picking up the grousing cat and hugging him to her chest instead. "I know what you're going to say."

"I doubt that."

Worry and fear were a potent mix. It threatened to send her running into the bedroom to gather her stuff and leave.

But she wouldn't.

Emma would have, but Spider refused.

"You want me to go someplace safe. Drop my investigation, and leave."

He crossed his arms, nicely sculpted biceps covering his deliciously muscled chest. He hadn't buttoned it. Why hadn't he? "That sounds about right. This just became a dangerous situation. I'll come over every day and check on the animals. I'll make sure no harm comes to them."

"No way."

"Emma—"

"No," she insisted. "Don't you get it? Whoever killed Kate is worried we're onto him. I'm not going to let him scare me away before she gets justice!"

"It's not worth your life." His voice was a firm, grumbling roar.

They stared at each other, neither willing to budge. Spider crossed her arms, arched a brow and said nothing, mimicking him.

Seconds passed.

He slid his arms apart, revealing his bare chest again, crippling her defences a smidgen. "You're very stubborn."

She lifted her chin. "I know."

His lips twitched. "All right then. If you won't leave, neither will I."

She frowned. "What do you mean?"

"I'm staying here with you."

Oh no, no, no. She was pretty sure having uninvited guests over would propel her from Worst House-sitter Ever into Terrible

Friend territory. She shook her head, even as he half-smiled and dropped onto the sofa.

"What are you doing? No. You can't stay." She tried to push his feet off the coffee table when he made himself comfortable. His legs were like steel beams that wouldn't give an inch.

"Not only did some maniac tape a threatening note to your door, your ex is a psychopath. I'm starting to wonder if he's been following you and knows what you've been doing. He might have left that note, hoping you'd turn to him for help." He shook his head, his eyes dark and dangerous. "I'm not leaving you alone, Emma. Not tonight."

She sighed. "Thank you for standing up for me, but I don't think Paul will be back. He won't risk losing his badge." Was Noah right? Could Paul have left that note? She'd only been joking when she'd insinuated that Noah was stalking her, but she had felt like someone had been watching her lately. She'd assumed it had been him, but what if it had been Paul?

"Not buying it." Noah spread his arms out wide. "You stay. I stay. That's the deal."

"Zach wouldn't like it."

"That didn't stop you before." He stretched his arms up and clasped his hands behind his head. "Remember the night I stayed in the guest room?"

"That was different."

"How?"

"It just was."

He shrugged. "Take it or leave it."

Letting him stay probably wasn't the major crime her conscience painted it as, but she wasn't comfortable with the idea for several reasons. No, this wasn't her house, but mostly, his presence had the ability to turn her into a sex-hungry blabbering imbecile. What if he wandered into Zach's office and saw that she had his house wired for sight and sound?

No, thank you.

Surely he wanted to leave and grab some extra clothes or something. Okay. She'd wait until he did and refuse to let him back in. Problem solved.

His eyes turned dark and hot as they scanned from her legs up to her chest – and stopped. Heat warmed her neck as she fidgeted, refusing to look down at her choice of sleepwear. It was a simple solid-white tank top paired with little grey shorts. No funny statements. No cartoon characters or superhero shields to draw attention to her bosom. Just plain and simple her.

The air sizzled. She knew she was a reasonably attractive woman and he was a man. A sexy, virile man who'd already proven he was interested.

Something about that thought flipped a switch in her brain as if her mind had finally finished processing all of the data that had been uploaded over the past few days. Noah had flirted, yes, but he'd always been careful not to cross a line with her. The only exception being the night she'd kneed him in the groin.

He knew the effect he had on her, and he used it to his advantage whenever it suited him.

What if *she* tried to tease *him*? Would it disorient him, scare him enough to make him leave?

Pulse racing, mouth dry, she licked her lips. Yes, she thought it might. She was willing to test the hypothesis.

It took every ounce of courage she could muster to drop her arms and saunter over to the sofa. Sinking down beside him, she stretched her bare legs out next to his, feigning a loud yawn. "Well, I suppose I'll sit here until you change your mind then."

His attention seemed glued to her legs now. "What?"

She reached an arm out along the back of the couch, leaned closer to him. "I'll wait. Here. Until you leave."

He shot up as if she'd poked him with a hot branding iron. His fingers worked the shirt buttons into place. "I'm not leaving."

Ah, so she did have an effect on him.

Good to know it wasn't one-sided.

"Suit yourself." Standing, she made a point to brush against him, letting her bare arm slide along his as she reached for the spiral notebook sitting on the counter beside where he stood. His skin was oh-so-hot to the touch.

"What are you doing?"

Smiling, she moved back to the sofa, propped her feet on the coffee table, and opened to a new page. "Figuring out who did this. It has to be someone we've talked to. Who else would know we're onto him?" She began making a list of all of the people she'd spoken to or questioned.

"Unless someone you talked to shared the information with the killer."

Him and his logical reasoning. Spoil-sport.

She tapped the end of the pen against her chin. "No. I think it's someone we've talked to. How else would they have known to follow me here?"

A frisson of terror chased away the sexual excitement that had been itching through her. Someone had been following her. Watching her. But for how long?

"You did leave your business card with the Abercrombies." Noah paced in front of her like a caged animal.

"So? It only has the office's address, and I haven't been to the office."

He rubbed the back of his neck. "I don't like this."

"Oh, I'm as happy about it as a pig in slop."

Frowning, he stopped pacing. "This is serious."

"You think? I'm the one being threatened. I didn't see anyone leave a note taped to your door." Which in itself seemed odd. Why target only her?

Her stomach suddenly felt as heavy as if someone had dumped a bag of rocks down her throat. A killer had followed her here, knew she was alone, and had been brazen enough to leave a note on the front door.

Paul.

It was starting to seem more and more likely that her ex was behind the threat.

"Emma." Noah lowered himself to the cushion beside her, watching her. "I won't let anything happen to you. Promise." His hand settled on her bare thigh. Not as a sexual advance, but more of a comforting gesture.

Sometimes he could be so sweet.

She swallowed, leaned forward, and kissed him softly, brushing her lips over his before kissing the corners of his mouth. His breath was warm as it mingled with hers.

"Emma."

Her name was both a plea and a warning. Placing his fingers under her chin, he leaned forward and pressed his mouth lightly to her lips. Spider's response was as immediate as it was instinctive. She leaned into him, thrusting her hands up and into the silky texture of his still-damp hair as the tip of his tongue delved forward, pushing between her lips and sending a shiver of pleasure down her spine.

She crawled forward, straddled him, pushed him backward against the cushions where he sat.

"Emma."

This time her name was a groan, tortured and full of promise. She let her fingertips slide down his face, trace the column of his throat, and dance along the exposed skin of his collarbone seeking the first button he'd fastened earlier. She undid it, popping the next one, and the one after that. Brushing the material aside and placing her palm over his bare chest, she relished the steady thump of his heart underneath, fast and strong.

All reason had abandoned her. She had to taste more of him. Feel him. Experience him in every way.

He drank from her lips like a man starved of love. Maybe he was. A moan escaped her control, and she sank into him, melting around him, offering him whatever he needed.

His fingers explored the skin exposed beneath the hem of her shirt, above the elastic of her shorts. Pushing her away suddenly, he pulled her tank top up and over her head, flinging the material to the side. He lifted his hands to cup her exposed breasts, and she gasped when he leaned forward and took one into his mouth, his tongue teasing her nipple with expert precision. Arching her back, she wrapped her arms around his head and let him feast on her. Liquid fire spread to her core.

Gently, he shoved her away. "We can't."

"Yes, we can." She leaned down to kiss those crazy words into oblivion. His hands firmly held her away.

"We. Can't."

His erection pressed against her thigh. He seemed every bit as turned on as she was, so why the heck was he putting on the brakes?

His chest struggled to reclaim air. Through gritted teeth, he managed, "I'm not prepared."

Reaching a hand between them, she stroked the solid, rigid length throbbing beneath the zip of his jeans. "I'd argue otherwise."

A desperate laugh escaped him. "I don't have a condom."

"Oh." She nipped at his mouth. "I do."

Actually, she'd seen a box of them in Zach's things the other day when she'd been looking for clothes to loan Noah. Still. She could replace it later.

He gripped her arms, closed his eyes, and kept her from touching him. "Emma, you're killing me. I'm trying to do the honourable thing here."

"That's no fun." She pretended to pout. Pulling away, she hopped to her feet. "Wait right here."

Entering Zach's bedroom felt like being dowsed with the proverbial cold shower. Her boss probably would not approve of her having sexy time with a near stranger on his sofa. Then again, who would tell him?

She spun and froze. Abbott stood in the doorway, watching her with intense interest. He shifted from one paw to the other and just … stared.

Spider covered her naked chest with one arm and hid the box of condoms behind her back with the other. "Hey kitty."

He sat like a statue, only moving his almond-shaped gaze from her face to her chest and back again.

Of course she was pet-sitting for a man who talked to animals. At least one dog was blind and couldn't have seen a thing. Costello was too dumb to probably know what he'd seen. The cat, however, would know everything.

Awkward.

"Listen, this isn't what it looks like." She cleared her throat when he didn't react. "Okay, so it is. What do you want not to talk? Tuna? I'll make sure you get lots of it."

More staring.

Spider moved sideways, dropped the condoms back in the drawer, and bumped it closed with her hip, all-the-while keeping her chest covered. "Nothing to tell. See? I put them back."

The cat lifted a paw and began licking it, brushing it over his ear and repeating the motion again and again. She hoped that was cat code for *we've got a deal.*

She sidled past him, not taking her eyes off the diabolical feline until she was out of the room. As flushed with unfulfilled desire as she was, she'd have to tell Noah they could continue this later. Preferably without the animals around and in another location … with condoms of their own.

She never got the chance.

When she rounded the corner, he was gone.

# Chapter 15

Noah paced in front of the window, long-lens camera in hand and cursed himself for being a coward.

He'd promised to stay and protect her, but what had he done? When things had gotten too intimate, he'd cut and run. Just like always.

It wasn't as if he'd been spooked by Emma's enthusiastic response to sex. He'd been with far more aggressive women and liked it. It had been the way his pulse had hummed when she touched him, his heart had skipped a few beats, his hands had shaken. Not to mention the unfamiliar sense of rightness he'd felt holding her.

Lifting the camera, he scanned the house across the street for signs of trouble, particularly of the redheaded variety. The morning sunlight made it easier to see, not that there was anything to catch his attention. All quiet. She still had the curtains closed.

He'd alternated between walking the perimeter of her house and spying from here all night. There had been no more signs of an intruder. Moving to his recently reformatted computer, he pulled up his email for about the twentieth time since he'd run out on Emma like some virgin schoolboy too terrified to go all the way.

His shoulders sank. Nothing in his inbox from her. No flirtatious messages. No snark. Not even an angry note accusing him of being an asshole.

Not long after he'd left her, he'd sent her a text message that had read, "You won. I'll keep watch from across the street. Call if you need me."

A few minutes later, she'd responded with "Definitely in need over here. Come back."

He hadn't responded to that, and she hadn't called.

Clicking out of his email, he tried doing a search on Connor Manning again. Call it ridiculous, but what if the psychic could ask Kate who murdered her? Seemed like the easiest solution to keeping Emma safe. Fifteen minutes later, he gave up on the pointless pursuit and went back to the window.

His heart tried tearing out of his ribcage at the sight in front of him. He swore and ran for the door, feet pounding against wood as he hurried down the steps to catch up with the woman who was driving him crazy.

"Emma! What are you doing?"

"It's called walking dogs. You should try it some time."

Both of the mutts ignored him, on a mission to drag her along after them. He had to jog to catch up. "You shouldn't be doing it alone. It's not safe."

"Oh really? I assumed I was perfectly safe. Why else would you run out on me after insisting on playing bodyguard?"

"Look at me." He grabbed her hand, wrangled one of the leashes away from her grip and stilled her. Her eyes, usually alive with interest, had dimmed. His chest ached, knowing that he was the reason. "I'm trying to do the honourable thing where you're concerned. You and me … it's no good."

"Why not?"

He clenched his jaw. "You deserve better. Let's leave it at that."

Fire sparked some life back in her blue gaze. "I don't remember asking for a commitment, Noah. I happen to find you attractive for some stupid reason. I thought you were at least mildly inter-ested in me. Why not have a little fun while we can? But no, you have to go and make it all crazy." She snorted and started walking again. "Men."

Her words startled him, but he couldn't deny they sent his pulse racing. Realizing he still held the cute blond mutt's leash, he let the dog jerk him forward. "So you're telling me you enjoy casual sex?" Cause he wasn't buying it.

"Not at the moment."

At the flippant response, he clenched his jaw. "Seems pretty odd you're willing to sleep with a guy you hated a few days ago."

She mumbled something he couldn't understand, so he grabbed her arm, made her look at him. "I said, 'I don't hate you.' I can count on one hand the people I hate, and that's a fallacy because none of them are actually real people." She held up a hand, lifting fingers for each name she vehemently stated. "Scrappy-Doo. Barney the Purple Dinosaur. Wesley Crusher – worst character in *Star Trek* history *ever*. That's it." She turned and began walking again. "I might have been mad at you for a few days, but I got over it. Mostly." She flicked a dismissive wave in his direction.

"Scrappy-Doo?" He stifled the laugh that threatened his demeanour. She probably wouldn't appreciate his amusement. His chest rose and fell on a breath instead. "You don't know how relieved I am not to be on your list with Scrappy-Doo. I *hated* that little guy."

"Who didn't?" Her lips twitched, betraying her own amusement.

"Okay."

"Okay?" She sent him a narrow-eyed sideways glance.

"If you're willing to give it a shot, let's see what happens."

She stopped, eyes wide, and faced him. "Seriously?"

He was a little shocked to realize he'd made the offer, too. Had he lost his effing mind?

"On one condition."

She rolled her eyes. "I should've known."

"I don't want either of us to be casual about this. I meant what I said. Let's give this – whatever this thing is between us – a real shot. Dinner. Movies. Whatever." A sickening wave of nausea threatened to turn his stomach, but he wanted this. He wanted to give her what she deserved, or give it his best effort. It felt right, and he was tired of fighting it. As an added benefit, it might be the only way to get close enough to her to keep her safe.

"Seriously?"

"If you say that one more time—"

"No. I'm in." She frowned. "But to be clear, you want to … date me? Cause I might be misreading the situation. I do that sometimes. Actually, I do it a lot, and I don't mmm—"

Her lips were still moving when he swallowed her words. She tasted like fresh mint and smelled like strawberries, and his heart leapt at the thrill of kissing her again. He pressed closer, lifted his hand to feel her hair and jerked sideways when the dog at the end of the leash lunged forward suddenly, barking like a maniac.

Noah dug his heels into the sidewalk to keep from going down. A short dark-haired woman in a tracksuit took a wide berth of the dog as she veered around them, swinging her arms in a robotic motion as she passed.

"Sorry!" Emma called, fighting to draw Charlie's leash closer to her side. A very becoming red crept up her face, making her freckles stand out. He looked forward to kissing each one.

They circled the neighbourhood, allowing the dogs to do their business, making sure to keep a safe enough distance so that the chemistry between them didn't explode.

Her expression had turned solemn the closer they grew to his house. "Noah, what are we going to do about that letter?"

He sobered. "Can you get in touch with Connor?"

Emma shook her head. "He said he'd be back, though. I'm not sure when."

Not good. "I'll think of something. I'm sorry I dragged you into this."

"I kind of pushed myself into it, so don't feel guilty." She arched a brow at him. "I think Kate tried to communicate with me because you weren't listening to her. Why did she choose me, though?"

"Maybe she likes you."

"That's a nice thought." She shrugged as she put the key in the door and pushed inside her current home. "Yeah. She probably recognized how awesome I am. It happens."

She was, indeed, awesome. "About this date. Got any plans for tonight?"

"Yes." She laughed at him. He had no idea what his expression had looked like, but if it showed the fleeting disappointment that shot through him, it was damn pitiful. "I have a standing date with the guys in my guild every Wednesday at eight. We kill trolls together. It's a thing." She unhooked Charlie's leash and smiled at him. "I suppose I could stand them up if a better invite came along."

"What would you consider a better invite?"

"Got any more of that lasagna?"

No, but he could. "My house. Seven o'clock?"

She bit her lip and nodded, eyes dancing with excitement. "I'll come over."

She acted as if she thought he was leaving her alone until then. Had she forgotten the danger she was in? Moving forward, eyeing her up and down, he stalked toward her, already imagining what her lips would feel like on his skin.

"Wait. Noah. We can't. Not here."

Sliding his hands around her waist, he pulled her into him, nipped her mouth. "Why not?"

"Um. Because." She pointed behind him and whispered, "The children are watching."

He turned and saw that both dogs and the cat were staring at them. "So? Let them watch. Maybe they'll learn something."

"You don't understand." Her hands gripped his biceps, but she didn't push back when he pressed her against the wall. Warm. Moist. Lush. That's how her mouth felt beneath his. She tore her lips away. "The cat will tell my boss about this."

Right. Collins could read minds or some such thing. "Your boss won't get mad about us kissing, will he? That's all this is."

"Mmmm." Another moan signalled her consent.

The problem was that kissing her made him want all sorts of things he shouldn't. Her hands gripping his hair, making sure he didn't pull away, made him want it more. Wrapping his hands around her thighs, he lifted her up high. Next thing he knew, his shirt was being pushed off his shoulders, her fingers leaving behind scorching heat where they explored his ribcage, his chest, his back.

Tearing his mouth from hers, he bit at her neck, licking the spot with his tongue. He slid his hand higher, beneath the hem of her shirt.

She moaned. "Noah."

*Ding dong. Ding dong.*

The doorbell and a chorus of frantic barks startled them apart. Emma hurried to straighten her clothes while he glanced around for his shirt. The two dogs whizzed around them like soldiers preparing for battle.

"Who is that?" Noah asked with ragged breathing.

She peeked out the window, and then shrieked. "It's my dad!" Picking his shirt off the floor, she threw it at him. "You have to go!" She pushed him toward the back door. "Hurry!"

A grin curved his mouth as he shrugged into the material. "Want me to hide in the bathroom until he leaves?"

Wide-eyed, she gaped at him. "No!"

He chuckled and bent down to steal a kiss. "I'll be back later. Don't. Go. Anywhere." He gestured at the doorknob. "Lock up. Make sure the alarm is on when he leaves."

"Go!" She shoved him out the back and slammed the door behind him.

What he wouldn't give to be a fly on the wall.

* * *

*Someone shoot me now.*

Checking one last time to make certain she looked presentable, Spider grabbed hold of Charlie's collar, took a deep breath, and opened the door. "Dad! What are you doing here?"

Frowning, he pushed past her into the room. "What took so long to answer the door?"

"Nothing." Charlie wiggled against her hold, so she let him go. "Um, I had to secure the animals."

"Hmph." Her father was dressed in his uniform, so she imagined he had stopped by on his way to work. Well, at least he shouldn't stay long. His gaze darted around the room, taking everything in with his eagle-eye precision, before resting on her. His eyes widened. "Good lord, what have you done to your hair now?"

She reached up a hand and patted the side of her head, wondering if Noah had mussed it all up or something. "Nothing. Why? What do you mean?"

"It's blue again. Partly." He shook his head. "Heaven help me."

Tossing his hat onto the coffee table, he sighed and sat down in the chair across from it. Wiping a hand down his face, he grimaced. "Had a call from Jack Lanier this morning. Wanted to tell me what happened here last night, thought I should know."

"Oh." Well, crap.

"I had a visit from Paul the day before that, told me he ran into you and some man together. I told him it was probably one of them boys you work with, nothing to worry about, but then I hear from Jack about this guy he keeps seeing you with." His blue eyes looked grim against his weathered face. "Figured I'd better come see what was what."

Crossing her arms, Spider pursed her lips. "Everything is fine."

His hand rubbed the material on his thigh, the way he always did when he was nervous. "This man – Noah West – you're not mixed up with him, are you?"

How did he know—? Wait. Jack must have told him all he knew about Noah. Figures. "We've gotten to be friends if that's what you mean." And possibly more if you hadn't interrupted. Something close to doubt nibbled at her conscience at the memory. Had she seriously agreed to date Noah? As in, give a relationship a chance? Was she out of her ever-loving mind? She had a plan, one that did not include a serious relationship. "And he might have asked me out," she admitted to her father.

He grimaced as if in pain. "Did he tell you about his past?"

She arched a brow. "Could you be more specific, please?"

"His father. Man's been in and out of prison most of his life. He's currently serving for DUI. Killed someone in the wreck. He's got a rap sheet a mile long."

She considered that information. "Noah does, or his father does?"

"His father."

She shrugged. "And?"

"Apples don't fall far from the tree." He pushed to his feet, obviously agitated by her lack of concern. "You stay away from him, find yourself a nice boy from a nice family."

"You mean like Paul? Cause that's not gonna happen."

"Paul's a good man. He's a good cop. You could do worse."

She shrugged, not wanting to go into great detail with her old man about what a good person Paul was now. It would only hurt him to know the young man he had put on a pedestal was hardly a saint. Aside from last night, the one and only time Paul had gotten physical with her was still fresh in her mind almost two years later. "I don't think you know him as well as you think you do. I didn't either."

"What's that mean?"

*Remember that black eye I had that time that I told you I ran into a door?* Yeah. That would go down well. "Let's just say I'm a little disturbed at the way he shows up at our house all the time. You know he only does it to check up on me, and I don't know. Some people might call that stalking."

"For Pete's sake, Emma. We play poker. Have for years. That didn't stop just because you two broke up." Her father jerked his head back. "Has he threatened you?"

"He's … scared me." The admission was difficult to make to her old man, who would probably dismiss her fears as an overreaction, just as she usually did. After last night, she wasn't so sure anymore. Then again, Paul and his father had been coming to poker night for as long as she could remember. Maybe she *was* overreacting, but... "Last night he really scared me, Dad."

His shoulders sank. "You can't blame the boy for carrying a torch."

"Dad." Her tone was pleading, hoping he would drop the topic of her ex. When it came to Paul, her normally very intuitive father had a serious case of blindness. If he took a moment to really assess the way Paul stared at her he'd see it wasn't an expression of pining away for a lost love. That *she* could handle. Anger always sparked in Paul's gaze as it followed her around the room. The same anger she'd witnessed seconds before the back of his hand had sent her crashing to the floor. She kept her distance. And so did he. But that didn't mean she felt comfortable when he was around.

Especially after last night.

"Fine." Her father held up his hand and turned. "I don't like you being here on your own. Why don't you pack up and come home? I'll tell the boys the house is off limits for now. We'll have poker night somewhere else. I'll talk to Paul. Tell him to leave you alone."

Her brow furrowed. "I don't want to come home. I like it here." She brushed a hand toward where Costello and Charlie lay on the carpet, watching them with interest. "I have responsibilities."

He pushed a hand through his whitening hair. "Bring the animals home, too. I don't care. It's not safe here, Emma."

"I'm not going."

"Emma." Her name was a warning.

"Dad." She gave it back to him.

"Hmph." Picking up his hat, he moved to the door. He surveyed the alarm pad in the entryway. "Hmph." Frowning at her, he pointed at the high-tech system. "You make sure you have this turned on at all times."

She resisted the urge to roll her eyes. "Yes, sir."

He opened the door to leave and froze.

Kellan stood on the other side of the door, finger poised to press the doorbell. Her blond Adonis of a co-worker's reaction to her father was almost comical. Eyes wide, mouth dropping open, his body stiffened. "Chief Fisher?"

Her father looked him up and down. "Murphy." Turning his head to frown at her, her father sighed. "Keep an eye on my daughter for me."

Without another word, he pushed past Kellan and strolled to his car.

"What? Wait. You're his *daughter*?" Kellan glared at her. "My old boss is your dad, and I'm just now learning this? What the hell, Spider? Does Zach know about this?"

No. No one at the firm did, and that's kind of how she'd planned to keep it. So much for that.

Kellan pushed inside, and she armed the alarm. "Explain yourself."

"Yes! He's my dad. What's the big deal?" She threw her hands up and went to the kitchen to fiddle with things and look busy.

"Why didn't you tell us?"

"Duh. Because I wanted to get the job in my own right, not because of any connection to my old man. He never tells me anything anyway."

Hands on his hips, Kellan looked absolutely shell-shocked. Poor baby. A giggle escaped her control.

"This isn't funny." He smiled at her and pointed at the door. "That man used to terrify me when I was on the force. And he's your dad?"

She doubled over in laughter.

"You punk." Kellan's chest shook with amusement.

"He's not so bad once you've seen him lounging around screaming at the TV in his underwear. Kind of hard to take him seriously after that."

Sliding his arm around her shoulders, he put her in a gentle headlock and scratched her hair. "Who knew we had such a comedian on the team?"

"Hey! Watch the hair!" She pulled away, patting it back into place. "What are you doing here anyway?"

This man was never going to see her as anything other than a little sister type. She might as well accept it. The thought didn't sting the way it once had. Memories of kissing Noah soothed the wound.

"I came to check in." He aimed a thumb toward the window. "Your guy was spying on you all night. Wasn't sure what that was about. Thought you should know."

"He was?" Her lips pulled wide in a smile.

"Yeah. That's a good thing? I thought I might need to go kick his ass."

She shrugged. Maybe letting Kellan in on the note was the wisest move here. Someone else should know, and he'd already become her partner-in-crime so to speak. She patted the cushions beside her. "Don't freak out. I have something to tell you."

When she was done, her co-worker's good looks were frozen in stern lines. "I suppose telling you to go home won't do any good."

"Nope. I'm staying."

To his credit, he didn't push the way everyone else had. Leaning back on the cushions, expression thoughtful, he nodded. "Then we need to find out who this guy is, and fast. Tell me what you've found so far."

She did, scribbling notes for him in her notebook.

"You did this on your own?" He held the piece of paper up. She grinned, and his expression looked impressed. "Good work." He tucked the notes into his pocket. "I'll run checks on everyone you've questioned. Too bad Alexandra isn't here to question Kate."

"Connor said he'd be back. If he doesn't come back, Alexandra will be back soon. One way or the other, we just have to wait."

Kellan nodded, but he didn't seem happy about it.

"Um, Kellan?" When he looked at her, she smiled. "I kind of have a date tonight. With Noah. At his place." As much as she adored Kellan, she didn't want an audience … or a sex tape floating around.

"Is that a good idea?"

"Probably not."

One side of his mouth kicked up into a grin. "Those are usually the most fun." He stood. "Come on. I'll draw a map showing where I put the cameras." He reached down and scrubbed the fur on Charlie's head. "Tell you what. I'll camp out here tonight, keep an eye on these guys. If anyone comes back hoping to cause trouble, they'll get a surprise." He didn't meet her gaze. "And, uh, I won't wait up if you know what I mean. Might even be safer if you stayed elsewhere tonight. Catch my drift?"

Bouncing to her feet, she leaned over and kissed his cheek. "Thank you."

He shook his head. "Just so you know, if he hurts you, I *will* kick his ass."

"Good."

Something told her Noah wouldn't – but if he did, she could handle him herself.

# Chapter 16

Slipping a fresh shirt over his head, Noah strode down the stairs to check on the lasagna baking in the oven. Learning to cook had served him well as a bachelor. The bonus was that it impressed the hell out of women. He stopped to glance out the window, wondering if Kellan Murphy was still over there with Emma. Her co-worker had been coming and going far too much this past week for Noah's liking. What was their relationship?

*Don't go there. You're not the jealous type.*

Yeah, well. Tell that to the green-eyed monster stomping around in his chest.

Rubbing his hands together, he focused instead on putting the finishing touches on their dinner. He lit a few candles since he knew women liked that sort of thing. Prayed he wasn't making a huge mistake that he'd later regret.

Daylight was already fading through the blinds in his kitchen, and as tired as he was, Noah was still acutely aware that someone had threatened her last night. Glancing at the clock, he went outside to meet her.

Plus, he was anxious to see her again.

He walked over there, wondering what she expected from him. He'd never dated much – not the old-fashioned open-doors-for-her, hold-her-hand kind of dating – and he felt ready to jump out of his skin at the slightest sound. He'd never seen his old man treat his mother with anything other than resentment, give or take a few tender moments. What if he did something wrong?

And why the hell did it matter so much?

He hit the doorbell and stepped back while a barking frenzy ensued.

The door jerked open, and Kellan Murphy stood there, the other man's steel gaze looking him up and down. He held a firm grip on the flighty dog's leash. Both man and dog presented a formidable barrier. This was another new one for him.

Noah lifted his chin, stood a little taller. "I'm here for Emma."

Kellan crossed his arms. Tilting his head back, he yelled, "Spider. Date's here."

Somewhat amused by the other man's protective stance – it was that of a brother, not a competitor – Noah felt himself relax. He held out his hand. "I'm Noah."

Kellan ignored the gesture. "West. I know."

He pulled his hand back. "And you're Kellan Murphy. Former Atlanta PD. Current security specialist at Collins Security Firm. I get it. You're pissed because I was looking into your company."

"What's done is done." The taller man shrugged. "Spider is like a sister. Capiche?"

Noah refused to look away. "Yeah."

"Then we're good." He stepped aside. "Come on in. I've had to endure at least an hour of 'Does this make me look fat?' while she tried on half of Atlanta's wardrobe and paraded around in front of me. She'll probably be a while. Beer?"

Noah shook his head and reached down to pet the blond mutt who, for once, didn't try to hump his leg in greeting. He noticed the duffle bag sitting beside the sofa. "Staying over?"

Nursing his bottle, the muscular private detective leaned against the wall. "Spider told me about the note. I figure it's a good idea to hang around and try to catch the asshole if he comes snooping again."

Funny how Emma had no qualms about letting this guy stay here when she'd all but thrown a hissy fit when he'd offered.

A door crashed open and a splinter of light spilled down the hallway. "I'm coming! One minute!" Emma called out.

The black and white cat sauntered in their direction, as bored as a lion in a zoo. The light turned off behind the animal as her voice carried down the hall. "Sorry! You didn't have to come get me. Am I late? I didn't think I was late."

Then she was there, and every cell in Noah's body immediately stood at attention. Even Murphy went still beside him. He didn't like the fact the man was noticing Emma as a woman.

The elegant black dress hugged her figure like a sheath, her cleavage proudly on display, the skirt falling no further than her knees. Her hair was pulled back neatly with a clip, emphasizing her pretty cheekbones. Only the combat boots rising above her ankles seemed familiar.

She pointed a finger at Kellan. "Don't you laugh!"

He wasn't. The other man was practically gawking at her, too. Stepping back, hands held up in surrender, he murmured, "I've just never seen you in a dress. You look … nice."

She put her hands on her hips and glared at him. "I knew you weren't paying attention when I asked how I looked. I tried on at least three dresses for you!"

"None that looked like that!"

Noah's fists clenched at his side, not liking the way Murphy was making cow eyes at his date. Not liking it at all.

Arching a skeptical brow at the other man, Emma marched forward, hooked her arm through Noah's and pulled him toward the door. "Thanks for watching the boys, Kellan. Don't wait up!"

Clearing his throat, Noah let her take the lead. He found his voice once they were crossing the street. "You look incredible."

She glanced down at herself. "You think so? I borrowed it from Hannah's closet."

"Your boss's wife knows we're on a date?"

"Uh-huh. She thinks you're a total hottie, by the way."

His head spun at that declaration. He hadn't expected the news of their … thing to spread so quickly. Talk about pressure.

She glanced over her shoulder toward the house they'd left. Red spread from her neck up. "Sorry about that. He wasn't awful to you, was he? I, um, didn't want to leave the animals alone. You know how in movies the killer always breaks in and boils the pet cat or rabbit as a threat while the person is gone?" She shuddered. "I'll be more comfortable now knowing they're safe."

Boiling rabbits? That stuff only happened in movies.

He slid his arm out of hers and entwined their fingers instead. He liked the feel of holding her hand. "Good. I intend to make tonight very memorable for both of us."

The colour crept higher into her cheeks, but she leaned into him. "I like the sound of that."

****

Dinner was every bit as delicious as Spider had expected, having sampled his, er, talents the other day. The conversation hadn't been half bad either. They discovered they enjoyed the same movies, had similar tastes in music, and agreed that Tolkien was one of the best writers to ever grace the planet. She had a feeling they would never agree on the age old question of which was better – *Star Wars* or *Star Trek* – but not everyone was perfect.

Sipping her glass of wine, she shifted uncomfortably in her seat and inspected the living room beyond Noah's shoulder, which was a task since he looked sexy as all get out tonight. Clean shaven, hair doing that thing where one mischievous lock curled over his forehead begging to be brushed back, dressed in a tight gray t-shirt and nice black slacks, he looked like a model ripped from the pages of *GQ* or something.

Focus on the cameras now. Focus on Noah later.

How in the heck was she going to disable the cameras without him knowing about it and before things, um, progressed? She was already ready to tackle him where he sat, and if that sultry gaze which he'd been pouring over her was any indication, he wouldn't have resisted. If only she was the type of woman who had no qualms about tackling him…

A swarm of butterflies had taken up residence in her stomach, and she knew she'd been talking too much. She always talked too much when she was nervous. Oh, no. Guys hated that, didn't they? Especially guys who oozed total hotness the way Noah did.

She was so out of her league here. Tilting her head back, she took a big gulp of wine to steady her nerves and remind herself Noah had invited her here. Several hours ago, he'd had her up against a wall, ready to—

Moist heat spread through her belly, killing at least half the butterflies and giving her a boost of courage. *You've got this.*

Setting her glass on the table, she stood. "I need to use your restroom please."

"It's around the corner."

"I thought it was upstairs." She needed it to be upstairs. In his bedroom, where one of the cameras was hidden.

"The one downstairs is closer." Smiling, he stood and gathered her empty plate with his.

"Of course it is." She laughed. "I'll be right back."

Glancing over her shoulder to make sure he wasn't following, she made a quick detour up the stairs to his bedroom, taking careful steps so that the usual *clunk clunk* of her boots didn't give away her destination. Clock. That's where Kellan said he'd put the camera.

And the clock was high up on the wall. Fabulous.

Blowing out a frustrated breath, she reached up on tiptoe, snagged the clock, found the camera, waved at Kellan in case he was watching and shut it off. Mission accomplished.

She almost dropped the thing trying to get it back on the wall, but she was pretty sure she had it placed back in the same position. After tugging the dress down where it had ridden up on her thighs, she brushed dust off her hands.

"That's one. Good job. Yay, me." She whispered the mantra to herself and stepped back to make certain it wasn't hanging crooked.

"One? You mean there are others?"

Well, crap.

*The Avengers' Black Widow would be so disappointed in you right now, Emma Marie Fisher.*

Turning, she saw Noah propped against the doorjamb, watching her, still looking sexy and dangerous. "I can explain."

Amusement sparkled in his eyes. "No need." He straightened and moved forward. "I deserved it." He rubbed a hand at the back of his neck. "If you could get rid of the other cameras, though, I'd appreciate it. I'm not into voyeurism."

"Wait. You're not mad?"

"How could I be?" He lifted his hands and shrugged. "Although I do feel obligated to point out that it's not exactly legal to bug the inside of someone's home without a warrant. You do know that?"

She snorted. "Of course." Actually, she'd had no idea. Maybe that's why they rarely did it.

He stood so close the scent of musky cologne teased her senses. Lifting a hand, he fingered the end of her hair, his knuckles brushing against her breast. "You really are something."

"Something good or ... something that needs to be reported to the police right away?"

His mouth curved in a sexy smile. "Good. Definitely good." He kissed her, murmuring, "We'll save the illegal stuff for our second date."

Her shoulders relaxed, immediately tensing again when he took another step closer and slid his hand up, into her hair, before cradling her face in his palm. His eyes were dark, hot, full of adoration as they grazed her lips. That look paired with his gentle touch caused a tingling heat to spread through her body and pool between her legs. He bent and took her lower lip between his, caressing her mouth open with his soft, insistent tongue. Her hands slid around his neck. Enjoying the slow, unrushed connection, her heart picked up its pace and her body melted against him.

Oh, how easy it would be to lose herself in this man.

Her fingers gripped his shoulders, so solid and broad, as he slid his arms around her and walked her backwards. She fell onto the bed and he came with her, covering her gently, careful not to crush her beneath his weight. She tugged at his shirt, pulled it free from his pants, wanting to trace every delicious line and curve on his chest while she had the chance. He pulled away long enough to pull the shirt over his head and fling it across the room.

"Touch me," he whispered in a voice so hoarse she barely recognized it. "Please."

He buried his face against her neck, teasing feather-light kisses down the column of her throat as his hands slid the hem of her dress up higher and higher. Her fingers explored his tanned chest up to his shoulders and back again, his skin taut and yet as soft as velvet, scorching hot to the touch. She could sense the power his muscles held, yet he touched her with such tenderness she choked out a whimper at the thought. No one had ever treated her with such consideration. It had never felt this way with Paul.

Her nipples were hard against his chest through the material she wore, and she wanted it off, now. "The dress," she managed to get out, and thankfully, he understood exactly what she wanted. He pushed away and helped undress her in a quick manoeuvre that betrayed the fact he'd done this before, probably numerous times, while she felt woefully inexperienced in comparison.

Shyness threatened to overcome her when she settled back down in only her matching black bra and panties, his heated gaze devouring the sight of her beneath him.

"You're beautiful, Emma. Look at me." His hand lifted her chin, forcing her to meet his eyes. "You're in control. Not me."

"I am?"

"Oh yeah." He rolled onto his back beside her. "Show me what you want."

She wanted to lick every bare part of him she could see and strip those pants off so she could explore further. She reached a trembling hand out, touched the rippled muscles at his abdomen and hesitated.

"I've never … been on top before."

Desire turned his eyes even darker. "I'm happy to be your first then. Come here."

She crawled on top of him, straddling his hips, careful where she touched, half afraid she'd do something ridiculous and hurt him and half afraid she'd do something dumb and embarrass both of them. Leaning forward, she started with a kiss, teasing his tongue with her own until a groan vibrated beneath her hands on his chest. Empowered, she let her hands wander lower, finding the button of his pants, undoing them, and sliding her fingertips beneath the zipper that contained a hard, prominent bulge. His fingers speared through her hair, gripping the back of her head, and stilling her.

"Be gentle with me. I'm … sensitive right now."

"Hmmm. You mean you don't like this?" It was a rhetorical question. He was obviously enjoying her attention.

Licking her lips, she lowered the zipper, watching him carefully for a reaction. His jaw clenched as he met her eyes. "I want these off."

"Then take them off."

Delighted to have permission, she sat up and began tugging them over his hips. He wore a pair of boxer briefs beneath that moulded to his body in a positively indecent fashion. She couldn't wait to get to that part of him. Later. Leaning over, she licked at his nipple, tearing a guttural groan from him and sending a thrill of pleasure spiralling down to her core. She trailed a line of kisses over his chest, licking and sucking the places that drew the strongest reaction from him. This was fun, exciting, empowering. She already couldn't wait to do it again.

Feeling bolder, she crawled lower, grabbed the hem of his briefs and slowly pulled them down. Wow. He was … magnificent.

Sliding her hand around his erection, she thrilled in his sharp intake of breath. She moved her hand up and down and began to stroke its velvety length, setting a pace he seemed to enjoy. Groaning, he took her hand in his.

"We'd better save that for another time." His voice was rough. Strained.

Oh. Poor man did look a bit tormented, veins standing out in his neck and all. She shifted to lie beside him, kissed his swollen lips in apology. "Too much?"

He slid his hand around to caress the nape of her neck. "I'd rather be inside you when I come."

Oh. She licked her lips. "Do you have – you know?"

Pushing up, he kicked his pants free and reached toward his nightstand. Spider felt heat warm her face, but she was too far-gone to let shyness ruin this for her now. Swallowing hard, she laid back against the pillows. His eyes asked a question when he looked at her, and she reached for his hand.

"Maybe we should save the whole me-on-top thing for later, too." Placing his hands on her bra, she murmured, "Finish undressing me."

Sheer joy leapt into his eyes. Curving a hand over her breast, his thumb toyed with her nipple through the bra. He leaned down, kissed her again, drank from her lips while he removed the material with her hardly noticing. The man had some skills, that was for sure. His lips moved down her neck, greedily finding a new target in no time. Her fingers tangled in his hair, holding his head to her breast to keep him there. She squirmed against him, crying out when his teeth nipped her nipple and his tongue licked the spot. His hands slid lower, curving around her bottom, slipping inside the elastic of her panties. She instinctively lifted her hips so he could drag them down and off her legs. Seconds later, she felt something pressing against her moist, hot centre, his fingertips teasing the entrance, all-the-while he teased his lips down the hollow of her stomach, moving lower and lower until she cried out, not certain she was ready for that level of intimacy yet.

He lifted his head, smiling encouragement at her, and lowered his mouth back to the inside of her thigh, trailing kisses until he reached her core. She cried out and clutched the comforter beneath her when his tongue licked her, long and sweet, before probing deeper. Sweet mercy. She'd never experienced anything like this toe-curling pleasure. There was one spot he kept finding that drove her near to madness.

When he was done and she was spiralling back down from a massive orgasm, he crawled up her to claim her mouth with his.

A moan rumbled through her chest as his fingers teased her some more, shifting so that his erection took their place. All it took was one smooth push and he was inside her, throbbing and hot and oh-so-good. She gasped, grasping his shoulders and whimpering softly as he took her, each stroke long and hard, filling her completely. Then he rolled so that she was on top.

"Finish it," he whispered into her ear, tonguing the lobe and sending a tremor through her body.

She rode him, slow at first, then harder, faster. Oh, yeah. She liked this position. Liked it a lot.

It didn't take much to push her over the edge again, and she cried out in pleasure, clenching around him and urging him to join her.

Seconds later, he did.

***

Spider lifted her head from his chest and glanced at the clock. Almost three in the morning, So much for texting Kellan to let him know she was staying here for the night. Sliding her hand around Noah's hip, she laid back down, grinning like Costello after he humped someone's leg. Had this really happened?

Drifting back to sleep with that thought, she jerked awake

sometime later. Only … she wasn't in Noah's bedroom anymore. It was dark. Trees surrounded her.

"Kate! Get back here!" A man's voice yelled in the distance.

She found herself running aimlessly into the darkness, her breathing ragged in her own ears. Hands suddenly gripped her shoulders from behind, and she struggled, feeling her nails connect with skin. She fell backwards and a sharp pain lanced through Spider's skull.

Gasping, rubbing at the back of her head, she sat straight up, blinking against the morning sunlight that cast shadows on the wall. Noah still slept undisturbed beside her. Leaning down, she kissed him softly and slid off the bed. After a trip to the bathroom, she picked up one of his shirts off the floor and slid it on. It took her a few minutes to find and disable the other cameras. Hopefully, Kellan didn't see her prancing around half dressed in the process. He obviously knew what had been going on, but still. She tucked the equipment into her bag and went in search of coffee.

The dream she'd had still troubled her, even as she sipped a fresh cup of joe and nibbled on whatever she could find that was edible. Was that the same dream Noah had been having, or different?

The area where Kate had been running had seemed familiar, and not because Emma had been having this same dream for the past two nights. Familiar as if she'd been there herself.

"Darn you, Connor. Where are you?"

She had a feeling this would go much easier if he were here to communicate with Kate on their behalf.

Or maybe…

What if they didn't need Connor to communicate with Kate? What if they had another tool at their disposal?

Setting her coffee aside, she hurried into Noah's office, found his computer and booted it up. She carried the laptop into his living room and planted herself on his couch, using the flash drives in her purse to restore his previous files while she waited for him to wake up and hear all about her brilliant idea.

*Ding dong.*

At the unexpected sound of the doorbell, she heard movement overhead, meaning Noah must have been as startled as she was.

*Ding dong.*

Know what? That was probably Kellan, coming to check on her after seeing that she was awake. Or perhaps Kate was attempting to reach out to her again. That ghost seemed to have an affinity for doorbells.

She put the laptop aside and hurried to answer it. Looking out the peephole, she saw no one and figured her hunch was right about Kate. She opened the door and said, "I'm glad you're here. I've got an idea on how we can – oh!"

An older woman with graying hair blinked in surprise. "Hello." She tried to look past Spider into the house. "I'm looking for my son. Noah West. Isn't this his address?"

Holy cannoli. It was his mom.

# Chapter 17

"Can I get you something to drink?" Spider glanced toward the stairs for about the tenth time since letting Holly – Noah's mother – and Larry Harwell – his stepfather – inside. She edged closer to the staircase, flames shooting up her face as she tried to tug the hem of Noah's shirt over her bare thighs, and wondered why in blazes he hadn't come down yet.

Already tidying up around the room, his mother had yet to meet Spider's gaze. "No, dear, we're fine."

Relieved, she gestured toward the kitchen anyway. "Help yourselves. I'll go get Noah."

She hurried up the steps, praying she didn't accidentally flash his parents in the process.

Noah was still sprawled across the bed tangled up in the sheets as if he'd been fighting with them for hours. Good grief. She hadn't worn him out that much, surely? She pounced on him. "Noah, wake up! Your mom is here!" Straddling him, she shook his shoulder.

He grumbled something incoherent.

She shook him again. "Noah? What's wrong with you?" His skin was hot to the touch, his face red. She pressed the back of her hand against his forehead. Oh, no. "Noah?"

His voice sounded weird as he whispered, more clearly, "Lake Allatoona. That's where my body is."

Spider sat back, shocked. "What did you say?"

"Old Highway 41. In the trees. My grave."

"Kate?" Oh. My. Gosh. Stemming back the tide of panic clawing at her chest, Spider leaned down. "Kate, your body is buried at Lake Allatoona? That's what you're telling me?"

Noah's eyes blinked open, slowly. "Emma?"

She shifted to his side, surveying his features closely. "Are you aware of what you just told me?"

"What?" He lifted a hand to his forehead and gave her a sad, pathetic smile. "Water?"

Bouncing out of bed, she found a cup by the bathroom sink. She handed him the drink. "Are you okay?"

His brow pulled together. "I've been dreaming. Different dreams. Intense."

"About Lake Allatoona, by any chance?"

"About a lake. I don't know which one."

"Noah, I think Kate just used your vocal chords to give me a clue. A big one. Huge!" She shook her head and held up her hand. "Hold that thought. You did hear me when I said your parents are here, right?"

He pushed up on one elbow, eyes widening. "What?"

"I, um, made the mistake of opening the door. I'm pretty sure your mom thinks I'm a total skank."

A husky chuckle escaped him. "I don't think my mom has a clue what a skank is." He tried pushing to his feet and fell back on the bed. "Whoa. Give me a second."

"You were fine last night. More than fine." His colour was strange. Splotchy.

"I don't know. I feel like hell now."

Oh, yeah. Kate had done something, used him somehow to get her that message.

She got him another glass of water and hovered around him, uncertain of what he needed. She found her underwear and dress and managed to slide them on, conscious of the fact she had an audience. She swore that she could feel heat where he looked at her.

"I've got to go call my father." She sat and tugged on her socks and boots. "Hopefully I can convince him to go search Lake Allatoona for Kate's body … although, I'm pretty sure it's out of his jurisdiction. I should try calling Alexandra, too. You don't look so good."

"Emma."

"Do you have any broth? I can heat you some broth. Maybe it will make you feel better." She pulled her laces tight and secured them.

"Emma, I'm fine. See?"

Glancing up, she saw that he was standing beside the bed, buttoning his slacks from the night before. "That was some recovery."

His weak smile betrayed the fact he didn't feel well. "You need to explain to me what you're jabbering on about, but I also need to talk to my mom."

"Okay. I can go and change and come back later – if you want?" Uncertainty halted her steps.

His hand settled on her arm. "Why don't you stay?"

"While you talk to your mom?" That seemed kind of serious. As in, official relationship stuff. But she really, really wanted to go talk to her dad.

He nodded and watched her closely while she processed the request. Oh, wow. Things were moving so fast between them. It felt … surreal. She smoothed out the wrinkles in the dress. Why, oh why, couldn't she be wearing jeans and a casual t-shirt right now? She would feel so much better about this if she were.

"Okay."

His eyes softened as he pressed a tender kiss against her lips. Closing her eyes, she leaned into him, thrilled at any chance to connect with him again. "Mmm. No!" She tore herself away. "Your mom."

He chuckled and finished dressing while she combed her hair.

That done, she stayed close to his side in case he needed her help getting down the stairs, but he seemed to grow stronger by the second.

"Noah, you look—" His mom took his face in her hands in greeting and frowned "—unhealthy. Have you been taking care of yourself?" She touched his forehead. "You're burning up!"

"Mom, I'm fine."

While his mother continued to fuss around him, he exchanged pleasantries with his stepfather. Spider did her best to stay behind Noah. Out of sight, out of mind.

"Mom, this is Emma." Reaching for her, he slid a reassuring arm around her waist and pulled her forward. "She's staying across the street for a few weeks. She's pretty special."

*Special … how special?*

His mother finally looked at her, but her smile didn't reach her eyes. "We've already met." Clearing her throat, the older woman turned away and found the chair by the window. "This is a nice house. It'll make a good studio for you."

Noah pulled Spider to the couch. "Mom, I'm glad to see you, but what are you both doing here? I thought you were touring the country in the RV? Wyoming, last I heard."

"Your mother got your messages." Larry took a seat on the other side of Noah. His hand grasped Noah's shoulder in a fatherly gesture. "Your brother called her first. She thought we should come see you. We got here as soon as we could."

Mrs. Harwell's face was turned toward the window. The poor woman looked ill with worry. Sighing, she finally turned and looked at them. "Emma, have you known my son very long?"

"Uh, well…" She glanced at Noah for assistance. *No, ma'am, only a week or so, and yes, we've already slept together.* Oh, geez. She hadn't said that out loud, had she?

"Mom." Noah's voice interrupted anything further Spider might have said. "If you're here, I assume what John told me is true."

His mother seemed ready to bolt. Her gaze kept flickering

towards Spider with uncertainty, and Spider wished she were anywhere else. Iran. North Korea. The moon. Bound to be vacations compared to this. Stomach churning, she placed a hand on her belly. *I am going to be so sick all over his carpet in a minute.* Maybe that's why Noah covered her other hand with his, pulling it to his knee and lacing their fingers together in a gesture of solidarity.

"Anything you have to say can be said in front of Emma. She's a part of this too now."

Whoa. He was not acting like a man skittish of relationships anymore. What the heck had Kate done to him?

Tears welled in his mother's eyes, and Spider felt an immediate urge to rush over and hug the woman. If this was miserable for her, how must his mother be feeling? How hard was this for Noah? Glancing at him, she squeezed her hand, trying to offer some support. This was about them, not her.

Suck it up.

"Yes, it's true." His mother's voice quavered. "After we had John, we tried for more children, but I never got pregnant again. I assumed we couldn't have any more, and your father—" She lowered her gaze to the hands clasped in her lap. "You know what he was like. When I had the opportunity to take you in, I realized it was worth staying with him if that allowed me to be eligible for the adoption. It was only later, after I got pregnant with Kristina, that I realized I could still have children."

The way Noah's fingers tightened around hers was almost painful, but Spider didn't pull away. She waited for him to speak, for his mother to continue, but the room fell uncomfortably silent. Noah's eyes glistened with unshed tears. His jaw muscles twitched. If only she could comfort him.

Clearing her throat, she leaned forward and spoke in a gentle tone. "Did you know Noah's birth mother?"

Wiping her eyes, Mrs. Harwell nodded. "Her name was Kate Levine. We were cousins, the only family each other had. She went missing when Noah was just a toddler. Social services found me, asked if I was willing to take him in until Kate reappeared. When it became clear that Kate wasn't coming home, we filed to adopt."

"Wait a minute. You knew Kate?" Noah asked.

"Not very well. Kate lived with her parents in Covington, and we rarely saw them." His mother rushed to her feet and knelt in front of him. "No matter what you're thinking, Noah, you will always be my little boy." She reached up and caressed his face, her own distorted with sorrow. "You *are* my son. That's why I never told you. I didn't see the need."

"It's okay, Mom. I understand." He brushed the other's woman hair behind one ear. "Thank you for taking me in." He swallowed so hard the sound echoed around the room. "I know this is hard for you, but I need to know more about my birth mother. Do you know what happened to her?"

"Only what the police told me." Her husband stood so she could sit beside Noah while she talked. In a trembling voice that grew stronger as she spoke, Mrs. Harwell reinforced everything they'd learned. "She was a good woman. The few memories I have of her – she was so kind."

"Didn't she have any other family?" Spider asked.

"She lost her parents not long before you were born." She told Noah. "Car accident. I saw her at the funeral. She was alone and pregnant. I offered for her to stay with us, but she was eager to attend college here in Atlanta. She was excited about making a home for you. She had some insurance money, so I thought she would be fine. I never forgave myself for not keeping in touch."

"And my father?" Noah managed softly.

His mother reached for her purse and pulled out an envelope. She handed it to him. He looked at the piece of paper and Spider leaned closer to peek at it too. "My birth certificate?"

His birth name had been William Noah Regner. Mother: Katherine Levine. Father: Christopher Regner.

"I only know his name from that. Kate said he wasn't ready to be a father, but she seemed okay with it." Mrs. Harwell pulled her son closer for a half hug. "I promise you, I did try to find him for you. Neither the social worker or I ever had any luck."

"Was my name Billy?"

She looked surprised. "That's what Kate called you. We decided to call you by your middle name instead, start afresh. You were so young, we didn't think you'd remember."

Noah's face had paled. "It's okay." He nodded and glanced at Spider. "I appreciate everything."

He didn't look as though he appreciated it. He looked absolutely devastated. Spider's arms itched to pull him into a bear-hug and squeeze.

His stepfather gave an obviously fake cough to break the tension. "Sweetheart, you should tell him about the boxes."

Hand on her chest, Mrs. Harwell forced a smile. "We stopped by our house and got them on the way here. Your ... mother's things. I've kept them in storage. It's everything she owned when she disappeared. We sold most of the furniture, so it's not much. I thought you might like to have it."

Noah frowned, his brow furrowing as he, too, stared at the carpet. She wondered what he was thinking.

Leaning around him, she asked, "Mrs. Harwell, do you mind if I ask? What do you think happened to Kate?"

Noah's mother shrugged. "I believe she's dead. I don't think she would have ever left Noah alone for so long otherwise."

Noah shifted away from them both and stood. Scrubbing a hand over his face, he turned and met Spider's gaze. "Why don't you go home and get changed? Make that call you wanted. Maybe you can come back later? Help me go through these boxes?"

He didn't want her to stay? Feeling hurt by the implication, she nodded. She wasn't clingy, so why did his dismissal bother her so much? The poor guy probably needed space to come to terms with all he'd learned. She couldn't even imagine.

Fine. She'd give them some privacy. A shower and change of

clothes would be awesome right now, anyway.

Besides, she needed to tell someone about Lake Allatoona.

"It was nice to meet you," she told the older couple before hurrying toward the door.

"Excuse me," Noah said behind her, and she felt his presence before she realized he had followed her onto the porch. "Emma, wait."

She turned. "Uh-huh."

"I'm sorry our time was interrupted."

She touched his arm. "Me too. Are you okay?"

"I'll be fine." Sighing, his knuckles brushed her hair behind her ear. His colour was more normal now. He no longer felt as hot to the touch either. "Promise me you'll come back. Two hours?"

Relief flooded through her. "I'll be here."

"Good." His expression sobered. "Promise me you'll be careful."

"Please." She rolled her eyes. "What kind of trouble can I get into over there?" She gestured across the street. Well, given her track record, it was a fair request. "Don't answer that." She pushed him toward his front door. "Go. Your mom needs you. Worry about her, not me."

His mouth slanted. "Two hours."

She gave him a thumb up. That would give her plenty of time to gather what she needed, call her dad, and touch base with Hannah for her daily check-in. He didn't know it yet, but she had a plan to solve this mystery once and for all.

***

Holy hell! He was adopted.

Noah had no idea how to handle that truth. Hearing it from his brother had been one thing – but from his mother? He'd experienced a myriad of emotions since she'd admitted everything. Confusion had turned to sadness. Sadness turned to frustration. Frustration turned to anger that had boiled to near overflowing in his chest, threatening to choke him. He'd had to excuse himself again to keep from screaming, "Why can't I just be normal? Why did you have to hide this from me?"

Why? Why? Why? So many questions in his head.

It didn't help that he still felt slightly feverish. No idea why. When he'd fallen asleep and started dreaming, he'd known right away he was in for a different experience. This time he'd watched as Kate tore away from her captor and escaped into woods. At some point, it hadn't been Kate he'd been watching run wild among the trees. It had been Emma. Waking up, he hadn't remembered all of the details, and he'd been mostly grateful for that. His body had felt like he'd been run over by a damn dump truck.

That feeling had faded throughout the day until all that lingered was a mild ache behind one eye.

And a swelling rage that demanded an outlet.

His fist found the target closest to him in the garage where he'd come to hide before his anger exploded and sent his mother to the loony bin. The cardboard box fell off the shelf and landed with a thud, the old clothes he'd intended to donate spilling out.

"Whoa. Don't make me call the Society for the Prevention of Cruelty to Cardboard in here."

He turned at the sound of Emma's teasing voice. His chest loosened its grip around his heart even as his pulse quickened at the sight of her. If he didn't know better, he'd say this amazing young woman with her funky hair and snarky mouth was a witch. How else could he explain the fact he immediately relaxed in her presence?

"Two hours," he reminded gruffly.

It had been at least three. Not that he'd been counting.

She shrugged and placed her messenger bag on an empty shelf. "Sorry. I got held up." Kneeling, she began scooping up the clothes and placing them back in the mangled box. "I take it things here haven't gone well?"

Rubbing his forehead, he shrugged and paced to the back of

the garage. "It's fine."

"Yeah, because you seem totally fine." She snorted, lifted the box, and placed it back on the shelf. His gaze raked over her. Jeans, Converse sneakers, and a tight-fitting green t-shirt that showed a pair of lemons and read, "If life gives you lemons, KEEP THEM. Because, hey, free lemons."

A chuckle tore out of his chest.

She tugged at the material. "It was this or my shirt with the ninja kitten that says 'Awwwssasin.' I figured this one was more fitting today."

He took a deep breath and stepped toward her. "Good choice."

"I do occasionally make them." She pushed up on tiptoe to kiss him. "You look better. Are you feeling better?"

He nodded.

"I called Alexandra because I was worried." Her eyes raked over him in concern. "She said you should probably rest. She doesn't think Kate possessed you, not exactly. But if Kate used you to speak to me, then Alexandra warned me you're probably feeling like hell. Are you?"

"I've felt better," he admitted. "But I feel a lot better than I did." He glanced at the boxes that held Kate's belongings.

"I called my dad. He thought I was crazy when I asked him to search the lake for Kate's body."

"You did what?"

"Oh, right. I haven't explained what you said this morning." Briefly, she told him about the words that had left his mouth; words he didn't remember saying. "My dad wasn't very receptive to it when I asked him to search the area based on a dream."

Noah frowned. "I doubt he would be."

Eyes skimming his face, she bit her lower lip and glanced over her shoulder. "Why aren't you inside with your parents, Noah?"

He grabbed her waist and pulled her closer. Something about her proximity warmed the cold ache of loneliness inside him, the one that had always been there, only he was now learning to recognize it. "I needed some space."

"I see." Her hands gripped his biceps and she lifted her pretty face up to his, eyes serious and searching. "She's still your mother. You know that, right?"

Of course he did. On some level, he knew nothing had really changed, except he now knew something he'd never known before. And the ramifications of that knowledge were staggering. For one, he wasn't Derek West's son. A swell of hope lifted his chest on that one major positive. Maybe he wasn't genetically predestined to be a philandering asshole after all. Maybe he stood a chance at a happy future with a loving family of his own someday.

He'd never allowed himself to hope for that possibility, had never even considered that he wanted it. Now he knew he did.

"Noah?"

He blinked down at Emma, remembered her question, and nodded. "I know."

She pulled away from him and picked up her bag. "Good. Now get in there and make sure she realizes it. She didn't drive halfway across the country to stare at your wallpaper. We can talk about finding Kate's body later."

She was right, but he still hesitated. He gestured toward the boxes he and Larry had pulled from their RV. "Those were Kate's. I haven't opened them yet."

"Oh." She slid her hand into his. Her voice was gentle when she pointed out, "They'll still be here later. Your mom – not so much. Come on."

"Bossy, arent'cha?"

"Darn right."

He allowed her to lead him out of the garage, and he couldn't help but notice his house looked a lot neater when they went inside. The vacuum was sitting out. That made him smile. That was his mom. Always cleaning when she was stressed, and Lord knows, they'd had one helluva clean trailer for a family with four rambunctious kids.

"Mom," he called to get her attention, and she stopped dusting to turn and look at him. Her eyes were puffy and red. Damn. He'd seen her look this way a lot, thanks to his no-good father.

No, not his father.

"Emma," she said in surprise. "I didn't realize you'd come back." His mom glanced between the two of them as if she were figuring out a puzzle.

"I hope you don't mind that I did."

"Of course not."

He felt a hand in the small of his back, urging him forward. "Noah wanted to talk to you." She stepped aside, sat her bag against the wall, and addressed his stepfather. "Mr. Harwell, would you like to help me make coffee for everyone? Maybe some sandwiches? I'm sure we could all use something."

Larry looked grateful for the reprieve, quickly moving to join her. The two of them disappeared toward the kitchen.

His mother smiled and twisted the rag in her grip. "She's lovely, Noah. I'm glad you've finally found someone. I was always worried…" She let the unspoken words hang between them. Not that she needed to finish. He was sure she'd been worried he'd end up like the man who had raised him.

He stepped forward. "She's afraid you don't like her."

"Don't like her?" She frowned. "I don't even know her."

He smiled.

"I know her and I like her. That's all you need to know." He took a deep breath. In and out. "Mom. Listen. This has been … confusing for me. I want you to know it doesn't mean anything between us has changed. You're still my mother."

Tears welled in her eyes, and she rushed forward, squeezing him around the waist so hard he knew she'd been suffering a hell of her own these past few hours. "You children – all of you – mean everything to me. No matter what else, Noah, you must believe that."

"I do. Don't worry." He let her hold him longer than was

comfortable, his side feeling pinched by the pressure of her embrace. When she finally pulled away, he took her hand. "It's going to take me a while to come terms with everything I've learned. Can you understand that?"

"Of course." She lifted a hand and caressed his face. "Take whatever time you need, son. Just don't shut us out. Please?"

"Never."

She smoothed out the wrinkles she'd caused in his shirt. "Now, tell me about Emma. How long have you two been dating?"

Dating? Hell. "Not long." He glanced toward the kitchen and heard himself speaking his thoughts aloud. "I'm worried I'm gonna screw things up. I've never felt this way about anyone before, and we didn't have the most conventional start."

"Good." His mother's smile grew wide. "When you fall, it's always scary at first. Trust your instincts, Noah. You'll be fine. You've always been a good judge of character."

"Have I?"

Nodding, she turned and finished the spot of dusting she'd abandoned earlier. "I'm sure you want us out of your hair so you can spend some time with her, so I'll finish this and tell Larry we need to hit the road."

"Aren't you staying?"

She turned back to him. "I wasn't certain how this day would end. We left the camper at a campground outside the city. We're driving back home tomorrow."

"You're welcome to stay." Truth was, he hoped they didn't.

"No, I think you need some time to take this all in." Her gaze strayed toward the kitchen. "I feel so much better now that I know you're not alone."

As if on cue, Emma and Larry came strolling through the hall, each carrying two mugs of coffee. His stepfather looked every bit as taken with his sexy neighbour as Noah felt.

"Holly, did you know that Emma here is the Atlanta police chief's daughter? She's a whip-smart young woman, works in computers. Isn't that something? Said she'd take a look at mine and see why it's been running so slow."

His mother looked suitably impressed. Emma pushed a mug against his hand and winked at him. "Ask Noah how good I am with computers. You should see what I did with his."

He laughed. That was one story he'd prefer to keep between them.

*Chapter 18*

Spider lifted one of the framed prints leaning against the wall and stared in awe at the beauty presented behind the glass. She'd been to New York City once, but she'd hadn't seen it through eyes like this.

The sky was painted violet against the backdrop of Times Square. A little boy gripped someone's hand out of the frame and gazed up in wonder at the neon lights and signs. The backdrop of Times Square was fascinating, but it was the expression on the child's face that carried her back to that feeling of discovering something wonderful for the first time.

It was such a beautiful picture.

"What do you think?"

Startled, she almost dropped the frame as she spun at the sound of Noah's voice. She hadn't realized he'd come back inside after seeing his parents off.

He nodded at the photo she held. "I took that one last year." He reached for one of the other prints propped against the wall. "This one is my favourite."

Taken from the harbour at sunset, the skyline of New York City was vibrant, rich in colours, and made the perfect image for a postcard or poster.

"They're amazing, Noah. I had no idea."

He set the frame back down. "I always try to take at least one

209

week every year to go somewhere I've never been. Somewhere I can go with my camera and explore. It started as a hobby, but…" He shrugged. "Hopefully, I can make money from it. We'll see."

Spider was pretty sure he had a bright career in front of him if these were any indication. "I always say I'm going to travel, but going to Dragoncon sucks all my vacation money away every year."

"Dragoncon. That's like Comic Con, only it's in Atlanta, right? I've never been."

Spider smiled. "It's so much fun! You and your camera would love it. All the cosplayers – people in costume," she clarified in case he didn't know. She got excited remembering it. "I've been known to stand in a corner and just take pictures for hours. Your pictures would probably be amazing."

"Do you cosplay?"

"Me?" She snorted. "I am not that talented, or patient. I would never be able to decide which character to cosplay as." She let her words trail off, wondering if she should admit such things. Too geeky? Probably not an attractive quality in a woman, not to a hottie like him.

He smiled. "Let's do it."

"Do what?"

"Go to Dragoncon. Let's plan on it. You don't mind if I tag along, do you?"

She'd be thrilled to have a companion. She usually went solo or met up with online friends. "Sure, but it's usually in September." That was almost six months away.

"Good. Maybe I can talk you into cosplaying by then. Sounds like it would be fun."

"*You* would cosplay?"

"Yeah." He drew out the response in a tone that suggested she was ridiculous for asking. Pushing a hand through his hair, he picked up some of the frames and carried them over to the dining room table.

Wait. He was making plans for them? Long-term plans?

Hope surged through her chest and caused her heart to do a Snoopy dance. He certainly seemed to be taking whatever this thing was between them seriously. She hadn't fully let herself trust that he would, choosing only to believe they'd share a week, maybe two, before he started trying to ditch her. She was ready for that. She could deal with that.

*Don't overthink this. Remember your five-year plan.*

Biting her lip, she picked up a couple of frames and followed him. "So how are you doing? Seriously, and don't tell me what you think I want to hear."

He didn't answer for several seconds. "I don't really know how to describe what I'm feeling."

She considered that. "Do you want to be alone?"

"No." He was emphatic.

She glanced around, wondering if she should suggest either of the ideas she'd been kicking around in her brain since this morning. Daylight still shone through the curtains, and it wouldn't be getting dark for at least a few more hours.

How could she ask him to go with her to search the area for his mother's body when he'd only just learned Kate *was* his mother?

"What are you thinking about?"

Her gaze darted to his, and she shook her head. "Nothing." She forced a smile. "What do you want to do with the rest of the day?"

His expression suggested he was deep in thought, but finally, he met her gaze. "This might sound crazy, but what if we went to this lake and took a look around? Would you be up for that?"

She almost blurted out an enthusiastic *yes*, but concern kept her in check. "Would *you*?"

He nodded. "I'd like to put this all behind me, and I don't think I'll be able to until I have more answers."

"Then let's go." She gestured toward the door. "I can have the boys packed up and ready in fifteen minutes. Meet me there?"

"You want to bring the pets? Emma, this isn't—"

"Hello! I'm not a total ditz." She frowned. "They always use dogs on TV to search for dead bodies. I happen to have two awesome canines at my disposal." She straightened. "Besides, Kellan has to work tonight, some charity party, so he can't watch them."

Rubbing at the back of his neck, Noah offered a smile in apology. "I think dogs have to be trained to find bodies."

"And one of the dogs in my care is blind. I figure that makes his sense of smell sharper than most." She crossed her arms. "Isn't it at least worth a try?"

He hesitated. "Let's do it."

Fifteen minutes later, exactly as she'd predicted, Spider had Charlie and Costello leashed up, Abbott secured in his carry cage, and plenty of fresh water, treats and other supplies for them bundled up in her bag. The dogs did happy little doggy dances at the door, eager to go for a ride, and the cat was already asleep.

Spider shrugged into her leather jacket in case it got cooler after dark and met Noah outside. "What kind of supplies should we bring? A shovel? Flashlights? What else?" She wrangled the animals into his jeep.

Noah paled a little. "I don't think we should worry with a shovel. We're only going to look around."

"But—"

He shook his head. "No shovels. I'll grab some flashlights in case we need them."

Crossing her arms, Spider hopped into the passenger seat. She was still pouting when he came out carrying two flashlights. How did he expect them to find an almost thirty-year-old grave without a shovel?

"You have your phone, right?"

Nodding, she pulled it out of her pocket and checked the battery life. It was almost at full charge since she'd left it plugged in all morning.

Once they were on the road, Noah relaxed. "I've never been to this lake. You?"

She nodded. "A few times when I was younger." Paul's family

had a cabin out there. "I've never been a water person. I prefer the mountains to the beach or lake."

Glancing in the rearview, he pulled onto the highway. "What kind of car does your ex drive?"

"Paul?" A horrible thought occurred to her, and she turned to look behind them. "He used to drive a truck."

"A red one?"

"Yes. Why?"

"I think he's following us. See that one back there? That him?"

Yes! Oh, for the love of—

Reaching for her phone, Spider scrolled through her contact list. Her finger hovered over her father's name before scrolling down to the number for Jack she'd added the night before. He answered quickly.

"I'm pretty sure Paul is following us. Is there anything you can do?"

The older man swore. "Where are you?"

"We're headed to Lake Allatoona. We just got on the highway."

Jack cleared his throat. "Is he on duty?"

"He's in his truck, if that's what you're asking." She looked in the side mirror to see if Paul was still behind them. He was. "What should we do?"

"Don't do anything." He swore again. "I'll call and talk some sense into him. If he doesn't stop following you in the next ten minutes, call me back." He hung up.

Spider risked a glance at the man beside her. His knuckles were showing white where he gripped the steering wheel, and he kept shifting his gaze between the road and the mirror.

"I'm sorry." She sighed. "I kind of have a lot of baggage."

Noah could have any woman he wanted. Pretty soon, he'd grow tired of having to deal with Paul making a nuisance of himself. Another reason she shouldn't let herself hope their fling was anything more than that.

She glanced at him, unable to help comparing him with her

psycho ex. Noah was nothing like Paul. He'd respected her need for distance when she'd been mad at him, had spent more time running away from her than chasing her and he'd been a kind, patient lover, more focused on her pleasure than his own. Could that mean his feelings for her extended beyond sexual chemistry? 'Cause hers certainly had begun to.

Noah's shoulders visibly relaxed, even as he frowned at her. "It's not your fault, Emma." He shifted in his seat. "Maybe we should save this for tomorrow."

"No!" No way was she letting Paul interfere again. "Jack will get him to leave us alone."

"Or he'll just let him know we're onto him so he can try something different."

Or that.

Every muscle in her body tensing, Spider sank into her seat and watched the red truck behind them as it followed in the side mirror. Finally, after what seemed like ages, the vehicle veered right onto an exit ramp.

She called Jack right away. "Thank you. What did you say to him?"

"That he was needed at work." Jack took a deep breath. "I didn't let on that you knew he was following you. Emma, the boy's probably still pining for you. That's all. Maybe he's just trying to keep an eye on you since you're seeing this new guy. I wouldn't jump to conclusions. Paul's not stupid. He knows your dad would have his hide if he did anything to hurt you."

Self-doubt chased the worry from her mind. "I don't know."

"If he gives you any more trouble, call me. You be careful, you hear?"

Hanging up with her father's friend, she still couldn't shake the feeling they were being followed. Paranoia settled like a bird in a nest in her stomach. Giving up this mission might have been the smartest option, but Noah wasn't the only one desperate for answers.

Spider needed them, too.

***

Noah grabbed one of the dog's leashes – the short, stubby one – and tested one of the flashlights.

Emma leaned into the car, murmuring promises to the cat that she'd return soon. Noah waited until she and the other dog were out to crack the windows and activate his car alarm. The cat should be fine. He didn't plan to go far.

"You're sure this is the spot?" he asked again.

She nodded, stumbling along after the larger dog that already had his nose to the ground following an invisible trail. "This is where you, or Kate, told us to look."

The area wasn't crowded. Only two other people mulled about the place, and they were packing up their things and leaving. The entrance sign had warned that this part of the park would be closing at 8 p.m., which was in less than an hour. A boat ramp led to the lake while grills and picnic tables under sheds lined the edge of the trees.

"We'll never find anything out here."

"Have some faith. We haven't even started looking yet." She frowned at him.

He swept his arm toward the forest. "Look at this place. If a body was hidden here, it would have already been found."

"Then I suggest we start further out where it would be easier to hide a body."

He let her lead the way, growing more and more doubtful by the minute. Neither dog seemed interested in anything except hiking their legs and peeing on everything. He finally stopped when shadows began to engulf the scenery. "We shouldn't go much further. We should get back to the cat."

She sighed, her expression etched in disappointment.

*Can't leave. Almost there.*

Whoa. Where had that thought come from?

Emma started to turn around, but he grabbed her arm. "Let's give it a few more minutes."

She searched his face. "Really?"

Nodding, he wiped a hand over his mouth and glanced down at the dog at her feet. He could hardly believe he was doing it, but he opened his mouth and said, "Kate. If you're with us, we could use some help."

Barking ripped the silence as Costello started huffing and bouncing toward the trees to their right.

Almost immediately, Charlie jerked his head down, caught scent of something, and started pulling hard to the right. Emma clung onto his leash and trailed after him. "Okay, Charlie, lay off the crack. You almost took my arm off."

They walked for several minutes, and it seemed Charlie was being led somewhere by something neither he nor Emma could identify. The blond chubby mutt kept looking up, tilting his head, and following the same path. Holy hell. What were the animals seeing?

The dog started circling a log, dug at the ground beside it, then lifted his leg and peed on the fallen tree. Frustrated, Noah was going to suggest they turn back when Charlie started digging at the ground again, pushing at the pine needles with his nose.

"He's found something." Emma knelt beside the dog and glanced up at Noah.

Costello shuffled over and started pawing at the ground, too. The ground was soft from a recent rain, and it didn't take long for them to make a dent in the spot. Emma turned her flashlight on and pointed it at the area they were focused on, even as something inside Noah cried out *This is it!*

The dogs dug and dug, kicking dirt all over the place until a small hole had formed. Both Costello and Charlie stuck their heads in the hole and tugged at something with their teeth. Emma pushed them quickly away.

"Noah, I see something!"

"What?" He knelt and used his hands to brush away dirt and pine needles.

She plucked something out of the hole. Long, yellowish-white. Definitely some kind of bone. "Is this what I think it is?"

His stomach was tied up in knots. "Yeah."

She arched a brow at him. "Bet you wish we had brought that shovel now, don'tcha?"

***

Spider's body was as heavy as a pile of bricks by the time they made it home after midnight, but her mind was still buzzing with nervous excitement over what they'd found.

The lake had been outside of her father's jurisdiction, but he'd called the appropriate authorities and then met them at the gravesite too. She was pretty certain he mainly wanted to size up Noah, but her father had been his usual take-charge gruff self, spending more time chatting with the officers at the scene than with her or Noah. They'd given a statement and left, with her father's parting comments weighing on her mind the entire drive back.

"It'll take them a while to do testing to identify the body. No telling who it is. I've asked them to keep me in the loop."

Spider didn't need test results to know whose body it was. Kate Levine. There was no doubt in her mind.

"Do you think they'll find any evidence at the grave site to prove who killed her?" Spider had asked.

"Doubt it," her father had said. "But you never know. They'll have a body, so that'll make it easier to press charges if they ever catch the suspect."

At least that was something.

Noah had been quiet on the drive back, pulling into Zach's driveway and following her inside without a word until he

217

informed her, "If Kellan isn't going to be around, I'm staying here tonight. No arguments."

She didn't want to be alone, but mostly, she didn't want him to be alone. She had no idea what was going on in that head of his. The man was stubbornly unreadable sometimes. But if she had to guess, he was sorting through some heavy feelings. They'd probably just found his birth mother's body, for Pete's sake.

When he returned, he put his things on the sofa. "Got any sheets I could borrow?"

"You want to sleep on the sofa?" She hadn't meant for her voice to sound quite so … shocked.

"It's probably better." He gestured toward the door. "I can keep an eye out from here without any—" He looked her over. "—distractions."

"You can stay in the guest room with me, or you can stay in another room if you prefer to sleep alone."

"The sofa is fine."

So this was it, then. The first of the inevitable excuses he'd give to untangle himself from her. Crossing her arms, she started to call him out on it, but no. The shadows under his eyes reminded her of the rough day he'd had. Piling more drama onto that would only justify his efforts to push her away.

"I'll grab you some sheets."

The relief that flittered across his expression would have been hurtful if she'd allowed it to be. Instead, she focused on making him as comfortable as possible while she went over everything that had happened tonight. She doubted she'd be able to sleep after all the excitement.

But when she fell into bed minutes later, she drifted off within minutes and Noah was the last thought on her mind.

* * *

Noah stared at the ceiling and came to a reluctant conclusion.

He wasn't cut out for this.

Emma deserved someone better, more stable in her life. Not someone who'd discovered everything he'd believed his entire life was a lie. The disapproval in her father's eyes tonight had sealed the deal. Last thing he wanted was to come between her and her old man, especially since the bond between them was obvious to anyone with eyes. Noah craved that kind of relationship and knew he'd never have it. The man whose sperm had given him life had wanted nothing to do with him, apparently. The man who'd raised him had only shown him fleeting moments of concern.

Something inside him was broken, and Emma deserved more. How could he ask her to hang around while he figured out how to be complete? Who knew if he could be?

She was kind, funny and loyal to a fault. She was everything he hadn't known he was looking for. How could he stand to lose her?

A shadow on the ceiling moved, snapping his body to alert. Seconds later, the cat jumped on top of him. Releasing the breath he'd been holding, he relaxed as the animal strolled up his body, stopping to stand on Noah's chest. Almond-shaped eyes stared down at him for several seconds until, finally, the cat sank down, sprawling across him as if he were a body pillow.

The animal's purr was soothing and, eyelids drooping, Noah let it lull him to sleep.

# Chapter 19

Spider wasn't certain how well her plan would go over with Noah, but that didn't stop her from setting everything up while he was busy showering upstairs.

It had taken her a while this morning to figure out if she had everything they needed to try her other plan – the one she hadn't shared with him yet – but she'd found an extra voice recorder in Zach's desk, downloaded and tested a few software applications, and called Alexandra to make sure they wouldn't be doing anything crazy like opening up portals to release evil flying monkeys or something.

When he'd suggested they make a trip over to his house to go through Kate's belongings, she'd seized the opportunity to put her plan into action. Guilt almost had her spilling out the details before he'd opened his door, but considering how quiet he'd been since last night, she'd figured he wasn't in the mood to hear them.

Noah took one step into the room and froze. "What's all this?"

"Umm." She bit her lower lip, wondering if she'd overstepped her boundary by touching his stuff. "Hear me out first." She walked over to her laptop, which was sitting next to his on the counter. She'd connected and anchored his DSLR camera and tripod to his machine and had positioned it to capture images in the central part of his living room. "I was thinking."

"Heaven help us."

"You're so not funny." She switched the camera on and aimed it at him to do a test check. His bemused expression filled the screen on his computer. Yep. It was working, which was beyond awesome since she had no idea what she was doing. "Remember how Kate scared me to death by typing those crazy words on my computer?"

He frowned. "I remember you mentioning something."

"Point is, she was able to communicate with me through the computer. You know, sort of like an Ouija board, I guess. Since Connor hasn't returned and Alexandra is knee-deep in family drama, I thought we'd try to reach out to Kate ourselves. If she could give us more details, like the name of her killer, we can solve this case once and for all."

He ran a hand over his face. "I don't know if this is such a good idea."

"Of course it is. Come here." She moved behind the counter, pulled up one of the new applications she'd found and retrieved her phone. Noah reluctantly moved behind her to see what she was doing. "See this?" She turned and held up her mobile.

"Your phone?" His voice was wary.

She opened up an app and smiled. "Not anymore. I just turned it into an EMF reader." She barely resisted the urge to give him two snaps and an "Oh, yeah!"

"I'm supposed to know what that means?"

She shook her head and turned away in disgust. "Haven't you ever watched a ghost-hunting show?"

"Not my thing. Sorry."

She sighed, typing fast to bring up the programs she'd installed to link her computer with her phone and record all of the information they captured. "Electromagnetic field detector. Supposedly, it can detect the presence of a ghost." She picked up her phone and stepped closer to show him the display. "See this? If there's a spike in the reading, that's an indication we're not alone."

"Or that you're standing next to some electrical equipment."

"Or that."

She noticed the weary lines creeping back into his features. "I suppose I should have waited to talk to you about this first." After all, Kate was his mother. It was easy to get caught up in the excitement of a ghost hunt without realizing the people on the other side were simply that. People.

She hadn't stopped to think how traumatic this might be for Noah either. It was probably far too soon to expect him to be okay with this. With any of this.

"Know what?" She sat her phone aside. "Let's not do this. We can wait—"

"No." He grabbed her hand to keep her from turning. "You've got everything set up. This was a good idea. I think."

"Are you sure?" She stepped closer, slipping her arms around his middle and watching his expression for any sign that he was only pacifying her. His shoulders sank as he slid his hands up and down her arms, half smiling.

"I'd like to get this mystery solved so I know you're safe and we can move on from all of this."

Moving on from all of this could mean moving on from her. A tiny nugget of doubt worried at her hope that he meant moving on *with* her rather than away from her.

He was a hard man to read, but she decided to take him at his word. The poor guy already had enough to deal with. "Right. Should we do it now, or do you need a little time to adjust?"

He shook his head. "What do I do?"

She reached for the voice recorder. "I might be overdoing things a bit, but I figure at least one of these has to work, right?" She turned the recorder on and placed it in his hand. "We ask Kate questions. Record everything. I'll be over here at the computers, so if she prefers typing her answers, I'll know it. The camera is also recording in case we can get anything that way."

"You're right. I think you're overdoing it just a little."

She shrugged. "Well, I'm hoping we only have to do this once."

"Right. Good plan."

Smiling, she handed him her phone and explained again the way to use it. "She's attached to you, so it's probably best if you ask the questions."

"Sure." He swallowed. "Do I walk around or what?"

Good question. "Maybe. Start in here and see what happens. Remember, if the reader spikes, stop and talk to her."

His face paled, but he clenched his jaw and nodded. Slowly, he moved to the other side of the room. Clearing his throat, he asked, "So … is anyone here?"

Spider's gaze focused on the displays linked to her computer. A blank Word document was open in the left-hand corner, available as a writing tool if Kate wanted it.

But absolutely nothing happened.

"Ask again," she urged him gently. "Walk around."

He paced to the other side of the room. "Anyone here? Kate?"

The digital meter jumped, and Spider gasped. "Did you see that?"

"Yeah." He glanced around the room. "Kate?"

It jumped again.

"So you're here. Good." He hesitated. "We want to help you. We think we know what happened, but we need some help figuring out your killer's name."

Spider nodded encouragement at him from her station.

He held out his hands in question. "How do I get her to tell me a name?"

The reader spiked, higher than before, and so did Spider's heartbeat. "Ask her to type it over here."

Before Noah had the chance, two letters appeared on the document.

JD.

Spider sucked in air and stepped back.

"What happened?" Noah hurried to see, his body tensing where it pressed against hers. He swore. "I don't suppose you can give us a last name?"

The letter C appeared in front of the blinking cursor. Nothing else.

"Kate?" Spider asked.

The letter O appeared twice as the screen flickered and went black. The steady hum of the power source faded to silent.

"What? No!" Spider tapped the space bar, hoping the machine had only gone to sleep, but it remained frustratingly dead. "Crap!" She hurried to her bag, hoping she'd brought her power cord. "Oh, I'm so stupid! I bet she drained the battery by pulling from its energy in order to type. Stupid! Why didn't I have it plugged in?"

"Camera's dead, too. So is your phone."

Seriously? Spider could kick herself for such an amateurish mistake. She'd seen enough of the shows with guys who ran around taunting spirits to know this had been a probability. She hurried to plug her laptop directly to the wall and drummed the touchpad impatiently while she waited for it to boot up again.

Noah's hand settled on her shoulder as he leaned over her from behind and wiggled the hand that held the voice recorder in front of her. "This still has juice."

Spider straightened. "I wonder if we captured anything."

"Only one way to find out." He hit rewind and then play.

Jostling sounds mixed with the white noise of distorted silence before Noah asked his first question. "Anyone here? Kate?"

A snakelike whisper could be heard.

"Holy hell." Noah jerked his head back. "Did someone say *yes*?"

Spider nodded. "I heard that, too."

Their voices from earlier followed. When Noah again asked, "Kate?" there was another distorted response. Unintelligible this time.

"I can't make out what she's saying." Noah pushed the recorder toward her.

"Me either. Here. Let's see if this works."

Her computer had rebooted, so she connected the voice

recorder, downloaded the raw wave file and inserted it into the program she'd used to decipher Kate's previous message on Noah's video. A few minutes later, she thought she had the proper sound waves alienated and digitized enough. She clicked play.

"Danger."

It was still hard to make out, but Spider would bet her month's salary that's what the word was.

"I can't believe this." Noah leaned against the counter and stared in shock at the wall. "Did we get anything else?"

They listened through the rest of the recording. Something faint in an urgent-sounding tone could be heard right after Noah's voice asked, "I don't suppose you can give us a last name?"

Spider worked her magic on that clip, amplified the volume, and listened carefully.

"Cot!"

She looked at Noah for clarification. "What do you hear?"

"Caw?"

"I hear cot."

"Replay it."

She did, and they couldn't come to an agreement on what the sound meant. Crossing his arms and leaning back against the counter, Noah glanced around the room. "We know she was writing C-O-O before the computer died. What last names would that be?"

"Cooper?"

"Cook," he offered.

She sighed and shut the lid on her laptop in frustration. "Have we talked to anyone with a name that begins with C-O-O?"

Noah's brow furrowed. "What was the name of that bartender? The one at the new restaurant that used to be Wally's?"

"I have no idea. I don't think I asked."

"Me either. Maybe one of us should."

A shot of adrenaline bolstered Spider's courage. "I bet it's him! Oh my gosh!" This had to be the lead they'd been looking for. She reached for her phone, but it was dead. "Dag nab it. I can't call them and ask his name."

"Wow."

She frowned at him. "What?"

"Your language is … wow."

"Shut up."

Chuckling, he reached for the landline. "Can you work your magic on Google and get me a number?"

She did, settling down in the chair beside him, biting her thumbnail while she listened to his side of the conversation. He thanked the person for their help and disconnected the call.

"Well."

Spider grabbed his arm and shook him. "What's his name?"

"Carl. Carl Spottswood."

"Carl!" She sprang to her feet, itching to replay the audio clip. "I suppose she could be saying Carl."

She leaned close to the speaker, but she swore she still heard "Cot!"

"Spot? Maybe we can't hear the rest. Spottswood?"

Noah shook his head. "Maybe, but I don't know. How does that make him J.D.?"

"A nickname?" Spider shrugged. "Let's ask her again."

Noah grabbed her before she could reset the equipment. "I think we should wait on Connor or your friend, or let the police handle things from here on out. We could end up chasing an innocent man because we mistake something we hear. Besides, I think I need a break."

She opened her mouth to argue, but quickly shut it again. Her heart turned over at the anguish in his handsome face. It was tempting to tell him to go take his break while she tried on her own, but Alexandra had warned her not to go solo on something like this. Something about attracting the wrong kind of energy by being alone and vulnerable.

"Fine. Do you want to go take a nap or something?"

He pulled her hip forward until it met his. "Or something."

"Oh."

"We have to be good around the pets later, right?"

"Uh-huh."

"The pets aren't here now."

"No, they aren't." Her voice was barely a whisper.

"This might sound crass, but I would really love to lose myself in you for a while. Forget about everything in my effed up life and soak in your warmth. Will you let me do that?"

She softly covered his cheek with her palm and loved the way his green eyes softened to hazel at her unspoken agreement. Relief made her muscles soften. She'd been so worried after last night that he hadn't wanted her anymore. He covered her hand with his, lacing their fingers, holding her gaze. Then he leaned down and kissed her, a lingering kiss that caused her to melt from the inside out.

She curled her hands around his shoulders and he lifted and carried her, refusing to remove his mouth from hers until he had no choice in order to lift her shirt up and over her head.

***

It was much later when Spider opened her eyes and realized the animals were overdue for their afternoon potty break. *Worst pet-sitter ever.* Noah's breathing was steady, his face relaxed in sleep, so she slid out of bed without disturbing him, got dressed, scribbled him a note and went to check on the animals.

Charlie and Costello danced around her as if she'd been gone three years rather than three hours, their tails wagging in happy doggy bliss. She squatted and gave them affectionate rubs in reward before letting them out back to do their business.

She tried calling Connor again, simply because she thought he might listen to her message and at least send her a text in reply. She explained everything that had happened this afternoon. And then added, because she thought it was funny, a fake shriek.

"Oh my gosh, Connor! I think … I think I see a red-eyed ghost coming at me. It's getting closer. Oh no! If only I knew a psychic or someone who knew about these things to help me!" Then she made a kissy sound into the phone and returned to her normal voice. "Call me."

She hit END and settled back on the comfy sofa, wondering if she had time to unwind with a quick game with her friends if any of them were online. She connected through the console and put her headgear on.

The familiar slashing sound of swordplay greeted her as she entered the game already in progress.

Foul-mouthed rants assaulted her ears, prompting her to tell her two friends, "What have I said about all of this swearing? Geez. I leave you guys alone for few days, and you've lost half our gold? What's wrong with you people? We're down three lives, too?"

She cut down two trolls, her blue-bearded masculine dwarf avatar twirling across the screen in combat.

"SpeedySpider! You're back!" SuperWiggles123 cheered through the earpiece.

"Hey. Hey. Told you she hadn't joined another team."

MartyMcFlyTimeTraveler's large giant-with-a-mohawk avatar came running over to her muscular dwarf. "Where were you the other night? We almost got slaughtered at the dam."

"Had a date."

"What? No!" He wailed. "You're supposed to marry me, remember?"

She snorted. "And what? Live in your parent's basement with you? With that filthy mouth of yours? No thanks."

MartyMcFlyTimeTraveler was a fourteen-year-old Catholic school student in Des Moines, Iowa. She knew because she'd done background checks on all of her online friends. A girl couldn't be too safe. Especially a girl gamer. As soon as guys heard her voice in the game, they were all over her. They probably fantasized all girl gamers looked like Mila Kunis or something. As if.

"Hey! I got plans. Career plans."

A troll dove out of some bushes toward them, and Spider flipped her dwarf backwards, stabbing the offender with an easy manoeuvre that saved them both.

An ear-piercing burst of static caused her to cry out in pain. "Check your microphones, boys. Someone's got issues."

"I didn't hear anything." SuperWiggles123 disagreed, but most of what he said was distorted.

"Me either," MMTT concurred.

As they continued to fight on screen, Spider adjusted her headphones.

A whispering sound seemed to be interfering with the game. "You guys don't hear that?"

"Nah. Just the sound of awesome slaughter as we head to the next level. Oh yeah!" MMTT chuckled.

Static and whispering. Spider pressed one of the headphones against her ear.

A soft whisper said, "Cop."

Holy guacamole. Spider's breath caught in her chest. Was Kate still trying to communicate with her?

"Oh yeah! Did you see that?" MMTT asked with delight.

"Shhh!" Spider shushed him. "Quiet for a sec."

She strained to hear Kate through the background noise of the game. Bursts of static sent stabs of pain through her ears, but she couldn't take the headphones off.

Another whispering sound that resembled the word "danger" came through.

Cop and danger?

"I don't know what you're trying to tell me," Spider said in frustration.

"I tried to tell you to look at my mad slaying skills, but you got an attitude." MMTT answered. "Never mind."

Spider groaned and disconnected the game. "Kate? Are you still there?"

Silence was the only sound through the device now.

Ripping the headphones off, Spider looked around, uncertain what to do.

Cop. Danger.

Was Kate trying to warn her about Paul?

## Chapter 20

Noah knelt in front of one of the boxes his mother had left him and hesitated before opening the flaps. Two medium-sized boxes. Whatever was inside was all his birth mother had owned. Pity stilled his movements; this seemed somehow intrusive all of a sudden. He felt no attachment to whatsoever was inside these boxes. He should, shouldn't he? They held his meagre heritage.

Blowing out a breath, he ripped the tape off one lid.

He'd seen Emma's note – "*Animal potty break. Come over when you wake up.*" – but he'd been drawn here to the garage instead, eager to see if these boxes held clues that could put an end to Kate's restlessness.

He hadn't been lying when he said he was ready to move past this. For the first time in his life, he was with a woman who inspired him to want better things. To believe he actually deserved them.

Yes, he should probably cut Emma loose, but he couldn't bring himself to. He didn't think she wanted him to either, and he was a selfish enough bastard to take advantage of the fact. If or when she wanted out, he'd let her go. But not until then.

Packaging paper crinkled as he drew it away, revealing a stack of framed photos. An eight by ten of Kate holding him as a baby revealed a happy, pretty woman and a smiling, toothless child. Mother and son.

Something stirred in his chest. He recognized the emotion. Regret – strong, heart-piercing regret.

"West."

He sprang to his feet, turning at the sound of his name.

Emma's officer friend Jack strolled toward him, hands clasping his belt-buckle on each side. "Just patrolling the neighbourhood. Saw you out here and thought I'd come see if there had been any more trouble."

Noah glanced at the framed photo in his hand and lowered it to his side. "No. No trouble. Everything's been quiet." Noah considered the man. "Thank you for helping Emma with her ex yesterday. I'm sorry you had to get in the middle of that."

He shifted uncomfortably. "She's a sweet kid." Wiping a hand over his mouth, he glanced toward the house across the street. "I heard what happened last night." He turned back and stared at the framed photo. "How did y'all figure out there was a body there?"

"You wouldn't believe me if I told you."

"You got any evidence pointing to who did it?"

Noah shook his head. "Not yet." He glanced back at the boxes. "I'm working on it though."

"Let me know if you do." The officer's narrow-eyed gaze dropped down to Noah's hand before skimming over the boxes around his feet. "Cleaning out the garage today?"

"Just going through some old things. They belonged to, uh, my birth mother."

Nodding, Jack frowned, his eyes again falling to Noah's hand. "Cute picture."

He forced a smile and lifted the photo. "Yeah. Guess I was a cute kid."

Something strange flickered in the older man's gaze as he scratched his neck. "Well, I'll leave you be. You have a good evening."

Noah watched Jack walk away before turning back to the boxes. Piling one on top of the other, he lifted and carried them inside, hitting *close* on the garage door as he did. Might be better to go through them with more privacy.

He looked through the various photos Kate had framed, not recognizing anyone other than her. Some other photos were piled inside an envelope. Lots of pictures of a baby – him, he presumed – and a few of Jennifer Abercrombie and Kate goofing off. He slipped through the pictures, stilling when he came to one from the bar. Wally's. A neon sign stated the restaurant's name in the background. Kate and a few people he didn't recognize posed around a small Christmas tree set up at the bar. Customers crowded around in the background.

One man stood out, not because Noah recognized him, but because of the way his gaze was intensely focused on Kate. Kind of creepy, actually.

He lifted the photo for closer inspection.

Young. Early twenties, probably. Thick, dark hair with long sideburns.

There was something about the man's profile that seemed … familiar. That's when Noah realized the man was in uniform.

A cop. Holy hell.

*Thud.*

The sound drew Noah's attention toward the stairs.

"Emma?" he called, wondering if she'd come back. He'd left the front door unlocked in case she got impatient and came looking for him.

A creak along the floorboard was his only response. He moved to his feet.

"Kate? That you?"

He slowly advanced toward the direction of the sound.

The feeling someone was behind him crept up his nerve endings before he could react. A dark blur moved in the corner of his eye, and he turned.

A slamming pain at the base of his skull robbed him of his eyesight. Stars burst through his vision seconds before his muscles crumbled beneath him.

And everything went black.

***

Glancing down the street, Spider didn't see Jack's patrol car anywhere. Well, that was odd. She'd peeked out the curtains and seen him walking around the side of Noah's house and decided to come talk to him.

She didn't know if Kate's latest warning was about Paul or not, but Spider was tired of hiding her fear of her ex from the proper authorities. Jack was a friend. She trusted him to advise her about the right thing to do.

She started to head up the front porch, but a strange feeling gripped her gut.

*Not safe.*

Where had that thought come from?

Stepping back, lingering in the front yard, she glanced around. The neighbourhood was quiet. No signs of activity.

*"Danger."*

Kate's warning whispered through her ear again, and Spider wasn't sure if it was a memory or a new sound.

Trusting that her instincts, at least, were spot on, she detoured the same way she'd seen Jack disappear. The back door looked pried open, and Spider's stomach sank to her feet like an anchor.

Whipping out her phone, she tried Noah again. Voicemail. Kate must have zapped his battery, too.

Had Jack seen someone trying to break into Noah's house? Had he gone inside to apprehend the suspect? Where was his backup? If anything had happened to Noah…

Ducking around the corner, she sank to her haunches and scrolled through her phone, quickly trying Kellan first. When she reached his voicemail, she considered dialing 9-1-1, but what if she was overreacting again?

234

Cop.

Danger.

Wait. Had Kate been warning her that a cop was somehow involved?

Jack?

Jack.

J.D.

Terror curdled in her stomach and threatened to force her lunch out.

That was crazy! She'd known Jack forever. He couldn't be.

Pushing to her feet, she edged her way around the house, peeking through windows until she glimpsed movement.

Through a slit in one blind, she saw Jack bending over Noah, wrapping duct tape around his hands. He finished, placed a strip over Noah's mouth, and then stood back, panting. He glanced toward the window where she was, and she ducked down and out of sight.

Oh. My. Gosh.

Jack *was* somehow involved in all of this.

Spider turned and clasped a hand over her mouth at the sight of the woman standing beside her. Kate Levine looked pale, her dark hair a striking contrast to her skin. She reached out a hand, ice cold, and grabbed Spider's arm, whispering, "You need to see."

The area surrounding Spider blurred as the scenery changed.

Suddenly she was in a restaurant, sitting across from a much younger version of Jack Lanier in a suit and tie.

"You're married?" The female voice sounded shocked and outraged at once. Spider stood, tossing her napkin onto the table. "I would have never come on this date if I'd known you were married, J.D."

"Kate, wait a minute!" Jack jumped to his feet as Spider turned to walk away.

Suddenly, she was standing in a room, and her hand – Kate's hand – held back curtains. Jack leaned against a streetlight on the sidewalk below, looking up at her. She let the curtains fall back into place as fear surged through her veins.

A sense of wooziness threatened to overtake Spider as she was back in Wally's – not the newly updated restaurant, but the old bar. She leaned over the bar top, confiding in her co-workers.

"I think I'm in love. He treats me like … you wouldn't believe." A quick glance to her left showed that Jack was nearby, frowning as he eavesdropped. Good. The words were a lie made up to deter his attention. A hint of fear gripped her chest every time she looked at him. He'd been following … showing up places he had no right being.

In a flash of light, Spider was wiping down a table when Jack's voice said, "Kate."

She turned to find him smiling at her. "I'm glad you found somebody. I just wanted you to know that. I want you to be happy."

Her clenched muscles relaxed a little. "Thank you, Jack."

"If you ever need anything…"

She wouldn't. Not from him. She was glad her white lie had had the proper effect. Maybe now she could concentrate on school, and Billy. Oh, how she loved her little boy.

The vision swam away again.

Suddenly, it was raining, and Spider's clothes were beginning to cling to her body. The bus wouldn't be there for another fifteen minutes. Glancing around for a place to get out of the downpour in the meantime, she saw a familiar car creeping up to the curb. The window rolled down, and Jack said, "Why don't you get in? I can give you a lift."

She shook her head. "No thank you. I'm waiting for the bus."

"Come on. Get in." When she didn't move, he added, "You don't want to catch a cold and give it to your kid, do you?"

Wavering, Spider felt the sting of heavier rain and moved toward the car. Maybe it would be okay. He hadn't been following her for a few days. Maybe…

Suddenly, Spider was back in the yard, standing behind Noah's house. She didn't need more visions to know how the story had ended. Sinking down, Spider wanted to curl into a ball and weep at the loss of her trust in her father's dear friend, her breathing loud and ragged, even to her own ears.

Noah!

She lifted her phone to check the time, uncertain how many minutes had passed. The experience had seemed to last several minutes, but according to the time, only one minute had gone by.

Surely Jack wouldn't have bound his hands and mouth if Noah was dead. He had to still be alive. He needed her help.

*Think!*

Fingers trembling, Spider calmly dialed 9-1-1, told the dispatcher what was happening, and ended the call. Best case scenario, the cops would be here in about five minutes.

Who was she kidding?

This was Atlanta. She'd be lucky if they got here in ten.

Raising up, she peeked through the blinds and saw Jack dragging Noah's body along the floor. Whatever he had planned probably wasn't good.

Spider sank down and considered her options. Call her father? Sneak in and find a way to conk Jack on the head? Simply wait here and pray that help arrived soon?

*Think. Think.*

How was she going to get Noah out of this alive?

***

The familiar dream started as it always did, with Kate accepting a ride from the man she called J.D.

Only this time, Noah saw the young man's face.

Younger, less weathered, about ten pounds slimmer, Officer Jack Lanier sat behind the wheel of the car, dressed in a plaid button-up shirt, the smell of alcohol strong on his breath as he leaned towards Noah – no, not to him – towards Kate.

The car doors clicked shut, only this time, the dream didn't end.

"J.D., what are you doing?" Kate demanded, fear etched on her face.

"Just wanted to take you somewhere. Real quick. It's pretty. You'll like it. I just wanna talk."

"J.D., I have to work! I'll lose my job. I can't afford to lose my job!"

"I'll take care of you. Don't worry."

Time seemed to pass in a blur of highway signage indicating Lake Allatoona was their destination as fear swelled in the car around Noah. The car eased to a stop, Jack put it in park, and he released the locks on the door. Scrambling to get away, Kate immediately went running along the edges of the lake into the green and orange trees surrounding it, leaves crunching beneath her feet, betraying her location.

"Kate! Don't be afraid! Come back!" Jack gave chase. Noah felt him not too far behind them. "I won't hurt you. I just wanted to spend time with you!"

Kate fell to her knees, crying out in pain.

"Kate! Get back here!"

Back on her feet, she ran aimlessly into the growing darkness, her breathing ragged in Noah's ears. Hands suddenly gripped her from behind. Screaming, Kate clawed at Jack's face as she twisted around and fell backwards, stumbling over a fallen tree limb.

A loud crack accompanied her last breath as her skull connected with a boulder. She lay motionless on the forest floor as Jack stood over her.

"Kate?" Jack bent and touched her face, a trail of blood along his cheek. "Kate!"

A wailing moan tore from him as he fell back, crying, "No! Oh, God, no!"

Noah's eyes slowly opened, heavy, drugged, reluctant to do his bidding. He struggled for consciousness as the interior of his car swam around him. He became just aware enough to realize his hands couldn't move and something was blocking his mouth.

Panic seized his chest. No! He struggled to free himself, hating the sensation he was trapped. Memories of his father locking him inside the closet gave him a shot of adrenaline. He had to get free.

Jack reached in front of him, put the key in the ignition, and cranked the engine.

"I'm sorry about this," Jack told him. "It was an accident – your mother. I panicked. Hid her body. I was married, you see? My wife had told me she was pregnant. She'd threatened to leave me if I chased other women. That's why I wanted to talk to Kate that day. She was the one I wanted to be with, but I had a kid coming. You know?"

Wiping a hand over his face, Jack stumbled back. "If my wife had ever found out I was with Kate at the lake that day, she would have taken my kid and left me. Kate scratched me. My DNA was under her fingernails. If she hadn't scratched me … no one would have believed it was an accident." He shook his head. "I could have lost everything. My family. My job. Can you understand that?"

Noah groaned and struggled against the duct tape.

"I tried to make up for it. Made sure I was a good husband and father. Never did anything wrong after that. Never even looked at another woman." Jack's voice was pleading. "Please understand I don't want to do this, but I don't know what else to do. I love my family. They mean everything to me."

Noah tried to yell "Then don't do this!" and struggled to move. His foot connected with the gas pedal, revving the engine loudly.

"If my family ever learned what I did…" Jack shook his head, pulled his trembling hand out of the car and slammed the door. "I'm up for retirement in a year. I'll lose my pension. I'll lose everything. You won't suffer this way. You'll just go to sleep. I'll come back and take off the tape. Everyone will assume it was suicide. No one will know." It was as if the older man was trying to convince himself more than anyone. He was too far gone to realize the holes in his plan.

If Noah could only talk to him, make him realize there was too much forensics evidence this time for Jack to get away with murder.

He tried again to scream for help, but the sound was too muffled.

Lethargy was beginning to seep in. He felt so drowsy…

Somewhere in the distance, he heard the screech of an alarm and thought of Emma. Lovely, feisty Emma. What would Jack do to her if she discovered his secret?

He struggled to stay awake, struggled to free himself, but sleep was too seductive. He felt himself sliding sideways. He'd think about it later … when he woke up.

***

Spider took a calming breath, knocked to be certain she made a ruckus – as if the alarm she'd activated at Zach and Hannah's wasn't loud enough – and squared her shoulders, her fingers slipping against the plastic casing she held behind her back. A trickle of sweat slid down her temple as she tried to slow her racing heartbeat. Glancing back at Zach's house she lifted the remote to the alarm and pressed to deactivate it, offering a mental apology to the animals who were probably cowering somewhere right now.

If the cops hadn't been on the way before, they would be now.

You. Can. Do. This.

Jack wouldn't expect her to go on the offence. She had the advantage here.

The floorboard creaked on the other side of the door, and her grip tightened. Swallowing, she yelled out, "Jack! I know you're in there. I know you killed Kate! It's over!"

The door opened. Jack, his face pale and anguished, looked at her.

Not giving him any chance to react, Spider lunged forward, whipping her hand around and pressing the stun gun her father had given her years ago against Jack's side. He shook uncontrollably as electricity zapped the air. When he bent over, she slammed her knee up and into his groin, sending him sprawling back onto the carpet in the entryway. He groaned in agony.

She grabbed the duct tape she'd seen him leave sitting out and quickly bound his hands and feet with it, the same as he'd done to Noah. Jack was nearly unconscious.

"Noah?" she called.

Knowing Jack was secure, she raced toward the garage, horror replacing fear as she opened the door and got a heavy whiff of fumes.

"Noah!" she screamed, hitting the *open* button on the garage door and hurrying to free him from his vehicle. He was slumped over, unconscious, his mouth taped shut. She ripped the tape off his mouth and slapped his face. "Noah? Noah, wake up!"

Hands gripped her shoulders from behind, and she shrieked, startled, turning to defend herself if needed.

"I've got this," Connor said, grabbing her hands between his. She moved so he could slide his arms under Noah's and drag him out of the car.

Together, they managed to carry him to the front lawn.

"Where have you been?" Spider demanded as she worked to free Noah's hands. Police sirens in the distance signalled help was on the way.

"Long story. Tell you later." Connor leaned down and pressed his ear to Noah's chest. He swore. "His pulse is weak, but it's there. The ambulance is on its way. Don't worry."

Noah moaned something incoherent, but didn't wake up.

A police car came speeding around the curve, blue lights casting an eerie glow over Noah's face. Tears welling in her eyes, Spider met Connor's gaze. "Kate?"

Connor nodded. "She's here. Her hand's on your shoulder."

Spider didn't feel a thing. "Good."

"Remind me never to piss you off." Smirking, he nodded toward the house.

She glared at him. "Could have used some help."

"You had it on your own. Nice work." He stood to go greet the officers now on the scene.

She searched Noah's face, cupping it in her palm, happy to feel the warmth returning there, comforted by the increasingly steady rise and fall of his chest. Love for him almost overwhelmed her. Wait. Love? The realization stole her breath and startled her.

She loved him.

Holy cow. Love. That was big. Huge!

"Emma!"

Her father's voice was followed by the slam of a car door, and she turned to see him striding, out of uniform, toward her across the lawn. She scrambled to her feet and flung herself into his arms, grateful when he squeezed her in return.

Her frantic phone call to her dad had been the last she'd made before setting her rescue plan in motion, rushing out the events she'd witnessed and begging him to come.

"Did he hurt you?" Her father's gruff voice sounded tortured.

"No, but I might have put him down kind of hard."

"Jack?" He looked skeptical. Pushing her aside, he marched up the steps, following his men into the house. She hung back, waiting, wondering what he'd think until curiosity got the best of her. Casting a glance at Noah, who was being attended to by the paramedics now, she hurried up the steps and found her father leaning over a still-unconscious Jack. Trussed up like a Thanksgiving turkey. In uniform.

"Well, I'll be," he said and glanced up to look at her, standing tentatively in the doorway, half-in, half-out, not certain if she should run or stand tall.

She pushed her shoulders back and met his eyes, standing her ground.

A half smile curved her old man's lips as he looked her up and down as if seeing her for the first time. Walking over, slowly, he engulfed her in another hug, patting her on the back. In a proud voice, he uttered the words she'd rarely heard him say.

"That's my girl."

She laughed and hugged him back, sobering only when she got another glimpse of Jack behind him. This was the man who'd once brought her a copy of Halo when she'd been too sick to go out on midnight launch and get a copy herself. He'd always been so kind.

How could he be a killer?

She sobered. "Dad, what's going to happen to him?"

"Don't know yet. Still not sure what the hell happened here." He pushed her toward the door. "Go ahead. Tell me everything you know."

And she did.

# Chapter 21

"You look like you need this."

Spider glanced up and saw a cup of something that smelled like hot chocolate inches from her face. She grabbed it with greedy hands and smiled at Connor, bless his heart. He sank into the waiting room seat beside her and sipped from his own cup. "How's he doing?"

He nodded toward the Emergency Room sign over the hallway where Noah rested.

"Fine. They're releasing him, but my father wanted to talk to him first. Alone."

"Ah. No wonder you look so messed up."

She smiled, wondering if she looked half as terrified as she felt. There was no telling what her father was asking Noah. About her. About them.

Her stomach rolled again and she groaned, lifting the mug and hoping the liquid soothed her nerves.

"Hey." Connor bumped her knee with his. "You saved someone's life tonight. Be proud of that."

A sad smile tugged at her lips in answer to his. "I still can't believe Jack was responsible for all of this."

"He flat-out panicked," Connor told her. "He'd worked to put his past behind him. When he realized Kate's body had been found … it dredged it all up again. All of the guilt and the fear." He shook his head. "He knew it was only a matter of time before Noah found something to reveal the truth."

"How do you know? Did you talk to him?"

"I hung around while they read him his rights and put him in the car. Picked up on a few things." He tapped the side of his head. "I don't think he would've hurt you, Emma. He went after Noah because he thought if Noah was out of the picture, you'd go back home and drop the investigation. Something tells me he doesn't know you very well, does he?"

That was something the old Emma might have done, but no. Jack didn't know Spider at all.

"If it makes you feel better, I think he would have ended up pulling Noah out of that car if you hadn't done it. Guilt was already eating him up."

That did make her feel a little better. "Is Kate here with Noah?"

Connor glanced around, smiled, and met her eyes again. "No. She's sitting here with us right now."

"With us?" Spider sat up straighter. "Why?"

"She wants me to tell you something. Something important." He stopped as if listening. "There's a guy named Paul. A cop. You know him."

Spider felt her body tense.

"Kate says to trust your instincts there. He's bad news. Talk to your father. Get him out of your life. She said you don't know it, but he's been following you, watching you more than you realize." His expression sobered. "She says that if she had trusted her instincts she might still be alive. She doesn't want to see the same thing happen to you."

Spider took a deep breath and nodded. "Thank you, Kate. I'll talk to my father."

Her gaze strayed down the hallway again. Her father had been in the room with Noah for an awfully long time.

"They're just talking about the case. That's all."

She blinked at him. "How do you do that?"

He raised his eyebrows.

"Knowing what I'm thinking." She gestured down the hall. "Knowing what they're talking about. It's … freaky."

"About that." He reached into his jacket and pulled out a piece of paper. "You've earned this."

She glanced at the IP address, username and password written in barely legible handwriting. "What's this?"

"You asked me about the Bellator de Lux, remember?"

"How could I forget? You ditched us after that."

"We have a lot to talk about. All of us do. When will Alexandra be back?"

She shrugged. "Soon. I think. She's got appointments lined up next week she hasn't asked anyone to cancel."

"Good." He sighed, glanced around, and moved to his feet. "Walk with me?"

Reluctant to leave her spot, she chewed her lip and stared toward the ER.

"I can tell you when they're done. Come on."

Intrigued, she moved to her feet and followed him. "How can you possibly know that? I was right about you being some kind of experimental soldier, wasn't I?"

"So, the Bellator de Lux," he reminded, and she zipped her lips, eager for any information. "You've figured out it's a lesser-known organization."

"If by lesser-known you mean secret, then yes," she couldn't help but insert sarcastically. She tacked on "Sorry" in case he was offended by the sarcasm.

His grin widened. "We're more of a network of people. Special people. People like me and Alexandra and your boss, Zachary Collins."

She stopped dead in her tracks. "Shut the front door! Alexandra and Zach are part of your group? No way."

Glancing around to see if anyone had overheard her, he grabbed her arm and tugged her forward. "No. Not yet." He bent closer. "The thing about a secret organization is that it's supposed to stay secret. Got that?"

Nodding, she made a zipping motion over her mouth. Then she immediately made an unzipping motion to ask, "I was right, wasn't I? It's a secret government organization. Black ops or something."

He heaved a sigh. "No. Privately funded by—"

"The Vatican! I knew it."

"No. Not the Vatican." His voice was growing impatient, although she sensed amusement in there somewhere. "By people who've been running the Bellator de Lux since before Rome fell."

"Seriously?"

"Seriously." He led her to a park bench in the courtyard and gestured for her to sit. "They're very selective about the type of people they involve. When I met Alexandra, I knew she was the best candidate we'd found in ages. Thing is, it's not my decision."

"Oh." Spider pinched her face at him. "Why are you telling me all this? Oh, no. You're going to kill me, aren't you? I know too much."

He chuckled and sat down beside her. "No. I'm not killing anyone. Would you shut up and listen?"

She pretended to zip her lips again.

"When I recommended Alexandra, it brought Zach to their attention, too. Thing is, they don't just walk up to your door and ask you to pay membership fees. They do an intense background check. Watch you for a while. Judge if you're a good fit. Only, they don't always do it themselves."

"I don't understand."

"Noah."

"Noah? Wait. He's a member?" That lying piece of—

Holding up his hand, Connor shook his head. "For such a smart girl, you jump to way too many conclusions. No, he's not a member. The Bellator – without my knowing, I might add – hired him to spy on Zach and Alexandra. They hired an attorney he was familiar with to be a middleman and fed him some line about an insurance claims case. Total nonsense. They always hire the best people they can find in the area. It's their way of making sure potential candidates can do what's needed. Last line of the application process, you could say."

The pieces of the puzzle began to slip into place. Except for a biggie.

She leaned closer. "So what exactly is the Bellator?"

"Don't worry. You're going to find out." He grinned.

"I am?" She wasn't sure if she liked that grin.

"You're the first person to get through their super secret firewall. You only have yourself to blame for bringing yourself to their attention."

Oh, crap. He *was* going to kill her.

He laughed. "No! They want you to work for them."

Oh, thank God. Her shoulders relaxed, and then tensed again. "But I like working for Zach."

"Keep doing it. I'm kind of hoping he'll take me on part-time. It was my suggestion that we make a base out of his agency, if he's willing. A place for other Bellators to come and go when they're in the area. It'll make a good cover."

That actually sounded kind of … cool.

"So it would be two jobs?" She really needed to be clear on this now that she was pretty certain she had a boyfriend. Priorities and all.

"We help people. There's a lot going on in the world that shouldn't be, and we're kind of the guys who go in and make things right. Sometimes it's ghosts or demons. Sometimes it's other people with abilities like us taking advantage of people who don't have the same skills. You choose your cases. I'm guessing the Bellator will pay Zach and his people well for whichever cases they work, so no second job. Just sort of expanding on your current one."

"That's what managers always say when they give you a promotion without a raise." She grumbled. "Okay. One more question. Can I tell Noah about my super secret new job as a superhero?"

He chuckled and stood. "That's up to you, but you need to ask yourself if he can be trusted. No one without reason can know about the Bellator, Spider. I'm serious."

She held up her hand and gave him a Scout's promise. Bouncing to her feet, beyond excited to share the news with Noah, she demanded, "Are they done talking yet?"

"I have no idea."

"But—"

"I only said that to get you to come with me. I have to be in close proximity to know what a person's thinking or saying."

She punched his arm. "You jerk!"

He laughed. "Come on."

"One more question."

"I'll believe that when I hear it."

Another punch to his arm. "Do you have a girlfriend or wife? Like, how do they deal with this? Does she feel left out?"

She didn't want to do anything to jeopardize her newfound relationship with Noah. It meant too much to her. Poor man had so much to deal with already.

"There's a woman out there," Connor began, only to hesitate. "I haven't met her yet, but I know she's the one. I've seen her up here." He tapped his head. "Until I meet her, I have no idea how she'll deal with everything. Can't help you there."

Spider stopped walking, grabbing his arm to make sure he stopped too. "That sounded all kinds of crazy."

"What I've seen of love, totally crazy."

He had a good point.

She looped her arm through his and dragged him toward the ER. "You intrigue me, Connor Manning. Tell me more."

***

"I think there's something you should know about your daughter, sir." Sitting on the edge of the hospital bed, Noah gripped the side

249

and forced himself to meet the eyes of the man sitting across from him. It was not the most ideal situation to do this, but having a near-death experience had improved his courage. He might as well. "I'm pretty sure I'm falling in love with her. You should be aware that I intend to get to know her better. A lot better."

"Hmph." Eyes so similar to Emma's looked him up and down. "She know that?"

"I haven't told her yet." He wasn't seeking the man's permission, but the proper thing to do was let her father know his intent. Hell. He was new to this. Maybe he was doing it wrong. Running a hand though his hair, he decided to put all of his cards on the table. "You're her father. She loves you. I don't want start off on the wrong foot with the man who raised her. That would be stupid, and she wouldn't thank me for it. She'd dump me, and I don't want to lose her." He took a deep breath. "Basically, I don't know what the hell I'm doing. She's got me all tied up in knots."

"Hmph." Something close to a smirk lifted the man's lips. "She's a handful."

Noah smiled. "Yes, sir. She is."

If the way Emma's father looked him squarely in the eyes with such an intimidating perusal was any indication, the city was a lot safer with this man overseeing its police force. Noah kept his chin level, refusing to look away, even though he wanted nothing more.

Chief Fisher finally moved to his feet. "You don't treat her right, you'll have me to deal with. You hear that?"

"Yes, sir." Noah stood to shake hands with the police chief, but the man didn't oblige.

"I'll go and let her know you're ready." The chief quickly moved out the door.

Noah had just sat in the chair the older man had abandoned when Emma stuck her pretty head through the doorway. He rose to meet her embrace.

They said nothing for several seconds, simply stood there, holding each other tightly, her warmth seeping into him and soothing that anxious, jittery feeling that had been threatening to return. Noah wondered if her father had had time to tell her what he'd said, but he guessed not. Chief Fisher had looked a little pole axed there at the end.

She lifted her head and looked at him. "How do you feel?"

"Killer headache. Otherwise, pretty good."

"Awesome." She pulled away. "Ready to go?"

He noticed someone lingering in the doorway and glanced up to find Connor Manning watching them. Noah held out his hand. "Thank you for pulling me out of that car. The chief told me the parts I didn't know."

Connor returned the gesture, his grip strong and firm. "Glad I could help, but Spider did most of the rescuing."

"Yeah, I know. I heard about what you did to Jack. Poor guy." He squeezed her to his side, proud as all hell.

Emma looked down, her eyes filling with a touch of sadness. "I hope he'll be okay. I didn't mean to hurt him."

He exchanged glances with Connor, whose eyes were narrowed, intensely focused on Noah's face. "I think Noah needs to explain what happened with Kate and how she died."

Noah would never get used to the other's man's uncanny knowledge. "I'll explain in the car. Okay?"

By the time he was finished explaining the events he'd dreamt, they were home – or at least, at the Collins house. "I'm glad it was an accident." Emma's sad expression had waned some. "I didn't think Jack could be a killer, but then again, he tried to kill you. Guess I *was* wrong about him."

Noah's tone was harsh. "If he hadn't kidnapped her for only God knows what purpose, she might still be here."

"True." She sighed and looked at him. "Will you stay with me tonight? I don't think you should go home yet."

He relaxed. "What if the animals see something they shouldn't?"

She shrugged. "I'll bribe them."

The growl of another car approached, and Noah had to force

himself not to kiss her on the front doorstep like a lovesick schoolboy. Connor parked his car at the curb and strode toward them.

"I asked him to follow us," Emma admitted. "Kate deserves some closure, don't you think?"

By the time Connor had left, Kate had been guided to cross over and find peace, Emma was bawling and Noah had shed more than a few tears himself. He hadn't seen the harm in Kate sticking around if she wanted, but Connor had explained what could happen if she did. Ghosts who lingered became warped and turned into demons over time. That wasn't something Kate had been willing to risk either.

He walked Connor to the door and thanked him.

"She wouldn't have gone if you didn't have Spider." Connor shared that detail in a quiet voice, just between the two of them. "She saw the same thing I did." He glanced at where Emma stood in the kitchen, feeding two hungry dogs and a grumpy cat. "You two belong together. Don't screw it up." Connor slapped his arm and walked away.

Noah shut the door behind him and ran a hand over his face.

That was at least the third person who'd threatened him if he broke Emma's heart. No pressure.

He pulled Emma with him onto the sofa and sank back into the fluffy cushions, closing his eyes, grateful for a moment's peace and quiet with her beside him. She cuddled into his side, smoothing her hand over her chest.

"Are you okay?" she asked softly. "About Kate, I mean."

There was sorrow and regret somewhere in his subconscious, but mostly, he felt numb about the whole thing. "A week ago, I knew who I was – or who I thought I was." He pressed her closer to his side, comforted by her proximity. "I never doubted where I came from, who my parents were, my family. I was always Derek West's son, doomed to repeat a lot of the same mistakes I'd seen him make."

"Why?"

He frowned. "What do you mean?"

"Why did you think you had to make the same mistakes he did? You're a different person."

"Because no matter how hard I tried to be different than him, I never felt it. Does that make sense?"

Lifting her head to look at him, she arched a brow. "Not so much."

"Just listen." He pressed her back down. "I always thought it was in my genes, that I had no choice, but now I know it's not in my genes. I do have a choice. I feel … disoriented. Like everything I once believed was wrong."

"Good, because it sounds like you need serious therapy if you believed any of that crap." She lifted her head and looked at him again. "My dad implied your father was an alcoholic."

He nodded, terrified her opinion of him had changed.

"Are you one too?"

"Of course not. I barely touch the stuff."

"You chose not to drink."

"Yes."

"Then you've always been able to choose not to be like him." She rolled her eyes before laying her head back on his shoulder. "What's changed?"

When she put it like that, he felt like a colossal idiot. Hadn't John told him pretty much the same? "Everything," he admitted. He didn't know how to make her understand when he wasn't certain he understood it himself.

"Noah, listen to me. I met your mother, the one who raised you. I kind of met the other one too. Fact is, you come from good people, people who love you. Just because fate handed you a rotten apple for a father doesn't define who you are. At least, not unless you allow it to."

Hope surged through his chest. "I hope you're right."

"Oh, I am. Get used to it."

That made him smile.

"Thanks for what you did today." He nuzzled her hair, inhaling the delicious scent of strawberries. "You saved my life."

"Eh." She snuggled closer. "I'll try not to remind you of it. Much."

He smiled. "Guess I owe you, huh?"

"I accept many forms of payment, including lasagna."

He sighed, feeling ridiculously happy for a man who'd almost died hours earlier. Because of her. All her. "You could do a lot better than me, you know?"

She lifted her head, met his eyes, and smiled. "I think you'll do just fine."

Lifting a trembling hand, he brushed a lock of blue and red hair behind her ear, caressing her face. "I'm gonna need help. This is all new to me."

Her eyes danced with mischief. "What? Making lasagna?"

"No. Being in love."

Her eyes widened, her mouth forming a very cute O. "Wait. Could you clarify that statement, because I think I blacked out for a second, so I might have imagined it."

He pulled her head down, kissed her, drinking in the taste of mint and hot chocolate that lingered on her lips. "I. Love. You. Crazy woman."

She sighed dreamily and sank into him. "Ditto."

Joy fluttered in his stomach. "To quote a wise and beautiful woman I know, I could use some clarification on that."

"I love you, too. I think." She wrinkled her nose at him. "This has all happened kind of fast. We haven't known each other very long."

"Yes, it has been fast." Worry chased away his smile. Was she having second thoughts?

"We have a lot to talk about."

"Such as?"

"I've recently had a kind-of job offer I need to tell you about." She made a dismissive gesture with her hand. "Never mind. We can talk about it later. You seriously love me?" Her tone sounded so hopeful, it chased away the worry eating through his thoughts.

"I seriously love you."

He was more certain now that he'd finally admitted it to her, and himself.

Squealing, she dove into him, pressing exuberant kisses across his face. Noah closed his arms around her, thrilled to have her in his arms any way he could get her.

As he found her mouth with his, he knew he'd finally buried the ghost of his father that had haunted him more than Kate ever had. He knew without a doubt he'd found what he'd always wanted, even if he hadn't known it. A woman who would accept and love him despite his many faults. A woman like Emma, who looked past his faults and saw the man he could become underneath.

He'd been searching for her for so long. Now that he'd found her, he wasn't about to let her go.

www.ingramcontent.com/pod-product-compliance
Lightning Source LLC
Chambersburg PA
CBHW010634100726
47900CB00011B/2823